Not Up for Debate

Emma Norman

For my one and only. Thank you for loving me, laughing with me, and believing in me. I love you to the moon and back.

Author Note

Dear reader, thank you so much for picking up Not Up for Debate! This book is a comedic romance, so most of the time it is very light, but there are a few topics that may be heavy to some individuals. Including anxiety and panic attacks, as well as alcoholism. Also, this story does include adult language and sexual scenes. It's a slow-burn romance, but if you prefer a closed door in the bedroom, skip chapter 30.

Prologue

You HAVE *GOT* TO be kidding me. There is no way this is actually happening right now. The only person in the entire world who could have ruined this vacation for me just sat down at my table. *This* man. This insanely irritating, completely irresistible man.

Chapter One
Three Weeks Earlier

I HAVE EVERYTHING FIGURED out.

I know that probably sounds a bit presumptuous, but looking back, my life has always followed a very predictable path.

Only child of a middle class family? Check.

Get good grades? Check.

Attend law school? Check.

Become one of the top corporate litigators in the entire country? Triple check.

I excel at perfection. Thrive under pressure. And rarely make mistakes.

My bookshelves are alphabetized by author, my closet is categorized by season, and I make lists like there is no tomorrow.

Basically, it all boils down to the fact that I always know what to expect and when to expect it.

Until this morning.

I honestly didn't see it coming when my boyfriend of three months, Rex—yes, his real name—decided to throw a bomb into my perfectly predictable life and break up with me.

Truthfully, I wasn't sad about it; it just totally caught me off guard. I don't like when things change course.

What makes it worse though, is that I had to rush out of my apartment and I barely made it to the office on time.

"Hi, Jane!" My wonderful but entirely too enthusiastic secretary, Kayla, says as I reach my office door. "Um…You're…Sorry, they already started a meeting in the conference room. You should probably get in there. Mr. Schwartz said it was super important." She hands me a steaming cup of coffee.

I give her the best smile I can muster while wondering to myself why in the hell I have to attend yet another lecture from my boss about the "future of our firm."

Seven other attorneys are gathered around the large conference table and from the exhausted looks on their faces, I'm guessing they all feel the same way too.

Slowly making my way to the only empty chair, I quietly put down my coffee and designer briefcase then sit.

Joe Schwartz, one of the named partners in our firm, Schwartz & Adler, is standing in front of the room going over slide after slide of profit numbers.

Minutes tick by, and I can feel my attention beginning to melt away like ice cream on a hot summer's day. I'm still partly listening to what he is saying, but my pen finds the corner of my legal pad and starts a little doodle before I know it.

Why does Mr. Schwartz talk so slow?

How could someone's mouth be so dry?

The complete lack of moisture in his mouth is screaming dehydration.

His lips are actually sticking to his teeth as he's talking.

The smacking between each of his words...*God, it's unbearable.*

Trying my best to push the mental images of parched lips out of my mind, I begin making a list of all the crap I have to get done when I get home from work. I need to do a few loads of laundry, get rid of Rex's stuff in my bathroom cabinet, I should probably restock my fridge since I didn't go grocery shopping yesterday and the only thing in there is some leftov—

"Isn't that right, Jane?"

I quickly snap my head up and stare at Mr. Schwartz with wide eyes. He looks at me expectantly as I slowly lift the end of my pen into my mouth, hoping it comes across as me just casually debating my answer.

"You know, Joe... Truthfully, if I'm being honest here, I think it goes without saying what I think about it."

After a brief pause, he grins his unnaturally white, perfectly veneered smile and says, "Jane, dear, you are absolutely right." He points a finger in my direction. "See, everyone, *that* is the point of view I would like everyone in this entire office to adopt. An outright, take-no-shit approach to the future of our firm."

I look around the room at my various coworkers and give a wary half-smile, not at all knowing what I just agreed with.

Joe slowly makes his way around the conference table and rests his giant, leathery hands on my shoulders.

Normally, I'm not one to hate being in the spotlight, but at this moment, I'm extremely aware of the fact that my out-of-nowhere breakup this morning took all of my time, and I currently have zero idea what my hair looks like right now.

The images popping up in my mind aren't reassuring, so I sit here awkwardly, smiling, while Joe begins kneading my shoulders with his large thumbs.

"That being said, Jane's no-nonsense attitude is exactly why *she* will be the one representing our new level-one client."

What?! Holy shit...

My jaw drops. This is a big deal. Like, a really big deal. Level-one clients are the mega-rich, the billionaires, the huge corporations that earn a lot of money, and *pay* a lot of money. As far as I can remember, these types of clients have only ever been represented by the partners.

My coworkers stare at me, mouths in straight lines, eyes barely blinking. I have the vague sense that I currently resemble a blow-up doll, so I try to close my mouth, but it just falls open again.

Joe continues with his speech. "As you all know, Howard Dumont of Dumont Luxury Resorts has been looking for a new firm to put on retainer. After some lengthy negotiations, he confirmed yesterday evening that he wants Schwartz & Adler to be in his corner during any future litigation," he says with a haughty grin.

My mind starts racing. Howard Dumont. The current talk of every major business magazine, Howard Dumont. The multi-billionaire hotshot, Howard Dumont.

I picture the well-dressed resort owner with his salt-and-pepper hair, large green eyes, and beautifully sculpted face. *Holy shit.*

Representing a client like Mr. Dumont is a life-changing step in my career. One that, yes, I've worked extremely hard for, and yes, having extremely wealthy clients is the reason I chose such a prestigious firm like Schwartz & Adler in the first place. But honestly, I didn't think it would happen this soon.

Here's the thing, it's not that I don't think I can handle it. I know without a doubt in my mind I am made for this. My initial shock comes solely from the fact that up until a few seconds ago, I would have put all my money on Joe Schwartz asking Mr. Colin Perfect-Pants to represent a level-one client over him asking me.

It's no secret Colin Clark is extremely qualified, but everyone at the firm knows I'm *more* qualified. I've had more high-profile clients, seen more days in court, and have a lot more wins than he has.

However, historically speaking, Joe has shown me that because Colin has a penis, he's somehow infinitely more capable than I am at being a corporate litigator. To hell with my very impressive—and extensive—resume.

My mind is reeling. I'll be honest, this completely out-of-character choice is making me suspicious. Something has to be going on. I start thinking about all of the possible reasons as to why Joe would choose me over Colin to represent Mr. Dumont.

One: Is Joe dying? *Oh gosh*, maybe he has cancer?

Two: Could be a midlife crisis. I hear that type of thing is common in men his age.

Three: Or, what if it's not Joe...maybe it has something to do with Colin.

Four: Could it be that Colin is dying? Is this Joe's way of letting him off the hook to spend more time with his family? *Oh man, now that is sad.*

I make a mental note to prepare to send some flowers to his wife; she really is a doll.

"Jane, I have full faith and confidence in your ability to work with Mr. Dumont." Joe nods earnestly and gives me a pat on my shoulder.

This admission makes me sit taller as a big stupid grin begins spreading across my face.

"Of course, this means that as a firm, we will now be bringing in a substantial amount of money. Which, in turn, opens up many growth opportunities for everyone across the board. Not only for us here in the Denver office but at our Manhattan office as well." Joe starts making his way back to the front of the conference room. "This brings me to the other big news of the day. For the past few months, Mr. Adler and I have been in talks about expanding our firm and creating a position for a new senior partner." Joe looks at me and winks. "At the moment, our exponential client growth and considerable increase in revenue is exceptionally significant. Team, we have made so many momentous moves in the right direction, and I'm proud knowing we're currently within the top fifteen law firms in the nation." Everyone claps, and Joe smiles.

When he reaches the front of the room, he turns to face us all. "Obviously, my partner and I are not blind to the fact that we couldn't have done this alone. We know we only have each one of you and your remarkable hard work to thank for that." He bows his head before looking me right in the eyes.

My breathing becomes heavy as I mentally prepare myself for the news. I honestly cannot believe that after my morning from hell, I could possibly be getting two pieces of life-altering news in one meeting. A meeting I didn't even want to attend in the first place, might I add.

Representing a high-profile client like Mr. Dumont is one thing, but the possibility of becoming a senior partner at thirty-one will change the direction of my life forever.

Tears of gratitude swell in my eyes and my cheeks begin to heat. I close my eyes, hoping to stave off the crying for at least another breath.

"So, all of this is to say, because of the tremendous growth we decided that Paul Adler will be permanently moving to our Manhattan office next week. This is so he can be there to help ease any growing pains that are sure to present themselves," Mr. Schwartz says, clasping his hands together.

My foot taps in anticipation, and my heart feels like it's going to beat out of my chest.

"Because Paul will not be in this office anymore, we both came to the conclusion that it was imperative to get the new partner set up here in Denver as soon as possible." Joe and I take a deep breath at the same time. "As of 6:30 this morning, our decision was made, and contracts were signed. I would like you all to please congratulate our very own Colin Clark as he has been promoted as Schwartz & Adler's newest partner!"

The room erupts into applause. My heart sinks down to my toes.

"This is such a colossal step forward for our firm, and I sincerely hope all of you are as excited as I am. This new partnership has already opened up so many opportunities for growth for others in our office. For example, Colin was going to be assigned the Dumont account, but because he will be busy with his new partner duties, our little Janie here gets to take a shot at it instead. Thank you, Jane, for taking this massive account. It's going to be exceptional!"

FFFFUUUUCCCCKKKK me. There it is.

Chapter Two

"You sure that's just coffee in there?" Jordyn whispers while slipping into the seat next to me.

I don't actually see her, since I'm currently face down on the bumpy not-functional-but-super-trendy table, but I'd know my best friend's mock condescending mom-talk anywhere.

"Because if it is just coffee, that's a damn shame, and I'm sure Daniel could remedy that for you real quick," she says with a snap, probably trying to get the attention of our favorite shop owner/server/best friend.

Taking a long, slow deep breath in, I manage out a muffled, "Thanks, but no thanks," on the exhale, breath fogging the table.

I turn my head to the side, uncomfortably squishing my ear, just in time to see Daniel give a yikes face and a little half-shrug to Jordyn before he hastily retreats from our table.

"Woah, there, sunshine. Your bubbly energy is scaring Daniel away. What's wrong, babe?" she says, scooting her chair closer to mine. "Did Rex keep you up all night again with his captivating football talk? Or were you two doing much more *captivating* things?" she teases, raising her eyebrows up and down.

This earns an even bigger muffled groan from me as I slowly roll my head back up onto my shoulders.

"First, it's not even *real* football talk, J. It's *fantasy* football. It's fake. Fake football. Second, Rex is a complete asshat, and we broke up this morning. Third, my life is in absolute shambles, and I'm really confused because things at work are both very good and very bad at the same time and I don't know what to do," I say with an exasperated pout and put my head back down on the table.

She reaches over and starts rubbing lazy circles up and down my back.

Jordyn's been my best friend for basically forever. We met when we were five years old, and her family moved to Fort Collins from Atlanta.

On the first day of kindergarten, we both showed up wearing the exact same light purple dress with little white polka dots. I know it doesn't sound like much, but to five-year-old little girls, this was as close to divine intervention as it could ever get.

Her rich brown skin and perfect black curls were a stark contrast to my pale skin and long blonde hair, but again, to five-year old-girls, none of that mattered. When her chocolate-colored eyes locked with my big blue ones, we knew we were best friends right then and there.

Neither of us said a word as we linked arms and made our way over to circle time. We silently took our seats next to each other and have been by each other's sides ever since. Whether it's making one another laugh until we cry or cry until we laugh, we know we'll be together forever.

"Jordyn, I haven't felt this awful in a long time," I say, turning my head, my cheek tragically squishing into the table. "I think I'm at one of those crossroads that everyone tells people in their thirties about all the time." I frown. "I feel like I have two choices. One, I can pretend like nothing happened and continue to work for the king of the men-are-awesome-women-suck club. Or two, I could do the complete opposite and quit said high-paying job I've worked my entire life for and go be a traveling free spirit who may or may not sleep in the nude." As I say this, I realize I should sit up like a normal person, because a string of drool begins to pool under my cheek.

Not even missing a beat, Jordyn grabs some napkins and cleans up my embarrassing puddle, then reaches over and dabs my chin.

If it was anybody else, I might be slightly humiliated, but honestly, she saw a lot worse during our college days.

She's the best. She'll help me make the right decision. She always knows what to do. She's the smartest and most knowledgeable best frie—

"Well, babe, I don't know what to tell you."

At this abrupt change of events, my poor head finds its way back onto the uncomfortable table. I'll add this to the list of things I wasn't expecting today. I let out another groan. "Jordyn, you weren't supposed to say that. You're supposed to say something like, 'Okay, my most princess-like-amazing-charismatic-best-friend-in-the-whole-entire-world, here is what you should do...' then you would sit here and tell me what I should do so I don't have to make any decisions for myself." Of course, I say all of this directly into the table, so all that Jordyn hears are more muffled grumbles.

She puts her hands on either side of my head and gently lifts up so that we are eye to eye.

"Is that too much to ask?" I say, defeated.

My head almost slips out of her hands when the smell of warm chocolate fills my nose. Daniel deposits the most beautiful brownie I've ever seen in between my face and the table.

"Just so we're clear, I don't usually condone the intake of carbs before noon, but you look like this might be the only thing keeping you from banging your head back into my very expensive table," Daniel says with a pretend frown.

"Your table sucks, but thank you for the brownie," I say through a mouthful of gooey gold.

Daniel pretends to scratch his nose while flipping me the bird, then walks away with a smug little smile on his face. I have good friends.

"Jane, forget about Rex. He's a dick and totally sucks," Jordyn says, wiping a drip of coffee off the side of her mug. "But, you're going to have to actually give me some insight as to what the hell is going on with your job, because right now I'm just wondering whose ass I'm going to need to kick first. Is it that one awful HR lady who forgot your birthday last year? Is it Joe? Oooo is it that Corbin guy?" Jordyn pauses and takes a sip of her coffee, waiting for me to answer. "I'm at a loss here, babe, so you have to fill me in before I start making assumptions. You and I both know where that has landed us before," she says, looking at me over the rim of her coffee cup.

"First off, his name is Colin not Corbin, and second, yes kick his ass because he was made partner this morning."

Jordyn's eyes grow wide as she registers what I just said. "Schwartz, Adler, and...CLARK? *That's* the direction they decided to take the firm? With that *vanilla bean* of a man? All jokes aside, Jane, I really do think they need a good ass kicking."

I give a half-smile at her obvious attempt to make me laugh.

"I honestly don't know what they were thinking. I mean, from what you've told me about Colin, he seems to be a fine attorney, but gosh, he's nowhere near your level." She puts her arm around my shoulder and gives me a gentle squeeze. "I'm so sorry, babe. Penis power sucks. It wins. It always wins."

From his spot at the espresso machine, Daniel gives us a thumbs up and grins.

"I swear, that man hears the word penis, and it's like the bat signal goes off," Jordyn adds. "He doesn't even know what we're talking about."

A laugh bubbles up from deep inside of me, and I feel my gloomy mood start to lighten. "Jordyn, being made a partner doesn't mean your name gets added to the firm. That's totally a misconception...Also, please tell me how you remembered Colin's last name but not his first?"

She shrugs and takes a too-big bite of my brownie. After a beat, she says, "So, what are you going to do?"

"Well...that brings me to the next part of my morning."

"Please, no more bad news," Jordyn says, then quickly adds, "Wait, before you say anything, I'm going to backtrack a bit and say that you and Rex breaking up is going into my good news pile. So, at this point, we are one for one. Just had to get that out there. Continue please."

I roll my eyes. "Our firm just acquired a huge client. Like a very rich, very famous client.

"Who?" she asks quickly. "Tell me. Who is it? Tell me now, Jane."

I let her squirm in her seat, while I slowly chew my brownie, and then follow it with a comically long sip of my coffee.

I put down my mug and look her in the eyes. "Howard Dumont."

"SHUT UP!" she yells and slaps both hands down on the table.

Daniel rushes our way, winding through other tables. "Seriously, you two, I don't know what you have against my tables, but if you don't calm down with the abuses, I'm going to have to ask you to leave. Or at least go sit outside, because *those* tables are from Ikea."

We both ignore him and continue with our conversation.

"Also, Joe made *me* head of the account." A smile grows on my face.

"WHAT?! Jane! *The* Howard Dumont is your client now? That's amazing! Seriously, who cares about stupid ol' partner? This is HUGE! I'm so freaking happy for you!"

Seeing the bright smile on my friend's face does something to me. Getting a client like Mr. Dumont is…it's incredible. To be representing a multi-billionaire at this point in my career is an opportunity that most attorneys can only ever dream of.

This might just be my chance. My chance to put my abilities to good use and show them that being organized and analytical is what makes me so great at my job. This opportunity is just a stepping-stone on my journey to more high-paying clients, more wins in court, and then eventually becoming a partner. Plenty of firms have multiple partners, so I'm sure once I prove myself, Joe will have to promote me.

This is good. This is actually *really* good. My smile grows wider.

"Oh, I forgot to tell you the best part." I playfully slap Jordyn's arm. "In a few weeks, I get to fly to Hawaii for ten days. Joe told me that Mr. Dumont said, and I quote, 'I would really like to meet my new attorney and treat them to all the beauties and luxuries that my magnificent resort offers.'"

Jordyn fans herself with her hand, pretending to swoon.

"I'm not even kidding, J. Since he's such a new client, there isn't too much to do, yet. It's literally just going to be a few introductory meetings and him signing a bunch of papers. So basically, that means I just get to spend ten days in paradise with my new famous client and work on my tan." I kick back my chair and bring my hands up behind my head.

"You've done it, Jane. Congratulations. You've made it." Jordyn grabs my hand and gives it a shake.

I look her in the eyes, as I try to let her words sink in. *Have I done it though?* Have I really "made it?" I've worked so hard for so long, I honestly thought I would feel different when I got here. I thought that when I finally accomplished my career goals, I would feel this overwhelming sense of accomplishment, but so far, I just have the same nagging thoughts in the back of my mind, questioning if I'm where I want to be. I take a deep breath, trying to shove my doubts aside.

Jordyn gets out her notebook and clicks her pen. "I'm so glad we have some time to plan this! We can go get your hair done, with more highlights this time. You'll need to get a new bikini or two. You're gonna need to get waxed."

"WAXED? No way. Jordyn, you know I don't mind some good trimming, primping, and prepping, but I have some hard lines that I will never cross."

"Well, I do have a few weeks to convince you that some hard lines we draw, we can erase just as easily." She winks then continues. "Listen to me, you're in your thirties now. You just went through a breakup, and to top it all off, you just got one of the highest profile clients your firm has ever had. Take these ten days in paradise to find yourself. Discover who this new Jane is, and what she wants."

She sets her notebook aside and gently grabs my hand in hers. "In between the work you'll have to do, please rest. Eat delicious tropical food, drink the water right out of a coconut, eat some big juicy pineapples. The world is your oyster, babe." Her smile gets bigger. "Also, for the love of God, please have some mouthwatering rebound sex with a beautiful Hawaiian hunk who you will never see again. Don't even think about stupid Rex or any of the past tools you've dated, for that matter, and I promise you will come back feeling refreshed and like a totally new woman."

At her words, I feel my heart start to beat with excitement.

"I mean it, Jane, enjoy yourself. You deserve it. Frankly, you deserve a lot more, but this will have to do for now."

"Okay, J. You've sold me." I flash a genuine smile.

Maybe this is just what I need.

There's a slight bounce in my step as I walk the two blocks back to my office. The mid-morning sun reflects off the windows of the downtown Denver office buildings, and the late January snow sparkles atop the parked cars lining the streets. It's magical.

I close my eyes for a minute and feel the cool air on my face.

What a crazy morning. I had absolutely no idea that when I woke up today things would unfold the way that they did. I broke up with Rex, I got an amazing high-profile client, I didn't get promoted.

Partner. I feel my stomach drop. I didn't get promoted to partner. Why didn't I, again? Sure, Colin is a good attorney, a great attorney actually, but on paper, the job should have been mine.

I pause and take a deep breath of cold winter air. I don't want to feel this way. I don't like feeling like I deserved something more than someone else. It feels really icky.

Even though the position should have been mine, that doesn't mean I automatically have to hate the guy who got it. I mean, it's true that he is pretty *vanilla*, as Jordyn would say, but he genuinely is a really good guy.

He's been a good friend to me the entire time we've worked together, and I do respect the hell out of him. I just hate that for some reason, Mr. Schwartz doesn't see what I bring to the table. I hate that I was overlooked. I've been working my ass off nonstop for him for years, and it's starting to seem like it's never going to be enough.

I know that having Howard Dumont as a client is amazing, but it still feels like a blow to my gut knowing I wasn't the first choice. Knowing that I only got it because I was passed over for a promotion. *I* only got it because *Colin* was promoted.

Inside I feel that internal struggle of feeling both grateful for the new opportunity but also super disappointed with how I got it.

The longer I walk, the longer I have to ruminate over the events that led me to where I am.

I go back and forth from feeling grateful, to confused, then circle back to grateful again.

Then the realization hits me, does it really even matter how I got the account? Or does it only matter how well I handle it and prove myself?

When I was talking with Jordyn, I decided I would give this my all. Regardless of how I got here, I'm going to give it everything I have. I will show Joe he shouldn't have looked me over. I have to.

I step into the elevator at my office building and take a deep breath. I can do this. I'm here for a reason. I earned this. I will prove to everyone I'm the woman for the job, and that I am not one to second-guess. I put on my brightest smile as the elevator door opens at my floor.

I make my way through the various desks and find myself at Colin's office door. I knock lightly, secretly hoping I've missed him, but then I hear him say, "It's open."

Stepping into his office, I see a very stressed Colin looking up at me from the massive piles of papers on his desk.

"Oh, Jane! Hi! Sorry, I thought you were my new assistant, Maddie. She went out quite a while ago to get me some lunch, and she hasn't made her way back yet. What can I do for you?"

I stand here thinking for a moment.

Did I even look at him in the meeting this morning?

Was he already this stressed, or are his new responsibilities getting to him?

I glance down and see the picture of his cute little family on his desk and the reality of how busy he is about to become hits me.

"Oh, it's nothing. Not really. I just...I went to the cafe down the street, and I thought I'd bring you back a brownie to say congratulations. Now to be clear, I'm a bit biased because the owner is one of my very best friends, and also because brownies just so happen to be my all-time favorite food, but I can say with full conviction that the brownie in this container is the best brownie you will ever eat in your entire life."

Colin takes the small container from my outstretched hands, and I see in his eyes just how exhausted he is.

"Thank you, Jane. This means a lot to me. More than you know, actually." He sets the container on his desk and stares at it. "When Joe and Paul called me into the office this morning, I had no clue that they were going to promote me to partner. When they told me the news, you were the first person I thought of. You and I both know that you deserve this position over me, Jane." He lifts his eyes, and the exhaustion is now mixed with doubt. "I was sure you'd be taking the rest of the day off to plot some revenge plan to take me down, not buying me a celebratory dessert." He attempts a small smile.

I laugh. "If I'm being honest, you're lucky that you're dealing with me right now and not my friend Jordyn. Because if I hadn't stopped her, you would be getting an ass-kicking right now instead of that brownie."

We both chuckle at this, and then the air grows silent.

"Look, Jane—"

"Colin, I—"

We both try to break the awkward stillness between us at the same time, and the shared embarrassment makes both of our cheeks redden.

He tries again. "We both know you were the shoe-in for partner. It all happened so fast that I felt myself agreeing to the promotion before I even had the chance to really think about it. I'm not sure I'm ready for this right now. I'm not sure if I can even do it." He sits in his chair and runs his hands through his perfect, blond hair.

I take a deep breath. I really don't feel like reassuring someone who got the job that I deserved to get, but what the hell, I can tell he needs it.

"You've accomplished a lot as an attorney already, and this is just something new you can learn how to manage. I mean, obviously it's going to be a lot, probably even more than we could begin to guess."

He looks up at me, and I can sense I might be making it worse, so I switch gears. "You have a solid team of attorneys underneath you who will help while you find your groove. I'm not saying I'm totally happy about the decision, but I know you can do it. Also, I'm here for you while you figure it all out."

"Thanks, Jane, I...just thank you."

"Don't sweat it." I turn, headed toward the door. But before I exit, I turn back to face him and add, "Just don't mess it up. Because then I'll feel reeeeeaaaalllly bad if the guy who got the promotion I wanted does a shit job."

Colin smiles and gives a little nod as I close the door behind me.

I lean the back of my head against it while I gather my thoughts and prepare myself for the crazy ride I'm about to go on.

Chapter Three

"NAME UNDER RESERVATION AND ID, please," says the lady at the airport check-in counter, not even looking up from her computer. I can definitely tell that she doesn't find this morning nearly as exciting as I do.

I don't even hesitate as I animatedly pull out my special "travel wallet." I made it years ago, and I mark it as one of my greatest achievements. It holds everything I could ever possibly need while traveling. It's so intricately organized I feel like I'm winning the perfect traveler award every time I get to show it off.

Handing her my ID, I attempt to make light conversation. "Hi, Sheila, my name is Jane. Oh, yep you already know that...duh, you have my ID. Ha, um...anyway, you know there was a couple of months last year when I tried to use the app for my boarding pass, instead of having one printed out, but it's so funny because I actually missed having the physical thing in my hand, ya know?" An awkward laugh escapes me.

Sheila doesn't look at me.

"I love this part, I really do. It's the beginning of the adventure, right? It's like, after this moment, it's real." I smile before adding in a spooky voice, "There's no turning back now."

"Ma'am, are you wanting to 'turn back,' is that what you're saying?"

"Oh! No! I was...just...never mind."

"The scale is ready. Place the bag you want to check up here, please."

Now I'm not saying I'm *not* an overpacker, but I don't think I pack nearly as much as some people do. However, there is a small chance it could be overweight.

"Your bag is overweight," Sheila says unamused.

Shit. "Okay...um... I'll just take some stuff out and put it in my personal bag. Is that okay?"

"Whatever you wanna do, Miss."

Heaving my heavy bag off the scale, I tip it on its side and zip it open. Sitting right on top of everything I so carefully packed, is a Costco-sized box of condoms Jordyn must have snuck into it when she brought me to the airport this morning.

My cheeks flush as I hear an unapproving sigh come from up above me. A nervous laugh escapes my mouth as I quickly grab the condoms—and a handful of whatever else I can—and hurriedly shove them deep into my open purse. "Oh, man, I'm...um...I don't...I think it should be at weight now." My cheeks are still burning as I zip my suitcase shut and hoist it back onto the scale.

The anticipation grows as the scale is calculating the weight. I can feel my now overfull purse slowly sliding down my shoulder, warning me that there is no more room for anything else to be stuffed.

Sheila gives a little nod, then proceeds to tag my bag and put it on her side of the counter. A rush of relief slides down my spine as she passes me my boarding pass and ID.

"Thank you!" I say, with a big smile as she sends me on my way.

As soon as I turn around, I hear her let out an exasperated sigh and mutter quietly, "It's too early in the morning for this shit."

I laugh and smile to myself. It's almost noon.

I. Love. Airports. All the smells, the sounds, the hustle and bustle of people going places. For as long as I can remember, the airport has always been my special place.

As I make my way through the security checkpoint, I think back to when I was younger—going to the airport meant that

I was on my way to visit my favorite person in the entire world, my grandma Lolly, or Nan, as I called her.

Every fall, my family would pack our bags and fly to Ohio to pay her a visit. We would stay there for a few days at a time, listening to her stories, and watching her sew. Those trips are some of the best memories I have. In fact, they mean everything to me.

When I was seven years old, I remember pulling up to her house in our rental car, my parents arguing itineraries in the front seat while my heart felt like it was going to explode out of my chest with excitement.

I grabbed my backpack to retrieve whatever homemade crafts I had made for her in the past year since we had last seen each other. I could feel the smile on my face growing wider and wider as my parents opened the trunk to get out our luggage.

"Jane, I don't know how you have this much energy after the flight we've just had, but my goodness it looks like you're about to dance out of your skin," my mom had said.

"I can't wait! Can I please go to the door? Please can I go knock by myself?"

"Go ahead."

The happy anticipation at the thought of seeing my Nan bubbled out of every part of my body.

She opened the door in her brightly colored muumuu of choice and pink foam curlers in her white-as-snow hair. She looked down at me and pretended not to know who I was.

"Excuse me, Dear, who are you? What do you want? I'm going to need you to leave because I'm expecting my beautiful granddaughter here any minute, and you're standing in her way."

"Nan! It's me!" I laughed hysterically.

"Oh no, darling girl, while you might have the same pretty blonde hair as she has, I'll have you know that my beautiful granddaughter is much smaller than you are! She's not nearly as tall as you. I'm sure of it. Now if you will excuse me..." She slowly closed the door as more laughter erupted from deep inside my belly.

I dropped my backpack and scrambled to find something that she could remember me by. "Nan, it's me, I swear!" My words came out too fast, as I tried to pick out a memory that only she and I shared. "Remember...remember when I was here last time, and you made me gush the chocolate milk out of my nose?!" My laugh grew, as she brought her hand to her mouth attempting to conceal her smile. "'Member it was 'cause you accidentally called your Mr. Popper Cat, 'MR. POOP-ER CAT!'"

"Oh my!" She clutched her chest, giggling. Then, she brought me in closer and wrapped her gentle warm arms around me. "You really are my Bird! My oh my, how you have grown, my sugar! I can't believe you're really here! I've missed you, my Birdie girl."

Her hug grew tighter as I breathed in her cozy vanilla and cinnamon scent. I never wanted her to let go. She kissed the top of my head and invited me into her home. My safe place.

These are the memories that play through my head every time I'm at the airport. The anticipation and joy of escaping reality envelops my entire body. I love airports, and I think I always will for that reason.

I finish getting through security and slowly make the long journey to my gate. I'm browsing through some of the special airport-only shops when the smell of hot, greasy French fries fills my nose, and my stomach rudely reminds me that it's time for lunch.

The boy at Shake Shack who takes my order is a mixture between Ozzy Osbourne and Kevin McCallister from *Home Alone*. The long, black hair and thick black eyeliner, paired with the surprisingly sweet demeanor and loveable smile, is so heartwarming I don't even mind when he charges me for the extra cheese sauces.

A warm rush of gratitude slides itself down my spine as I take my tray to the table. Funny enough, something as simple as a giant burger with crispy fries and extra cheese sauce is what finally starts to put this whole thing into perspective.

I'm so freaking lucky—I have a stable job that pays incredibly well, and I'm on my way to Hawaii for ten whole days to meet an attractive billionaire resort owner, while also getting to drink piña coladas on the beach. Wow.

I take a big, juicy bite of my burger as I hear the cutest little laugh escape from the booth to my right. Still chewing, I turn my head and see a little girl with curly red piggy tales and a unicorn backpack whispering something into her dad's ear. He pulls a pretend look of surprise at the "secret" she just revealed to him, which makes her completely lose it and burst into the biggest belly laugh I've ever heard.

Hearing her laugh so hard makes me start to laugh. Now, this is cute when a three-year-old does it, but when a thirty-one-year-old woman who has just taken a bite of a burger does it, I'm sure it looks quite sad.

The girl and her dad look right at me, and it's at this point I can't differentiate if they're laughing *at* me or if we're all laughing together, but it honestly makes no difference. The three of us laugh so hard for so long that it becomes another point I add onto my airports-are-the-most-magical-places-in-the-world list.

After my meal, I grab my bags and continue the journey to my gate. It's no surprise however, that before I even come close, I find myself at an airport bookstore. I don't need a new book. I don't need a new book. I one-hundred percent don't need a new book.

In my personal bag alone, I have two books, and then a third and fourth in my checked bag. Let's not even mention the shelves at my apartment that are overflowing with countless hopeful to-be-reads.

I walk past the bookstore entrance, pretending to myself I'm not going to walk in, but who am I kidding, my foot crosses the threshold before my mind even registers what's happening.

Lazily scanning the shelves, I spy my favorite book in the entire world. I carefully take it off the shelf and hold it tightly to my chest. I know it's silly because obviously this isn't even the special copy my Nan gave me, but the effect it has on me is the same.

I mean, of course I did bring my special copy of *To Kill a Mockingbird* with me, but that doesn't stop me from seriously thinking about buying the one right here in my hands. I have multiple copies of it at home, but it almost feels like sacrilege to set it back down on the shelf.

"That's a fantastic book."

I turn to see what type of mouth this beautiful sentence just came from, when I come face to face with not only a beautiful mouth but an entire beautiful man staring back at me. The handsome stranger's mouth widens into a smile and says, "It really is a great book. The movie is far better, but it's still worth a read, for sure," the not-so-handsome-anymore man says with a wink.

I flinch back and swallow hard as I try to register what he just said. Standing here in horrified silence, I notice a worried crease popping up on his otherwise smooth forehead.

Before he can speak again, my years of debate team and law classes shove themselves to the front of my brain and the word vomit begins.

"I am, without a question in my mind, convinced that this book right here is what shaped the way Americans think about injustice, racism, and most of all, *humanity itself*. It holds one of the single most important lines in classic modern American literature, and I quote, 'You never really understand a person until you consider things from his point of view...until you climb into his skin and walk around in it.' The movie, while I admit it was a fantastic film that gave us a visual representation of the important story, didn't portray the complete picture of compassion and growth that the book did. So, all of this is to say that the movie is never better than the book. Ever. No matter the movie. No matter the book."

Mr. Stranger purses his lips, dips his head, and saunters off to find someone much less intense when it comes to books than I am. Good riddance. Who wants to talk to a guy who believes that any movie version of a book is better than the actual book anyway? Not me, that's who.

I question it again, but I realize I don't need two copies of this book on my ten-day vacation, so I tenderly place it back on the shelf and give a little reassuring *pat pat* on its cover when my phone buzzes. The notification that pops up informs me that my gate has changed, and I better haul ass to the other side of the terminal before boarding starts.

The exhilarating thought of paradise rushes through my brain. Tropical air is waiting for me. Blue skies and sandy beaches are just a few hours away.

The plane ride was uncomplicated and uneventful, which just so happens to be my favorite type of plane ride. I listened to a few new podcast episodes, drank two ice cold Diet Pepsis, and put together some important documents for Mr. Dumont to look over during our dinner tonight.

"Do you have any exciting things planned while you're here, Miss?" My Uber driver peeks at me from the rearview mirror.

We drive with all the windows down and the sunroof open, so the smell of fresh ocean air washes over me as we drive to the resort.

"Work mostly, but I'm hopefully going to get some much-needed sunshine and rest too."

"Sounds like my kind of vacation. What do you do for work, if you don't mind me asking?"

I take in a deep breath of that warm salty air and say confidently, "I'm an attorney. My firm just acquired Howard

Dumont, the owner of Dumont Luxury Resorts as our client, so I'm here just to get things rolling."

"Woah, big time, Miss! I don't know if you'll have much time to rest then," he says with his welcoming Hawaiian grin. "But if you do find yourself hungry while you're here, you be sure to go visit my brudda Leo down at Kekoa Family Poke. It's the best poke you'll ever eat, and if you tell them that Liam sent you, they'll only charge you double the price." He laughs.

"If the poke is as good as you say it is, then paying double sounds fair." I chuckle to myself and rest my head on the seat behind me. I am in heaven. I can feel the tension in my muscles melting away with each passing mile.

We pull up to the resort, and my eyeballs feel like they are about to fall right out of my head. When I heard the term "luxury resorts," a clear picture popped into my head. But now, that picture in my mind looks like a Best Western compared to the grandeur that is currently in front of me.

I step out of the Uber, and Liam gets out to help me with my bags. "Nice digs, huh?"

Words are having a hard time coming out of my mouth, so I just stare wide-eyed at the mammoth resort in front of me.

"Have a good vacation, Miss, and get yourself a pair of slippahs while you're here. Those tennis shoes will be full of sand before you even get into the building."

I look down at my shoes and let out a laugh. "Oh, I definitely will. Thanks for all your help, Liam."

"No problem, Miss. A Hui Hou." He gives me his big happy smile before getting into his car and driving off.

I turn back to the resort, and I'm met with the most drop-dead gorgeous woman I've ever laid eyes upon. Her thick, dark hair is almost to her waist and her tawny-colored eyes are mesmerizing. She gently places a necklace of brightly colored flowers around my neck and welcomes me graciously into the resort.

A rush of cool air hits me as I enter through the glass doors. The giant lobby is full of people coming and going. Families in swimsuits with little kids running around their feet, wealthy businessmen sporting cheesy Hawaiian-print shirts, and gorgeous women in long, breezy dresses and sun-kissed skin.

I feel severely out of place in my leggings and running shoes, but what can I say, comfort trumps beauty when I travel.

The check-in goes smoothly and a very handsome bellhop grabs my bags from behind me before I even have the chance to protest. He leads the way to the elevators with a smile on his face, and I can tell the next ten days are going to go by much too fast.

Once I'm alone inside my room, I rush over to the balcony and slide open the doors. Stepping out into the warm air, I gaze at the beautiful blue water glistening in the sunlight down below. Giant green palms sway in the breeze, and I hear people laughing on the beach. I could get used to this.

Turning back into my room, I take a running leap and Superman-dive onto the fluffy, white bed, and inhale the fresh laundry scent. I can't believe I'm really here.

My body sinks deeper into the soft downy comforter, and my long day of travel finally catches up to me. I turn to look at the clock on the nightstand and feel a sense of relief rush through me. It's only 6:30. At home it's nearly ten p.m., which means I would most definitely be in bed ready for sleep. No wonder I feel extra tired.

I have some time before I need to get ready for my dinner with Mr. Dumont, so I'm going to bask in the light of this moment and, for the first time in a long time, rest. I lay still and close my eyes, a small smile still on my lips. My heart feels so full.

Chapter Four

I FINISH OFF THE fancy drink in my hand, then quickly gulp down an entire second one directly after. Holy cow, this virgin mojito is the best drink I've ever tasted. I made the executive decision to forego the alcohol at the moment to ensure my *right-headedness* when I meet Mr. Dumont for the first time.

I've been told many times I have a tendency to become a bit giddy and flirtatious when I drink, and I need to make sure that I avoid that happening at all costs tonight. *God, could you imagine?* A shudder rolls down my spine.

With her head held high and a wide smile on her face, the hostess slowly walked me to the corner of the dimly lit restaurant and sat me down at Mr. Dumont's personal table.

There is absolutely no question that this is the best seat in the house. The giant grand piano is in full view, but the music is quiet enough for me to still hear myself think. It's just me, myself, and I in this cozy, little bubble. The best part, however, is that I'm surrounded by floor-to-ceiling windows overlooking the crystal blue water glistening down below.

The sun is just beginning to set, and I can see families playing in the sand and couples walking hand in hand on the water's edge. Watching these little scenes of happiness unfold tugs at something in my heart, and I can't look away. The way they all seem so comfortable with each other. The way each of them is smiling and laughing, like they don't have a care in the world. I never had a family life like that. I never got to feel so uninhibited and secure. I want that. So bad.

There is one family with a little boy who lugs bucket after bucket of sand up to where his family is sitting and continues to pour each of them onto his dad's big laughing belly. The little sister, who looks to be about two, sits in her mama's lap while she reads her a story. They all look so in love. So content and happy. It's beautiful.

I slowly turn my attention to a couple standing down by the water, letting the waves lap against their feet. The young man's arms are around the woman's slender shoulders as they gaze out into the water, just as the sun begins to dip under the horizon. My mind wanders to what they could be talking about. Getting married? Having kids of their own? The important questions that have somehow eluded me in every relationship I've been in.

If that were Rex and me down there, he would be whispering sweet nothings in my ear about some sports something or other, and I would be mulling over my never-ending laundry list of to-dos. Romantic indeed.

I feel my phone buzz from inside my purse, and I know it's from Jordyn before I even look.

Jordyn

> How's paradise babe?

Jane

> I'm in heaven, J. How's the snow? Haha

Jordyn

> Not funny. I'm freezing my ass off over here!

> Hey, how's Richie Rich Resort Owner? Have you asked him yet if he's looking for a second wife?

> Please tell him I'm extremely witty, very single, and FANTASTIC in bed. kthxbye

Jane

> Lol. I'll leave that part up to you.

I haven't even met him yet. I'm actually waiting for him right now.

Also, I'm drinking a super fancy drink and eating some super fancy bread. If you couldn't tell, I'm being super fancy right now.

Jordyn

What a life you lead my friend.

Get back to your glamorous dinner and please don't forget about us little people when you're sitting pretty.

PS I'm expecting full details when you're done. Love you.

Before sliding my phone back into my bag, I check the time and I'm shocked to find out that Mr. Dumont is more than twenty minutes late. My anxiety-prone mind starts to go through a list of reasons this could be.

Am I at the wrong resort restaurant? Did I get the time wrong? Did something bad happen to him? Before I dig myself too deep into a worry hole, I decide to set a timer to remind myself to start really worrying in ten minutes when he's thirty minutes late. *Classic.* Setting a timer to worry. I could possibly be a crazy person.

I'm mid-sip of my drink when a handsome man in a suit approaches my table with a troubled look on his face. Oh no, this can't be good.

"Excuse me, are you Ms. Robins? From Schwartz & Adler?"

"Yes, I am, is everything alright?"

He hands me a wireless telephone. "I have a call for you from Mr. Dumont."

I straighten my dress and check my breath into my hand (like an idiot because it's a phone call), then clear my throat.

"Hello, this is Jane Robins."

"Jane! This is Howard Dumont. It's lovely to finally get to talk to you. Hey, I'm incredibly sorry, but I've had an emergency investor meeting that was called at my Thailand Resort. I'm currently 35,000 feet up in the air. I'm sorry to miss our meeting."

"Oh, Mr. Dumont, it's really no problem. I'm sure we can arrange another time to get together when you make it back."

"Jane, this mess is going to take quite a while. I'm not entirely sure when I'll be back on the island."

The color leeches out of my face. No more vacation for me then. Back to reality. Back to the snow. I can literally feel the ocean teasing me from outside the window.

"Alright, no problem, Mr. Dumont. I'll catch a flight first thing in the morning and hopefully be back in the office by tomorrow evening. I'll work out a time with your assistant for us to jump on a quick Zoom call to get things started. Does that work for you?"

"Tomorrow?" he says gruffly.

Okay, wow. This isn't going as planned.

"Jane, I planned for you to stay ten days at my resort, and that means you'd better be staying ten days at my resort. Just because my investors think I have nothing better to do than fly across the ocean at the drop of a hat, doesn't mean you need to change your plans. I just got off the phone with the partners at your firm, and they agree with my decision. Enjoy your vacation, and we'll touch base again when I have all this other stuff figured out."

Then he just hangs up. Not another word. Like he didn't just drop a grenade right into my lap by saying that I get to take ten entire days off from real life. *A vacation*—just me, the blue ocean, and pure unadulterated bliss.

Passing the phone back to the suited man, I ask him to bring me an actual mojito this time, with double the alcohol, and the biggest brownie they offer. He nods with a knowing smile and heads to the kitchen.

Pulling my phone back out of my purse, I enthusiastically press the cancel button on my worry timer. *God, that feels good.*

I close my eyes and start dreaming of all the wonderful things I'm going to do over the next few days. I picture the mountain of books I'll read, the various desserts I'll get to eat, the tropical drinks I'll get to try. My mouth starts to water and a smile blooms on my face.

I just begin to envision the hard washboard abs of the man I'm going to have my vacation fling with, when I hear the chair across from me scootch out from underneath the table. I abruptly open my eyes to see who's joining me.

No. This can't be happening. Not now.

You have got to be kidding me. Literally the only person in the entire world who could have ruined this vacation for me just sat down at my table. This man. This handsome, charismatic, insanely irritating, completely irresistible man.

He sits across from me with those stupid, beautiful dimples, and a twinkle in his big, brown eyes.

Noah Riley.

"Hi, Jane. It's been a long time."

Chapter Five
Fourteen Years Earlier

Fort Collins, Colorado

My ancient locker is stuck again. I've already entered the combo three times, and it still won't open.

Saying a quick prayer to the locker gods and putting my fingers up to try one last time, the tall redhead boy whose locker is right next to mine saunters up. I pause what I'm doing and watch him, interested in what he's going to do when his decides not to open either. But then, I swear to God, it opens without him even touching it.

I purse my lips and glare at him. I'm not entirely sure why, but I feel slightly offended by the locker's obvious show of favoritism.

Glancing from him to his locker, the idea pops into my head that maybe I could just ask him if I can leave my books in his locker until tomorrow. I open my mouth to speak, then quickly shut it again, remembering the fact I've never even said one word to this kid, so asking him to use his locker would be horrifically awkward.

Crap. I really don't want to bring my heavy backpack to the debate tournament. It seriously weighs like four-hundred pounds with all my books in it. I start looking around the hallway for a place I can stash my books when the kid slams his locker shut. The force of his closing makes mine pop open effortlessly. *Thanks, guy.*

After quickly piling my books inside my locker, I race to the bus, praying to the transportation gods that it hasn't left without me. Oh man, could you imagine if I missed the first debate of the year? A shiver creeps down my spine at the thought. That wouldn't be good at all.

I make it to the bus just as the doors close. *Great.* I hesitantly bring my hand up and give a little knock on the glass door, hoping the driver sees me before she takes off, and I'm completely out of luck.

My reflection in the door stares back at me, and I can tell that my hair is a mess from my impromptu jogging session. I try my best to smooth it down as the bus driver opens the door and slowly eyes me up and down. From the look on her face, I can't tell if she's questioning if I'm on the debate team, or if she's questioning her career choice. But either way, she's definitely annoyed.

Giving her the friendliest smile I can possibly muster, I step onto the bus and make my way to my seat in the front row.

The bus ride is bumpy and extremely loud. Students are shouting over the roar of the engine, and music is playing from one of the CD players someone brought along.

Even with all the chaos happening around me, I don't stop going over my arguments for the upcoming debate. This is the first tournament of my senior year, and I couldn't be more excited.

Coach Christensen informed us in class that depending on how we do today, he will be picking the captain for this year's team.

Becoming the debate team captain is basically all that I've thought about all summer long. I know it's not the most important thing in the world, but honestly, it would look great on my college applications. My dream is to go to law school and becoming captain would make it that much easier to get into the exact program I want, and to me, *that*'s the most important thing in the world.

I can't wait to graduate. I can't wait to be an attorney in some big city somewhere with good friends and coffee by the bucketloads. I can't wait to live in some shiney new apartment on the high floor of some tall modern building, with all of my own things. I can't wait to start my life.

But first, I have to win this debate and become team captain. I can do it too. I know I can. I was up all night putting together my notes and finalizing every little detail. It's extremely important that everything looks and feels absolutely perfect. I have all my thoughts organized in my special color-coded binder with everything marked and highlighted just the way I like it.

I repeat my talking points over and over in my mind until I can recite them forward and backward without any pauses in between. At this point, there is no way I'm losing this. I'm too good at what I do. Debate just comes naturally to me. It's like I don't even have to think about it. I know what to say and when to say it and always have.

Just pulling up to Fossil Ridge High School, it's easy to see how much nicer it is than our school. It was only built a few years ago, so everything is all shiny and new.

Walking through the front doors, I'm hit with the strongest rich kid vibes I've ever felt in my life. Every single kid sitting in the large common area is absolutely stunning. I'm not kidding when I say that each one of them looks like they could have a contract with Abercrombie & Fitch. Long blonde hair, low-waisted jeans, polos with the collars flipped up, and Oakley sunglasses on the top of their heads.

Sure, there are some preppy rich kids at my school who dress like this, but it's definitely not *everyone*.

A blush creeps over my entire body. I feel so out of place. Sure, our whole team is dressed perfectly fine and none of us are really hurting for money, but it's pretty clear none of us fit in with this crowd.

The Fossil Ridge students stare as our group moves to the auditorium. God, I feel so uncomfortable. I feel like I have a sign around my neck that says, "Howdy partners. I'm new 'round here. Mind showing a poor ol' country girl like myself 'round these parts?"

Heat starts in my toes and rolls its way up my spine. I'm suddenly very hot. The feelings of inadequacy paired with the anticipation for my upcoming debate have scrambled all my thoughts.

Sweat begins to prickle on my scalp; I need some fresh air, pronto. I look at my watch and realize we still have a bit before the tournament begins, so I wander the halls looking for a way outside.

When I open the door, the sweet Colorado air hits me immediately. I take a deep breath in, and my nerves instantly start to dissipate. I shake out my hands trying to get the blood back into them.

You got this, Jane. You can do this. You're going to kick Fossil Ridge's ass. Asses? Doesn't matter. You're going to win this tournament and become team captain.

I jump around a bit, feeling pumped. Then, out of nowhere, I hear someone behind me clear their throat. I freeze. *Crap. Of course I'm not alone.*

Closing my eyes, hoping to God that they just leave and let me steep in my utter embarrassment on my own, I hold my breath and don't move a muscle.

I don't hear anything. No movement, no talking, no more clearing of the throat. Nothing. *Did I imagine it*? I turn my head, and that's the moment I come face to face with the most attractive guy I've ever seen in my life.

His wavy, chestnut-colored hair and smooth bronze skin are glowing in the warm afternoon light. His jaw is sharp, and his lips are full. *Holy crap, he's hot.* Those nerves I just tried so hard to get rid of, return with a vengeance.

"Oh, sorry, I didn't know anyone was out here. I was just hot…like temperature hot, not like looks hot. I just felt, like, really warm, so I decided to come out and get some fresh air." I breath in a shaky breath, awkwardly fanning myself. "Whew, that's better. Well, I'm going to head back inside now."

I reach for the handle but before I can open the door, I hear him scoff. "Maybe you're hot because you're wearing a turtleneck in August."

Wow, attractive and rude. That's a new one…

I turn my attention back to him. He's staring at me with big, dark brown eyes and a perfectly crooked smile.

"First of all, it's obviously not a *turtleneck*. It's a light crewneck sweatshirt. They're two entirely different things. Second, it's my favorite crewneck sweatshirt, and I wear it to all my special competitions because it's super lucky and helps me win. Third, it's not even that hot of a sweatshirt, and I can take it off if I want to." I cross my arms over my chest.

He raises his eyebrows and does nothing to hide the smirk on his face.

"Oh, come on! I have a shirt under it! Ugh, that's totally beside the point anyway...I was hot because I was nervous about my debate coming up, so I came out to get some air. Clearly that didn't work because now I'm even more hot because a stupid boy is being rude and presumptuous to me." I say all of this with an exasperated huff, pulling my sweatshirt off over my head.

"You're on Poudre High's debate team?" Stupid-hot-rude-boy asks me.

"Yes." I scowl, smoothing down my hair.

"Cool. I'll see you in there then." He grabs the door handle and steps inside the school.

Well, this is just great.

The auditorium we're competing in is absolutely massive. It's clearly state-of-the art, and the acoustics are fantastic. The debaters could whisper into their microphones, and I'm sure it would be heard loud and clear in the back row.

It looks like the Fossil Ridge team brought about eighteen kids or so, which is a good thing because our school brought sixteen. That means our entire team will all have the chance to show Coach what we got.

I look to my left for the umpteenth time to peek at what stupid-hot-rude-boy is doing. Since it's only been about ten seconds since the last time I checked, he's still just staring forward, watching the current debate unfolding on the stage.

This annoys me. No one, and I mean *no one*, is that interested in the politics of water usage in our town. Also, I don't think he's looked through the crowd even once to see if he could spot me. Not that I would even want him to search for me, because he's so obviously full of himself, but nevertheless, it's irritating that he hasn't even looked away from the stage once.

The competitors on stage finish up with their last rebuttal, and the winner is announced. So far, Poudre is in the lead with only one more debate of the night to go. My debate. It's finally my chance to shine.

I walk up onto the stage and take my place. I move the microphone down to my level, take out my notes, and inhale a big, deep breath to center myself.

I look over at my opponent and see that it's none other than stupid-hot-rude-boy at the podium opposite mine. My fists clench the papers in my hands.

Stepping forward, the moderator begins. "Okay, ladies and gentlemen, this is going to be our last debate of the tournament. First, on the affirmative side, we'll be hearing from the Fossil Ridge debate team captain, and then following the cross-examination we'll hear from Poudre High. Fossil Ridge, are you ready to begin?"

Hot-rude-boy nods his head and brings his microphone closer to his mouth. "Thank you, Mr. Nielson. Before I begin, I would just like to introduce myself. My name is Noah Riley, and as debate team captain, I would like to thank you all for coming here to Fossil Ridge this afternoon. This has been a wonderful tournament so far, and now that it's my turn, I'm excited to settle the score and see which school ends up taking the win." He flashes the audience a big, bright smile, then turns his attention on me and winks. *What. A. Dick.*

That's it. That's all it takes for all of my hard work and preparations from the night before to go flying right out the window. This freaking boy has gotten me so worked up that the debate that follows is a complete catastrophe. The worst part of it all is that he knows it too.

The level of confidence he exudes is amazing. He goes through each of his arguments with absolute ease and does it all while grinning ear to ear. He's so convincing that I find myself nodding and agreeing with every point that he makes. *What a mess.*

At the end of the debate, the moderator comes back on stage and announces Noah Riley as the winner of our round. If this was any other debate, I would put up a fight if I felt like I deserved the win, but this is certainly not one of those times.

My shoulders drop, accepting my defeat.

Noah turns and walks over to me with that stupid, dimpled grin of his. He shakes my hand before bringing me in close. He slowly bends down and whispers in my ear, "Looks like it's time to get a new sweatshirt."

Chapter Six

Now

"WHAT THE HELL ARE you doing here?!" I yell, although I'm really trying my best not to. I rip the napkin off my lap and throw it down on the table. A few people from the surrounding tables glance our way, probably hoping to witness something they can tell their friends about later.

"Nice to see you again too." He flashes me a beautiful white smile.

Shit.

The way he's able to talk so calmly, when I feel as though I'm about to pop like a can of biscuits, is so incredibly frustrating. I close my eyes and curl my hands into fists on the table. With each passing second, my anger increases, and I feel my blood pressure starting to rise.

Why is he here, why is he here, *why the fuck is he here*?

I clench my jaw, and my heart continues to beat faster and faster.

I open my eyes, hoping he'll be gone, but of course I'm not that lucky. There he is. Noah Riley, all grown up and staring at me with those same piercing brown eyes that he had all those years ago. I want a minute to take him in. This adult version of the boy I used to know.

If I thought he was attractive when he was younger, that was nothing compared to what I'm staring at now. The past fourteen years have clearly been good to him. His broad shoulders strain against the crisp lines of his beautifully tailored suit. His once shaggy skater-boy hair is now expertly cut and styled to perfection.

Slowly tracing the line down his face, I feel my breath catch as I take in his offensively sharp jaw covered with short, neat facial hair that is practically begging to be touched.

Nope. Nope. Nope. I shake the uncouth thoughts from my poor, confused mind. I shoot him a glare, daring him to speak. But much to my dismay, he doesn't say a single word. He just continues staring at me, waiting for me to break. *Fine then.*

"Noah, really. What are you doing here? In Hawaii? At this specific restaurant? Right now?"

The corner of his mouth twitches. "I was just going to ask you the same thing." His smile grows, but I don't take the bait. "You look great by the way."

He stares at me intently, the cocky smile still on his face. He raises his eyebrows waiting for me to talk, but when I don't budge, he continues instead. "I work for a law firm in

New York, and we recently acquired the owner of this resort as a client. The partners at my firm put me in charge of his account. I'm *here* because I'm supposed to be meeting him and a colleague here," he says smugly, looking around. "However, I don't see him here yet. I'm a bit late because my flight just got in, but I was sure they would beat me here."

What the actual hell?! My mind is racing, and my heart feels like it's going to beat out of my chest. "Ha ha. Very funny, Noah. First, I want you to tell me exactly how and why you know all this information about me, and then I would like you to tell me the *real* reason why you're here."

He pauses from looking around and stares at me, his brows scrunched together. Utter confusion is written all over his face.

"Noah, you can stop with the pretend, 'I don't know what you're talking about' crap and tell me what's going on."

"Jane," he says, one eyebrow raised. "I'm not pretending anything. I honestly don't know what you're talking about."

I raise my hands to my face and knead my temples with my fingers. Ugh. Why does every interaction with this man have to be so frustrating?

"Okay, then." I take a deep breath, attempting to gather my composure. "I'll start." I speak slowly, "I, Jane Robins, am a top attorney for a law firm in Denver called Schwartz & Adler. I, Jane Robins, was put in charge of a new client named Howard Dumont who owns this resort. I, Jane Robins, was asked, by Mr. Dumont himself, to fly here to Hawaii to go over some introductory information and client documents."

Noah's eyes grow wide. He looks genuinely perplexed. "You work for Schwartz & Adler?"

I nod my head.

"*I* work for Schwartz & Adler," he says slowly.

A burst of laughter erupts out of me. It's too loud and too stark for this nice of a restaurant, but at this point, it's completely out of my control.

Of course, he would work for the same firm that I work for. Of course, he would be put on the freaking top-tier client that I just got and have been working my entire career for. Of course, he would be the one sitting across from me at this beautiful, romantic restaurant in the middle of fucking paradise after I just learned I wouldn't have to worry about anything for ten whole days. Of course. Of course. Of course. This is how it is with him. Every. Single. Time.

The already awkward tension between us grows larger as my nervous laugh subsides, and the two of us are left sitting in a charged silence. My mind is going a million miles a minute, and I see the gears turning behind his eyes as well.

We both sit, still as statues, neither one of us knowing what to do next. Where do we even start? Where do we go from here? Who should ask questions first? What are the questions we even need to ask?

I look up from the table and gaze into his eyes. He swallows hard but doesn't speak, so I continue. "Okay. So, if what you're saying is true, then we both work for Schwartz & Adler. I guess that's not too crazy, because honestly, I've never even talked to anyone from our New York office, let alone met them in person. So, I guess it is possible you could work there." I stare at him, hoping he'll give me something, anything to help me figure this out, but his face remains neutral. "That leads me to the part I can't quite wrap my head around...how did you know about Mr. Dumont? Last month, Schwartz announced to our entire office that I would be taking the Dumont account. He never once mentioned that someone from the New York office would be working on it with me."

His eyebrows raise, and he just shrugs his shoulders. "I really have no idea what is going on here. I was sitting in my office yesterday afternoon when Adler informed me that both he and Schwartz needed me to fly to Hawaii ASAP to meet with my new client, Mr. Dumont, and go over strategies for the upcoming year. Truthfully, I didn't get much more than that. He did mention that someone from the Denver office would also be on the account, but he never said who. He definitely didn't tell me it would be you."

Ouch. Why did that sting?

"By the way, where is he?" he says, checking his watch. His very *expensive* watch.

I look at Noah, completely baffled by this entire situation.

Why did the partners ask someone, just yesterday, to join the account? Do they not think I can do this? Do they think I'm incapable of handling everything? Why didn't Joe mention any of this to me? I shake the thoughts out of my head and try to concentrate on what I should do next.

Sitting up straighter, I cross my legs. "Mr. Dumont's not coming. He got called away to Thailand last minute and doesn't know when he'll be back."

Noah's brows pinch together. "Well, okay, then. What does that mean for us?"

Us? Ick. I do not enjoy being an *us* with Noah Riley. History has taken care of that for me. "I don't know what it means for *you*, but I just got off the phone with Mr. Dumont, and he said that *I* get to stay here for the next ten days and have the paid vacation of a lifetime. So, that's exactly what I'm going to do. I don't really care what you decide to do."

Liar.

I am a bold-faced liar. As a matter of fact, I care entirely too much about what he does. Even just knowing he's here on the same island as me, feels like it changes everything.

"Okay, then, I guess I'll call Adler to see what he wants *me* to do." He folds his arms across his chest.

"Good idea," I say, folding my arms across my chest too.

A moment of tense silence passes between us, before Noah speaks again. His voice is quieter, like he's trying to work something out in his mind. "So...if they say that I should stay...does that mean we have to...do we work together? Do you, like, want to get together and talk?"

"NO!" The word rips itself loudly from my mouth and all other commotion in the restaurant goes quiet. This isn't going well.

The silence stretches for another uncomfortable minute, but the hushed conversations around us slowly begin to come alive again. Albeit they are now all about the crazy yelling blonde girl and tall, dark, and handsome man arguing in the corner, but hey, at least now there's some noise.

"Noah, if you're going to be staying, then there are going to be some pretty hard lines that we DO NOT cross." I draw both a metaphorical and literal line with my finger on the table.

The corner of his mouth lifts into a smirk. "Please go on..."

I narrow my eyes at him and throw my hands up in surrender. "You know what, let's just stay as far away from each other as we possibly can and pretend like this whole thing never happened. You do your thing, and I'll very happily do mine. When we're back on the mainland, we'll tell Joe and Paul that you should be taken off the Dumont account. Then, we never, ever have to see or talk to one another ever again. Sound good?"

"Woah, woah, woah. Rewind just a bit. Why am *I* the one that needs to be taken off the account? The partners told me to come. They clearly know that my experience is needed to handle Mr. Dumont. Why don't *you* ask to be taken off, since *you're* the one that obviously can't handle working with someone else." He sits in his chair with a smug smile on his face.

God, he's such an asshole. I don't know how he does it, but he knows exactly what to say to push all my buttons and get me all worked up. He's insufferable.

The way he makes me feel all my emotions to the highest degree is something that no other person has ever done before, or since. No matter what, the minute this man enters my orbit, every little thing I've ever felt in my entire life hits me like a brick, and I feel it all at the same time.

The last time we saw each other, all those years ago, broke me. I'm not sure I could do that again. I don't even *want* to do that again. I thought I was done with this, with him. But yet, here we are. My chest starts to constrict. I can feel my heart beating deep inside my temples.

"Noah, I'm not doing this with you right now. I'm not going to be seeing, talking to, or even thinking about you for the next ten days. After the ten days are up, I'll go to Joe myself and tell him there's absolutely *no way* we can work together. Then, it'll be up to him and Paul to work out. Okay?" I say through gritted teeth.

He nods.

"Good. That settles it then. While we're here, just mind your own business, and I'll mind mine."

The second these words leave my mouth, our attractive young waiter, timidly, approaches our table. He gently sets down my beautiful brownie and much needed non-virgin mojito, then asks quietly if we want to hear the specials.

"No, thank you, just the check please," I say with a half-hearted smile, at the same time as Noah says, "Yes, that sounds great."

Our poor waiter does a little dance of indecision. He takes a step like he's about to leave our table, and then takes that exact same step back.

Putting him out of his misery, I quickly grab a fifty-dollar bill out of my wallet and put it under my drink glass. "I'll just leave this here then. Thank you." I slide my chair out from the table, as the waiter begins to explain the specials to Noah.

"Aren't you going to finish your drink before you go?" Noah asks, voice oozing smugness.

God, please stop me from punching this man in the face.

Closing my eyes, pursing my lips, and shaking my head, I try harder than I've ever tried in my entire life to find that inner "zen" my therapist has tried to drill into my head. Deep breath in, and a long, slow breath out.

I open my eyes and carefully stare into his. There is mischief dancing behind those deep brown eyes, and I hope he can see that I'm not going to play.

We hold this tense stare while our waiter pointlessly continues listing the specials no one is going to be eating.

My eyes narrow as I curve my mouth into a sly smile. I stand, grab my drink, and pound it down in one gulp. "Keep the change."

The satisfaction I felt when walking away from Noah doesn't last nearly as long as I would have liked.

While walking back to my room, an entire ocean's worth of emotions crash through me and threaten to spill over. It's been years since I've laid eyes on that man, and my brain can't comprehend everything that just happened.

I feel like I'm on a rollercoaster ride. Going from mad, to happy, to nervous, to irate, to annoyed, to excited, to sad, so on and so forth, until I can't make sense of anything anymore.

I know the speed at which I downed my drink isn't helping matters either. The heat of the alcohol sitting in my empty stomach burns, and I realize I didn't even get to eat my brownie.

Now I'm even more upset.

Getting back to my suite, I fling my heels off at the door. I walk farther into the room and smile happily at the gorgeous bed staring back at me.

Plopping my butt down onto the fluffy comforter, I try again to process the insane plot twist that my life just took. Ten days in Hawaii?! No work to do? Noah Fucking Riley?! *What. A. Shitshow.*

I do my best to push it all out of my mind and decide to leave it for Tomorrow Jane to unravel.

I struggle to pull my tight-fitting dress over my head. It takes longer than it should because I'm sitting and absolutely refuse to get up, so when I do finally wriggle myself free, I feel a wave of triumph.

Shoes off. Check.

Dress off. Check.

Makeup off. Not check. *Damn.*

From my place atop the bed, I look around the room for the makeup bag I flung haphazardly after I was done getting ready for the super fancy dinner I was supposed to attend with my new, super-rich client. Spoiler alert, that didn't happen.

I spot it on the floor next to the full-length mirror just to the left of me. The rum in my system is making my head feel swimmy, and I don't want to get up from my cozy spot in bed, so I slide down and reach as far as I possibly can without having to leave my warm little nest. *Got it*! *Triumphant again*!

Taking out the makeup wipes, I try to focus on the positive things that could happen while I'm here.

Gently wiping my eyes, I imagine all the yummy tropical drinks I'll get to have, the numerous exotic fish I might get to see, and all the impossibly hot men I'll hopefully get to meet. I bite back the smile blooming on my face. See, three positive things. I'm so good at this. These thoughts will definitely help me forget all the Noah mess that happened tonight.

I finish removing my makeup, switch off the lamp next to me, then squish down deeper into the glorious bed.

As my head hits the soft pillow, a small chuckle escapes me. I'm so glad I'm not in a movie right now or this situation would be so much worse.

Noah and I would have to share this room, but there would only be one bed, and we would end up fighting about who would sleep on the bed and who would take the couch...who knows what would happen?

My laughter is replaced with a small sense of dread. That would be the worst.

As long as Noah and I stay far away from each other, absolutely nothing can go wrong.

Chapter Seven
Then

T HE LAST DEBATE TOURNAMENT was a complete and utter disaster. I've rehashed the entire event countless times, and I get more and more irate every time I think about it.

Whenever I close my eyes, I see Noah and that smug little smile he gave me when he won. *Looks like it's time to get a new sweatshirt.* I still haven't come up with a good comeback for that little nugget of nastiness, but I sure am trying.

These past few weeks, I've been doing some sleuthing about jerkface Noah Riley, and here is what I've gathered so far. I was immediately able to tell that he's popular. In every picture on his MySpace page, he's surrounded by tons of friends. And girls. Tons of girls.

His pictures are full of him and friends hanging out at the lake, playing soccer, having bonfires, or camping. How can someone be such a social butterfly while also making time for being debate team captain? It doesn't make any sense to me. And, it makes me angry.

Although I made a total fool of myself during the last debate, Coach still made me our team captain. He said he was proud of me for competing, even though I was so clearly *under the weather*. However, as you know, I definitely was not *under the weather*, I just happened to be completely disoriented by a very attractive asshole. But, of course, I didn't share this embarrassing teenage girl fact with my coach, because I was just made team captain, and I didn't want to spoil it.

"This lunch looks especially inedible," Jordyn says, scrunching up her face. Shoving aside her lunch tray, she grabs my hands from across the cafeteria table and smiles big, showing all of her beautifully straight teeth.

"What's going on?" I say, confusion coloring my face.

"Tyler..." she says slowly with a smile blooming on her lips, "invited me to the lake next weekend to hang out with him and some of his soccer friends. I want you to come with me!"

Tyler is Jordyn's boyfriend. He's two years older than us and is on the boys' soccer team at Colorado State.

Jordyn got an early acceptance and full-ride soccer scholarship to go there next year, so she had to go to some orientation thing, and Tyler happened to be the one leading it.

She's so freakishly good at soccer that Tyler spent some *extra* time with her, if you know what I mean, and Jordyn fell hard right then and there. They've basically been connected at the hip ever since. They're so adorably in love that sometimes it makes me question if there's something wrong with me.

I don't date much. It's not that I'm against it, I just don't really do it. I mean, I've gone out with some guys here and there, but the dates have never really gotten romantic.

I know it's my fault, because the thought of having to pay attention to a boyfriend, on top of everything else I already have on my plate, sounds exhausting.

I'm graduating this year, which will be the most important thing that has ever happened to me. I've been looking forward to getting out of here for as long as I can remember, and I want to be on my own and start my life. So, boyfriends will just have to wait.

My entire life has had one focus, one goal. I have to get the best grades possible, so that I'll be accepted into an Ivy League.

Both of my parents attended Ivy League schools, which, to them, means if I choose anything else, I'm a complete and absolute failure.

My parents are the type of parents who have only ever paid attention to me if I do something wrong; something that doesn't match their priorities. Or, in other words, as long as I act one-hundred percent perfect at all times, they pretty much ignore me.

Don't get me wrong, they're good to me and have always made sure that I get everything I need, they just totally suck at showing me any type of affection. I don't think the sayings, *I love you*, *you're doing great,* or God forbid, *I'm proud of you,* have ever been uttered in our household.

Truthfully, I don't even call them Mom and Dad anymore. I've called them Carol and Dan for as long as I can remember, because Mom and Dad just don't sound right.

That type of affection is reserved solely for my Nan. She's Dan's mom, and she's the best person I've ever met. My Nan is the one who pushes me to do things for myself. She's always been my biggest cheerleader, and I want to make her proud.

She's the reason I'll do everything in my power to keep getting good grades. She's the reason I know I'll eventually get my dream job and make tons of money. I'll do it for her.

I just have to make sure that no one gets in the way of me accomplishing these goals. No more boys making me flustered during a debate and making me lose. No more Noah Riley.

"Will there be boys there?" I ask Jordyn, feigning interest in the mystery meat on my tray.

"Is that a real question?" She looks at me, arms crossed, and pure sass on her face. "Of course there will be boys there. What do you think I meant when I said Tyler and his soccer friends? He's bringing some of the guys from his team, and a few other friends from school."

With big, brown puppy dog eyes, she continues, "Please, please, please...I don't want to be the only girl there. I can only handle so much soccer talk, Jane." She shakes her head, hoping I'm on her side, but from the look on her face, I'm guessing she can tell I'm not sold yet. "Look, I'll even let you bring a book! Your favorite book! Or homework! I mean, I don't know why you would even want to, but hey, I won't stop you. Please come. Please."

"Okay, okay. I'll come. But you're not setting me up with anyone, and I'm going to bring my debate notes to go over. Deal?" I raise my eyebrows and offer her my hand.

"You're so weird. But okay. We have a deal!" She says happily, grabbing my hand and shaking it fiercely. "We have a deal."

The rest of the school day is boring and uneventful. The only thing on my mind is the debate tournament happening this afternoon.

I'm not one of those people who hates public speaking. I love it, actually. There's nothing I take more delight in than standing in front of people, telling them what I think. But after how my last debate went, I'm not so sure that's the case anymore.

I stand by my locker checking and rechecking all my notes, memorizing every argument, and trying my best to kick these nerves, but it's proving to be difficult. My stomach bubbles with an overwhelming feeling of impending doom.

It's so strange, because I know I'm a good debater. I know I have tons of skill and knowledge, but my confidence is shaky since I lost to Noah. That debate was the only one I've ever lost, and I don't like it. I especially don't like how quickly he was able to get under my skin; I'll never let that happen again. Grabbing my jacket out of my locker, I head down the hall.

I take my seat in our old auditorium and close my eyes. *Visualize the prize,* as Dan would say. I roll my neck back and forth and take a few deep breaths. Say what you will about how outdated our school is, but the A/C in this place is top-notch. It's only September, but goosebumps start prickling up my arms.

The squeaky seat next to mine folds down, and I turn my head to see Noah Riley setting his bag down on the floor next to mine. *No, no, no, no, no.*

"What are you doing here?" I ask, horrified.

"I'm sitting down," he says *too* nonchalantly.

Well, he has another thing coming, because I happen to be very *chalant.*

"You can't sit here. This section of the auditorium is for Poudre kids ONLY. Your school sits over there." I point to the right side of the auditorium, pretending to look as unbothered as someone who is in fact very bothered can look.

He doesn't even turn his head to follow where I'm pointing. A slow, smug, little smile blooms on his mouth. His *perfect* mouth.

"Gosh, I would, but my coach told me to sit next to the person I was going to debate against. So that's why I'm sitting right here." He bends down and unpacks his notebook from his backpack.

"What?! My coach said I was debating against a girl named Trina! You're cute and all, but you definitely don't look like a 'Trina' to me."

This earns me a little laugh. The sound makes me both annoyed and flushed at the same time. This isn't going well. "Trina woke up this morning throwing her guts up, so our coach said that since I'm team captain, it's my duty to step in for her today."

My heart is beating out of my chest. This is just great. My vision starts to tunnel. I don't want to go against him again. I don't want to make a fool of myself in front of everyone again. I worked so hard on this debate, and I really thought I would redeem myself.

Just as I start to spiral, Coach Christensen calls my name to come up to the stage.

Noah turns his head and gives me a little smirk of superiority. "We're up."

I turn to study his face. He's looking at me like he knows he's under my skin, like he knows that he gets me all worked up and...he enjoys it. He honestly thinks he has the upper hand in whatever this little thing is that we have going on. Well, it ends here.

His pretentious smile is all I need to feel a flood of self-confidence come rushing back into my body. I'm prepared for this. I'm good at what I do. I can do this.

I stand up and unzip my jacket to reveal my lucky crewneck sweatshirt underneath. A wide genuine grin spreads across Noah's face.

"Ready when you are," I say, as I walk toward the stage.

Chapter Eight
Now

I WAKE UP TO warm, bright sunshine hitting my face. Rolling over in bed, I listen to the sound of the ocean lapping against the shore through my open window. A smile plays on my lips, and I bask in utter bliss before opening my eyes.

This bed. This bed is the best bed I've ever slept in. Ever. In my entire life. Don't even get me started on the pillows and the comforter. I bring the bedding up to my nose and breathe in the fresh cotton scent. Heaven. I've died and gone to heaven.

I open my eyes and am instantly reminded of the mojito I slammed before I went to bed. My head is pounding. It's not fair.

When I was in college, I could take shot after shot of God knows what and wake up for an early class the next morning. Now, I have one little mojito and my head feels like it's getting crushed between two rocks. Man, thirty-one is a bitch.

Water. That's what I need.

Yikes, I can't remember if I had any water at all yesterday. I had two Diet Pepsis on the plane, a Diet Pepsi when I got here, and then nothing until the mojito at dinner with Noah...No...*Oh, God,* No!

Images from last night begin popping into my head. Noah Riley. Noah Riley is here. In this perfect place. In this beautiful hotel. On this amazing island.

I rub my eyes wanting everything to be a figment of my imagination, but the reality of the situation hits me as the very real conversation we had last night replays in my mind.

He lives in New York City...he works for the same company I work for...he's assigned to the Dumont case...Did he mention anywhere if he's married or has a girlfriend?

My stomach flips. Woah, no. I *do not* care about that. Right now, I only care that he's here ruining my perfect vacation. I need to talk to Jordyn; I need to tell her what's going on.

I reach over to the nightstand expecting to find my phone, but my hand hits the bare table instead. *Shit.* Where is it? I look around, studying the disheveled room, trying to puzzle the pieces of the night back together.

I remember I had my phone at dinner in my purse. From where I'm at in bed, I don't see my purse anywhere, and my heartbeat picks up, hoping I didn't leave it at the table.

Fumbling out of bed, I desperately try to find it. I walk into the bathroom, not there. I search my suitcase, not there. *God, what if I left it there?* I put my hands on my hips and spot it hanging on the hook by the front door.

Relief washes over me. Thank you, Past Jane, that is the perfect place to put your purse. I hurry and pull out my phone, check for any missed notifications, then promptly trip on the heels that I carelessly flung when I walked through the door last night. Bad job, Past Jane. That is not the perfect place to put those shoes.

I lay on the ground and stare up at the ceiling. Thoughts of Noah flood my mind. How does he do this? It's been more than a decade, and somehow he is still able to ruin my life.

I press Jordyn's contact info, and my fingers drum on the back of my phone in anticipation waiting for her to answer. Thank God she picks up on the second ring.

"Hi! Holy cow, what took you so long? I've been waiting for you to call me! How was the meeting? How was Mr. Dumont? Was he nice? Is he funny? I was reading an article about him last night, and it said he can be really funny, which I was so surprised about because rich hot men aren't usually very funny, ya know? By the way, please tell me he's as hot in person as he is in pictures..."

I should have thought about what I was going to say to her *before* I decided to call her.

Jordyn knows my past with Noah, and I'm not entirely sure how she's going to react when I let her know that it was him who sat across from me at dinner last night instead of Mr. Dumont.

"Hello?" she says.

"Mr. Dumont wasn't at dinner last night. He got called away to Thailand at the last minute."

"Wait, what? What does that mean? When do you get to meet him then?"

Continuing to stare up at the ceiling, I pinch the bridge of my nose between my finger and thumb. What am I going to say....

"I'm not sure on an exact date. It's a 'his office will call my office type of thing,'" I say, feeling a pit in my stomach.

There's a brief silence on the other end of the line before Jordyn whispers, "Jane, what's wrong? You're not telling me something." She sounds concerned. Fine, I just need to get it over with.

I scrunch up my face, take a deep breath, then blurt out, "Noah is here."

"Who?"

"Noah Riley. Is here. In Hawaii."

"What?!? *Why*? What the *hell*? Did you talk to him? Did he talk to you?" She speaks fast, sounding as flustered as I feel.

"Oh, we definitely talked," I say with a groan. "Jordyn, he works for Schwartz & Adler, in our New York office."

"What? No!"

"Yes! And to make it even worse, he was also assigned to the Dumont account."

"Shut up right now. I have to sit down. Jane, you've got to be kidding me. This isn't, like, a real thing, right?"

"Oh, J, I so wish I was kidding you right now. The restaurant was gorgeous, my dress was stunning, and everything was just so fucking perfect. Then, I got a call from Mr. Dumont telling me that he wasn't even in Hawaii and didn't know when he was going to get back. I was totally bummed thinking that meant I had to leave, but then he shocked me by saying I get to stay here, and I don't have to do any work for ten days." All of this pours out of me so fast, I have to take a beat to catch my breath. "I was so freaking happy. I ordered myself a fancy drink and a probably very delicious brownie, and that's when everything came crumbling down."

"The brownie?" she says, trying to follow my story.

"No, Jordyn. That's the exact moment that Noah sat down and shattered all of my hopes and dreams and ruined my entire life. Again." I softly bang the back of my head on the floor.

"*Fuck.* Jane, I'm so sorry. What are you going to do?"

"Not leave my room for the next ten days, order copious amounts of wine and brownies, and probably binge *The Office.*"

"Oh, stop it! No, you're not."

"You're right. I've watched *The Office* too many times. Maybe it's time for *Seinfeld* again."

"Jane, stop! You cannot let him ruin your vacation."

"He already did. Just knowing he's here ruins everything. I came to Hawaii thinking this entire experience was going to be it. My big chance to impress the partners, do a fantastic job, and get a stunning tan at the same time. Then, Mr. Dumont had to go and get himself called away to a far away place, and then the devil spawn himself had to sit down at my table. The literal *one* person in the entire world who could have made everything worse, waltzed right into the room, and acted like we didn't even have a past." I let out a huff. "It just sucks, Jordyn." Tears begin to form in my eyes. "It just came out of nowhere. I hate it when plans change." I slowly stand up from the ground and walk over to the balcony.

"I know you do...and I know it's easier said than done, but you have got to stop letting people affect you so much. Noah doesn't mean anything to you anymore. He's just some random guy that needs to get off of your account. Jane, I know this entire situation is stupid. Really, *really* stupid, but you've dealt with stupid before." She lets out a small laugh. "Just look at it this way, you were told that you basically get to have a ten-day paid vacation," she says, trying her damnedest to lift my spirits. "Just try to relax for the rest of the time you're there, and then you can figure out the Noah stuff when you get home. It's a problem for Later Jane to fix."

"Later Jane doesn't want to have to fix it, either," I say under my breath.

"I heard that, and I know. But Later Jane will have *me* there to help her," Jordyn says, happily. "Just please, for the love of all things holy, don't make any rash decisions while you're upset. Don't call the partners, don't overwork, don't overthink everything. I promise I'll be here when you get home to help you figure out what you can say to the partners to get him off the account and totally out of your life forever. Again."

"Promise?"

"I swear. I'll be at the airport right as you land. I'll bring Daniel too. He's been extra sassy lately because his new employee, Jessica, was apparently caught stealing tons of sugar from the back pantry."

"Wait, what? She was stealing sugar?" I chuckle.

"Yup. Like over twenty-five pounds a week. It doesn't make any sense. We were talking about it last night, and we both came to the conclusion that she must be snorting it or something. I mean, she's always so peppy, ya know? We honestly can't figure out why a seventeen-year-old girl could possibly need that much sugar." We both laugh. "Anyway, Daniel has had a major attitude the last few days because of it, so it will be good to get him away from the café. Maybe we can grab dinner on the way home, then we'll come up with our Noah-attack plan. Deal?"

"Sounds good." I take a deep, healing breath. "I miss you guys. Thanks for talking to me, J. We will get it all figured out."

"Of course we will. We always do. For now, just relax. Go down to the beach and get your tan on. If you do happen to see Noah, tell him to go kick rocks."

After the phone call, I stare more intently out at the vast ocean and let her words sink in. I don't owe anything to Noah. I don't even know him anymore, and he doesn't get to ruin this vacation for me.

I walk over to my suitcase and take out my beach bag. I add my sunglasses, towel, and *To Kill a Mockingbird*, then proceed to put on the cutest and skimpiest red bikini I own. You know, just in case.

Chapter Nine
Then

I LOOK LIKE A six-year-old on her way to her first swimming party. The bright blue of my one-piece swimsuit in combination with my substantial lack of curves, reinforces my point even further.

The longer I stare at myself scrutinizing every little detail, the worse it gets. My hands drop heavy to my sides, and I let out an upset groan. This sucks.

My feet drag on the carpet as I make my way over to my closet. Please, for the love of God, let there be some sort of cover-up in here that can salvage this unfortunate situation.

I flip through item after item, and nothing immediately stands out. *Gosh, this is so dumb.* Why can't I just wear a cute little bikini like everybody else? I growl in frustration and fling my hands up in the air.

Oh, right, because my mother actually threatened to kick me out of the house if I ever wore a two-piece. "If you think that I would ever let my only daughter out of the house, wearing only her bra and underwear, then you obviously don't know me very well, Jane. If that's something you want to do, then you don't need to live under my roof with my rules."

She really said that. Over a swimsuit. The worst part is, I have no doubt in my mind that she would have done it. She really would have kicked me out of the house if I went against her rules and wore a bikini instead of this *Little House on the Prairie* smock that I'm currently sporting.

I move back to the mirror and gaze at the reflection staring back at me. Whatever minuscule feelings of wanting to go to the lake I had in the first place have all been entirely erased.

I look like a blueberry. An Amish blueberry.

Another moan escapes me as I rush back to my closet, hoping something cute appeared in the ten seconds since I last checked.

Nope. Nothing new. I let out a string of silent curses while again moving through item by item in my closet. I pass over a "cute-as-a-button" shirt my Nan got me sophomore year and end up with a plain black tee and jean shorts. It's nothing special, but at least it covers my suit.

Jordyn said that boys are going to be there. However, she failed to mention if she knew the boys, or if we're both going into this blind. Wait, scratch that, she'll have Tyler and I'll be the awkward third wheel.

I take one more look in the mirror before I head out. I look fine. Totally fine. My long blonde hair falls loose down my back, and my freckles peek through on the bridge of my nose.

I'm not terrible-looking by any means, so if any of these new boys don't talk to me today, it's their loss. I cock my head and shrug my shoulders. That would leave me with more time for my homework, anyway.

We pull up to the lake, and it takes my breath away. The deep blue water juxtaposed with the vibrant green of the pine trees is something right out of a nature book. I've lived in Fort Collins all my life, and I can't believe I've never been here before. It's stunning.

Jordyn spots Tyler the minute we get out of the car, and they run into each other's arms like two long-lost lovers reuniting after years apart. She was literally just over at his house before we came here. They've only been apart for, like, three hours tops.

When their attention shifts to me, I dramatically roll my eyes and pretend to gag myself. Jordyn flips me the bird and gives Tyler a big sloppy kiss.

"Hey, Jane! Glad you could make it!" Tyler smiles, grabbing me in a full-on bear hug and lifting me off the ground.

"Thanks! Jordyn promised I could work on my homework if I came."

He gently drops me back down and pats me on the back. "Oh, Jane, there are some guys here who would be happy to keep your mind occupied on much more exciting things than *homework*." He wiggles his eyebrows up and down and grins wide at Jordyn. "If you know what I mean."

"Ew, Tyler!" Jordyn shoves his shoulder. "Jane doesn't even know any of the guys here. She can do her lame ol' homework if she wants to." Jordyn links arms with me, and Tyler gives her a little smack on the butt. She sticks her tongue out at him as we start making our way down the rocky beach.

"This is it," Jordyn says. "If we sit right here, I can stare at Tyler's perfect ass while he plays volleyball." She sets her bag and towel on the ground, then proceeds to take off her swimsuit cover.

Safe to say I don't need to worry about us wearing the same swimsuit. She's in a tiny, hot pink bikini that compliments her warm, brown skin perfectly. Her *assets* are clearly out to play, and all the boys around us pause what they're doing to admire the show. I instinctively hug my towel tighter to my chest.

"Let's go get in the water and cool off before we lay out," Jordyn says.

"You go ahead. I'm going to set up my stuff first, then I'll jump in."

She nods before running down to the water, as I slowly take off my shorts. When I can see that no one is paying attention to me, I quickly take off my shirt and hope that everyone is still staring at Jordyn.

I stand on the beach, my blue one-piece swimsuit on full display, and no one even cares. *Huh*. I smile to myself. Maybe I do overthink things sometimes.

I begin to fan my towel out in front of me, bending over to smooth out a folded corner. Just as I'm about to stand up, someone runs into my bent-over bum and knocks me face-first into the sand.

I quickly stand up, brush the dust off my face, and turn around to see who so rudely bumped into me.

Noah Riley. *Fucking typical.*

"Oh, Jane! Jane? I'm so sorry I didn't mean to... Uh..." his apology is stopped short as he looks me up and down.

The heat rushes to my cheeks, and I debate digging a me-sized hole and crawling deep inside of it to hide. I snatch up my sand-covered towel and wrap it tightly around myself. "Noah, what the hell are you doing here?"

"Well, hello to you too." He drops the volleyball he just caught and rests his foot on top of it. "I'm here with my brother, Tyler, and some of our friends. We come here every weekend to play some volleyball, at least until it gets too cold. Hey, I really am sorry I bumped into you, are you okay?"

Tyler? Tyler...Riley? The realization hits me over the head like a thousand-pound brick. "Of course you'd be Tyler's brother. The same Tyler who's been dating *my* best friend, Jordyn, for months."

"Wait, Jordyn's your friend?" he says, seemingly surprised.

"Yes, why? Is that hard to believe or something?" I clutch my sandy towel tighter.

"No, not at all. It's just that she's over at my house, like, every second of every day. I didn't think she could have time for a friend, because she's so obnoxiously all over my brother all the time." He dribbles the volleyball back and forth between his feet.

"Um, excuse me? Tyler is all over her just as much as she's all over him, thank you very much. Also, I will have you know that in those few and far between moments when they're not all over each other, Jordyn is at *my* house doing all sorts of fun things." Why am I justifying myself to him like this? I sound like a third-grader.

"I don't doubt it," he says, the corner of his mouth edging up slightly.

The silence that follows is damn near unbearable. I shuffle my feet trying to think of something snappy to say to make him go away, but before I get anything out, he cuts in and says, "So, um...this is the best time of year to jump in the lake. Most people would say that summertime is the best time, but I've been coming here since I was little, and September is where it's at. The water feels great and the sun is still warm, but the trees are just starting to turn colors." He smiles at me, and my knees wobble slightly. "If you want, I'd be happy to show you the places with the least number of rocks."

"Oh, nope, sorry. I was just about to leave. That's what I was doing when you, you know, bumped into me." Remembering this fact, my knees suddenly feel very steady.

Noah opens his mouth to reply but is cut short as a pair of cold, wet arms wrap around my middle and take my towel.

"Where are you going? We just got here?" Jordyn says, drying her wet body with *my* towel.

Noah dips his head, trying to suppress a smile. After a beat, he lifts his eyes to mine and says, "I'll catch ya later, Jane. Oh, by the way, I like your suit." With this, he turns and begins walking away toward the rest of his group.

That hole of embarrassment, that I thought about digging earlier, better be big enough for me to live in for the rest of my life because, at this point, I don't think I'll be able to move from this spot ever again.

Chapter Ten
Now

T HE LIGHT BREEZE GENTLY tosses the loose strands of hair around my face as I leisurely walk down the beach toward the umbrellas.

The warm sunshine wraps around my body and envelopes me like a big, cozy blanket. Why the hell has it taken me so long to get to Hawaii?

Oh, right, I'm a busy attorney who has no time to actually enjoy the life I've worked so hard to achieve.

I let out a heavy sigh and look toward the beautiful clear blue sky.

My entire life has been one big rat race to get me here, right where I am. I've always done everything right. I've never had a rebellious streak, I always say please and thank you, I even hold the door open for people behind me.

And, if I'm being fair, it *has* paid off.

In school, when they ask you where you see yourself in ten years, this is it. This is exactly what I had in mind. But it's hard, because it still feels like something is missing.

I walk my gaze down from the sky, and my eyes are instantly drawn to a mother holding the hand of her little boy as he toddles into the waves.

She's grinning from ear to ear, and I can hear his little squeals of joy as his toes finally touch the water. I watch as his chubby little hands test the water, tentatively at first, but then it quickly turns into a free for all.

The mom gets down on his level, and they both take turns splashing each other, until I see him plunge his hands deeper in the water and come up with little fists full of wet sand.

His big, baby eyes are full of light as he looks right at his mama and smears the sand on both of her cheeks. I can tell that she's shocked, but her surprise immediately evolves into happy determination.

She reaches her own hands down into the water, and then wipes a hand full of wet sand on her son's bare toddler belly. This adorable little boy laughs so uncontrollably that he can barely even catch his breath. The mom falls out of her squat onto her bum, and they both continue with their mini sand fight.

My nose begins to sting, as tears line the bottom of my eyes. The beauty of motherhood is something else. Something that I can feel my heart aching for, but something that I don't know if I'll ever get to achieve. I don't want to do it alone.

Every goal I've reached, every career achievement I've ever made, I've done on my own. Never in my adult life have I had to rely on anyone else, so to now be faced with a desire so strong but knowing I don't want to do it by myself, knowing that I want someone to share it with, knowing I want a *family*, is hard.

I'm also hesitant to go down this motherhood path, because if I'm being honest, I'm not even sure I'd make a good mother in the first place. I don't think it's a part of my genetic makeup or whatever. My mom certainly isn't one to be modeled after.

My shoulders drop, and I slow down my walking pace. My thoughts are going so many different directions right now, and it's hard to find a middle ground. On one hand, all I want is to be a mother, but on the other hand, I know for a fact that I don't want to throw away the amazing career I've worked so hard for.

I stop my walking, and freeze in place. It would kill me to watch everything I've accomplished go right down the drain. I'm proud of what I've done and who I am.

There are so many parts of me that want to continue doing it, but being an attorney is hard. Extremely hard. It takes so much time already, and if I do ever become partner, even more of my time would be dedicated to my work. I can't see myself having enough time to add being a mother on top of it all.

Looking back up at the sky, I take a deep breath. Despite all of that though, I really do want it. I want to be a mom, and I really hope it happens for me someday. But as of right now, the only thing that is certain is my career. I can focus on being the damn good attorney that I know I am.

Suddenly, I get a heavy sinking feeling deep in my gut and am reminded of the giant man-sized hurdle in my way.

There's absolutely no way in hell Noah and I can work together. No way. If, for some reason, I'm not able to convince the partners to take Noah off the account, everything would fall apart; it would be a complete disaster.

Noah and I don't know how to communicate outside of constantly arguing with one another. We've never seen eye to eye, and I don't see that fixing itself anytime soon. Also, on top of all that, he's just an asshole, and I don't like him. *I don't.*

My pulse quickens, and I shake my head, trying to get rid of the unease creeping into my body. I roll my shoulders back trying to loosen my neck and inhale a deep, healing breath. I hear the echoes of Jordyn's reassuring voice telling me this is a problem for Later Jane to handle. Not Today Jane.

I take off my sandals and keep walking down the beach, feeling the warm sand under my feet. It's settled then. Today Jane gets to rest and watch the tide come in.

When I get to the part of the beach where I want to relax, I see a lady asleep under the large umbrellas. She's the epitome of pure relaxation as she snoozes the time away.

As I wiggle my coverup over my head, it snags on my bun, which causes my sunglasses to fall off my face and into the sand.

When I turn to pick them up, I stub my toe on the corner of one of the chairs. This is going well.

The chairs under the large umbrellas are remarkably comfortable, and I melt into mine the moment I sit down. The cool ocean breeze drifts my way and I close my eyes, desperately trying to find that sweet spot of bliss my sleeping neighbor has found.

The gentle crashing of the waves and the sound of palm trees swaying high above my head calms all the nerves that have riddled my body since last night. Feeling the tension in my shoulders loosen, a feeling of warm contentment blooms in my chest. I smile, letting myself get fully lost in this moment.

I slowly open my heavy eyes, and that's when I see him. Noah, casually walking down the length of the beach, bare feet in the water, beach towel in hand. My throat constricts and my heart picks up speed. *My God*, he is gorgeous.

He fucking knows it too. He's always known how attractive he is and that he can use that attractiveness to his advantage. The way he walks with his broad shoulders held high and his chest puffed out is the way only a man who has immeasurable self-confidence could walk.

I would have thought that with age, this show of self-centeredness would have diminished some, but like most things with Noah Riley, that has apparently not been the case. If anything, he seems even more cocky and arrogant than he did in high school. *God*, he really is an asshole. A gorgeous asshole who just looked my way. *Shit, Shit, Shit.*

My heart is pounding out of my chest and my toes start to tingle. I close my eyes tightly and pray he doesn't see me, or if he does, I'm hoping he thinks I'm asleep and won't come over here. We have a deal. He minds his business, and I mind mine. He better not break it.

I can feel my blood pressure rising. *What if he does come over here? What does my body look like right now?* I move down a bit in the chair and lay my head on the soft cushion. I turn slightly and cross my ankles. *I'm so glad I shaved my legs before I walked down here, good choice, Past Jane.* With my eyes still closed, I take out my bun and let my hair fall around my shoulders. *Do I look sexy? I really hope I look sexy.* I lightly rest my right hand on my bare lower stomach and position my left hand palm up by my face. *Do I look like I'm sleeping? If I'm sleeping, he won't talk to me, right? This position is so not comfortable right now. What the hell am I doing, sexy sleeping? I may have lost my mind.*

"There's no way you're relaxed sitting like that," I hear him say, condescension dripping from his mouth.

I don't move, wishing he would just get the point and leave me alone.

"Are you even asleep?" A slight chuckle leaves him. "Oh, I see. You're playing possum."

Playing possum? Who the hell does this guy think he is?

"Jane," he pauses, "I can tell you're not sleeping. You're pretending." He says it slower this time, like a dad who just caught his child cheating in a game.

I open one eye and stare up at him. My brows furrow as I see a "gotcha" grin spread across his face.

"I will have you know that possums do not *pretend*. When they're scared, they go into something called tonic immobility. Their poor little bodies enter a completely catatonic state in response to fear. It's actually very sad, just so you know." I stare up at him and cross my arms over my chest.

He's standing close to me. So close that I can see each grain of sand on his tan legs. His eyes narrow as his gaze beats down on me. I stay silent, but I cock my head to the side and raise my eyebrows. Goading him to argue with me.

"Can I ask you how you know so much about possums?" He says with a satisfied smile.

I open my mouth to say something, ready to defend my knowledge of completely useless facts, but nothing comes out. I close my mouth again, pursing my lips. "Noah, why are you here? I thought we had a deal. I leave you alone, and you leave me alone. So far, only one of us has kept their side of the bargain. I'll give you a hint, it's definitely not you." I swing both of my feet over the edge of the chair and slide on my sandals.

He grabs the corner of the chair closest to mine and pulls it over. He sets his stuff down and sits.

The air around us grows tense. We're knee-to-knee now. There's less than an inch between us, but I can feel the electricity in that tiny, empty space. I catch a glimpse of his eyes as they trace the lines of my body. *God, I'm so glad I wore this bikini.* His eyes linger a beat too long at my chest, and his shoulders lift with a deep inhale. My core tightens, and a small bead of sweat rolls down my spine.

"First, let me tell you my good news," he says, gaze returning to my eyes. "*Our* boss, Mr. Paul Adler called first thing this morning and told me that I, too, get to stay here for the next nine days. You know, since it's already been paid for." I see a playful gleam in his eye. "Looks like we *both* get to enjoy a vacation." He relaxes back into his chair and crosses his ankles. "In other news, I just came down to the beach to read for a bit. I honestly didn't know you'd be here."

"Well, I came down to the beach to read too, and I was here first. So, you can go find another place to read. The beach is big Noah. You'll figure it out."

"Very true, but...this is the only place that has these nice big, comfy chairs and umbrellas. So, I think I'd like to stay right here." He pats the spot next to him. "I'll scoot my chair back over there, and you can continue with your *pretend sleeping* or whatever it was that you were doing," he says with eyebrows raised. He picks up his book and searches for his page.

"Ya know what?" I say flinging my hands up in the air in surrender. I'm an adult, I have no problem being the bigger person. "Fine. You stay here. I'll just go back up to my room." I don't even listen for his answer as I gather up my beach bag. I clench my jaw and hurriedly stuff my things inside.

As I turn to walk away, I have this little nudging feeling at the base of my neck. "Look, before I go, I just have to ask, what book are you reading?"

He looks up from his page and shuts the cover slightly so I can read what it says. *To Kill a Mockingbird.* Ha, should have seen that one coming.

Chapter Eleven
Now

WHAT THE HELL AM I supposed to do? The door to my room clicks shut behind me.

My body feels heavy as I plod my way over to the bed. Before I get there, I catch sight of my reflection in the floor-length mirror on the opposite wall.

Sliding over the coffee table, I move to the mirror and stand for a moment really looking at myself. Starting at my head, I slowly move down, observing every little detail.

This red bikini is, honestly, doing wonders for me. The color is sassy and fun, and my boobs look totally awesome. I turn, peeking behind my shoulder and yeah, my ass looks pretty darn awesome too. A satisfied smile creeps up on my face as I think about Noah seeing me in this suit.

I've changed a lot since we last saw each other. When we were younger, I was severely lacking in the curves department, but that hasn't been a problem since my freshman year of college.

I don't know if it was the late-night pizza-fueled study sessions, or all the early morning sugary coffees, but my curves came and definitely stayed. I happily welcomed them with a much-anticipated shopping spree at Victoria's Secret. Looking back, that's probably where my unhealthy obsession with pretty lingerie began.

There's nothing I love more than the feeling of silky panties against my bare skin. It's made even better when they match perfectly with my bra. It feels special, like a beautiful little secret that's only mine to know. I mean, I'm not going to lie, it also feels incredibly sexy when a man takes my clothes off and gets to be let in on my little secret. When he steps back to see the whole picture and takes a heavy sigh, I think in that moment, we both feel powerful.

I don't know if it's the tropical atmosphere or the complete lack of anything even remotely sexual happening in weeks, but for some god forsaken reason, images of Noah suddenly pop into my head. Him looking me up and down, eyes wide, and breath quick. A bite of his bottom lip, a small smile appearing just enough to see his dimples peeking through... *Nope. Nope. Not doing this right now....* I hurriedly step out of view from the mirror and jump-dive onto the bed.

Covering my face with the pillow, I try to erase the troublesome feelings emerging from inside of me. The thoughts of Noah being turned on, the blood moving through his veins going toward... *It's not working*. I squeeze the pillow harder into my face, hoping that maybe I can just squish the thoughts out of my head. After a while though, I start to feel lightheaded, and I question if a person could smother themselves to death or if it requires someone else to do it. I add this to my things-to-Google-later list.

Throwing the pillow off my face, I again find myself staring up at the ornate ceiling above me. The last time I was looking at this ceiling I was happy and full of gratitude, but this time, it's pure desperation. The absolute desperation of trying to cool the steamy feelings currently attempting to rip themselves free from my body. It takes a bit, but after a minute, I resign myself to just re-work the thoughts instead of trying to get rid of them completely.

I close my eyes and start with trying to turn Noah into a different man. I change his dark brown tousled hair into dirty blond beachy locks. I change his sultry, brown eyes to moody hazel ones, and his sharp chiseled jaw into one covered with long sandy facial hair.

I can feel it starting to work, so I keep going. I imagine this new mystery man coming out of the foam-tipped waves holding a surfboard and making his way toward me. When he finally reaches me, I can see the water trailing lines down his tan chest and disappearing into the band of his swim shorts. He's so close to me that I can feel the heat of his breath on my lips.

This is good. I can work with this. My fingers find themselves lazily dipping inside the seam of my red bikini and find the slick wet warmth that's there. I slowly begin teasing myself as I keep the fantasy of my Hawaiian surfer-boy playing in my mind. I work myself for a moment and find an all too quick but pleasurable release. Afterward, I feel myself being pulled into a deep, content sleep.

I shoot out of the bed, and my eyes are heavy as I scan the room. *Where am I? What day is it? Why am I only wearing a bikini?* This is how I know I just had a really solid nap. You know those deep naps where you wake up and don't even remember your own name? This was one of those naps. I honestly can't even remember the last time I had a nap, let alone one this good.

I smile and stretch my arms up wide above my head. A big, satisfied yawn escapes my mouth as I roll my head from side to side.

Brief images of Noah try to wiggle themselves into my mind, but I quickly shoo them away, because I don't want them anywhere near me. I have to keep my head on straight, and when he's in my mind, all semblance of reasoning and rationality go straight out the window.

Moving my legs to the side of the bed and shoulders in small circles, I try to wake up my body. I move my neck up and down, stretching my spine while repeating some happy little mantras.

I'm not usually one for self-help, but my therapist pointed out that's exactly part of my problem. I proceeded to argue with her, saying that I didn't need to say silly little things to myself, especially if they aren't true, but she just shook her head and passed me the list.

I am thankful for today.

I am proud of myself.

I deserve to be happy.

I can do whatever I set my mind to.

I am enough.

This last one is extremely difficult to say. It's just three little words, but I can rarely get them out. Never in my life have I felt *enough*. Never.

I've always tried so hard to do everything right, to make all the right choices and never do anything wrong. But it's hard to feel like I've ever done enough. It's hard to understand that just existing is enough.

Truthfully, I think a lot of women feel this way. We're constantly trying to do more, trying to *be* more. Running around like chickens with our heads cut off, trying to rise to these invisible expectations that no one is even holding us to except for ourselves. It's a race that we all enter, but no one ever wins. It's exhausting.

So, I've told all of this to my therapist, and she told me that I need to stop putting so much pressure on myself. She said I need to repeat these mantras twice a day until I actually believe them. Until I feel they are true.

It's actually sort of funny because I only started saying them after I was told to, not because I actually thought they would do any good. I was sure I would be the one stand-alone case in which mantras and positive-thinking wouldn't work. I was sure that after a few months, I would waltz right into my therapist's office and proclaim, "See! I told you! I told you I'm a loser! See! I told you I'm not enough! See! I failed again!"

But, if I'm being one-hundred percent honest, I think I can feel them starting to work. I can feel the little nuggets of truth that they hold. The beauty and magic of each word. I can feel my thankfulness for each little moment of my day. I can recognize the accomplishments that I've made and feel the pride in what I've achieved. It's taken some tough self-evaluation, but so far, it's been worth it.

The air in the hotel room is chilly, and I can feel small goosebumps start to prickle up on my skin. I realize I need to pee, so I find my way to the bathroom. I quickly look in the mirror and cue jump scare. Holy shit, I look like a hot freaking mess. All pre-nap sexy thoughts have completely disappeared.

My hair is sticking out at odd angles. My mascara is smudged all around my face, and I have a visible crusty line of drool dried on the corner of my mouth. How long was I out?

The shower head spurts to life as I try to find the correct temperature. I sit on the side of the giant bathtub and wait for the water to warm up.

The hotel phone rings, and I rush to pick it up. "Hello?"

"Aloha, Miss Jane! This is Melani from the front desk, calling to remind you of your massage in fifteen minutes." I turn to the clock on the table and again am shocked at how long I passed out for. It's already almost four o'clock.

"Massage? I'm sorry, I don't think I scheduled a massage."

"Oh, no, you didn't. Mr. Dumont ordered a massage package for you down in our spa."

I don't say anything. Fifteen minutes for me to transform from looking like I just completed a frat party walk of shame into someone ready to meet another living human being is cutting it close.

"Of course, if you would like to cancel, you're more than welcome to," Melani says in her beautiful sing-song voice.

Again, I'm silent. I'm thinking of something to say. Do I go down looking like the walking dead, or do I skip it and risk it getting back to Mr. Dumont and him thinking that I think I'm too good for his resort? I drum my fingers on the phone receiver debating what I should do. When was the last time I got a massage? I move my neck from side to side taking inventory, and I hear a little pop as the bones move together. "Okay, I'll be down there in fifteen. Thank you for the reminder."

"Perfect. I'll let them know. Enjoy your evening."

I hang up the phone and strip down. The water better be warm.

I wash, I scrub, I lather, I rinse (I do not repeat), and I, again, thank Past Jane for already shaving her legs. I jump out of the shower, put on a comfy little two-piece set, and some sandals, then hurry down to get my massage. That was the fastest shower I've ever taken in my life. I deserve a medal.

By the time I reach the spa, my hair seems to be wetter than when I left my room. I'm used to the dry air of Denver, so this humidity is a whole new ballgame. I bend over and flip my hair over my head. I do my best at trying to wring it out, but it's not doing much. *Oh well. Maybe it looks like I just took a dip in the ocean.* I shrug my shoulders and fling my head back up and put it into a messy bun on top of my head. I open the giant glass doors that say, "Dumont Luxury Spa," and that's when I see Noah sitting in the waiting room, his head in his book.

I'm just about to run as fast as I can back up to my room, because who needs a stupid massage anyway, when I hear an adorable little voice from the front desk say, "Aloha! You must be Jane! We can get your massage started now." My gaze switches from the front desk girl to Noah and notice his eyebrows raise slightly, but he doesn't acknowledge me. I wonder if he's even heard this little exchange. Maybe I can just slip right into my massage without even having to talk to him at all.

I whisper, "Yes, um.. Hi! Sorry I'm a bit late. I was... um... working." I see her eyes shift and look at my very damp hair as it drips onto my shoulder.

She smiles and says, "Oh, it's totally no problem at all. Your husband hasn't been waiting long. I'll just go ahead and go get the couples' room ready for you two." I don't even have time to catch my breath from the spit that I'm currently choking on before she turns and walks away down the hall, leaving me in the waiting room.

As soon as she said the word *husband*, I heard the distinct sound of a book shutting coming from behind me. I turn and see him glaring at me with wide brown eyes and eyebrows raised so high they practically disappear into his hairline.

"What did you do?" I say as I narrow my eyes and point my finger at him.

"*Me*? Nothing! What about you? What did *you* do?" His eyes drill into mine. "When I got here, she just told me we needed to wait for the other member of the party before we could begin. I thought she was talking about the massage therapist, I definitely didn't think it was *you*." *Ouch. Again.* He stands and moves closer to me.

In the past few days since our reunion, we haven't both been standing at the same time. So, it's at this precise moment that I remember just how much taller he is than me. I suddenly feel very small.

He stands still, staring me down, not moving a muscle. I do my best not to break my neck while staring right back up at him. Being this close to him, I notice lines on his face that weren't there when we were younger, lines that have appeared during all our years apart. My heart is thumping out of my chest. We've reached a stand-off. I really want this massage, and I am not going to let him ruin this for me.

I break first. I close my eyes and feel the air rush into my lungs as I take a deep breath through my nose. "Ya know what? It's okay. When that nice girl comes back, we'll just tell her that she's *very* mistaken, and we're definitely not married. In fact, we will tell her that we're the most not married people that have ever entered this spa. We could even tell her that we don't even know each other. Better yet, we could tell her we despise each other and want our massages to be in the farthest rooms away from one another as possible. That's perfect. That's exactly what we'll do." I nod, satisfied. "You're going to say it to her though, because I feel bad that she just got the couples' room ready, and we're not even going to be using it."

He doesn't move, but a hint of a smile tugs at his lips. "I heard you tell her you were working. Why is your hair all wet if you were working?"

Before I can explode, the spa girl comes back into the room. "Okay, Mr. and Mrs. Schwartz, your spa suite is ready. I just have to say that this is going to be the best spa experience of your lives. I wasn't, like, really sure what kind of massage you were going to want since the reservation literally just said Schwartz, Jane and Noah. It literally didn't have anything else. Usually it says something like, 'Couples' massage/facial/oils' etc... like usually it has a ton more information, but yours has basically nothing." She wrinkles her perfect non-wrinkled forehead. "But, since your reservation was created by Mr. Dumont himself, I knew that meant that you two must be, like, totally special." I nudge Noah with my elbow to say something, but he just stands by my side, smiling like a big ol' idiot.

"This is only my third, no fourth, real day working here, and I just really want to make sure that I make a good impression. So, I'm rolling out the red carpet for you guys! It's so totally cool that you're friends with Mr. Dumont." I see her cute little face light up, clearly pleased with herself. "Okay, so you two are in for a serious treat. I told Sven and Anya that you guys get it all. Seriously, I want you to get everything," she says animatedly. "Basically that means you're going to get a mixture of the light and slow Swedish massage, we'll throw in some aromatherapy, then continue with some deep tissue work, scalp massage, and of course, hot stones as well."

Hot stones? Oh God, I love me some hot stones. Did she also say deep tissue? It's like I can feel the knots in my neck turn to butter with just the mere mention of the words. I feel my knees start to buckle themselves and reach my hand out to steady myself on Noah's forearm.

He looks down at it, and I see a pleased little smile growing on his face. "Oh, that all sounds so wonderful, but Ashley, is it?" He says, glancing down at her name tag. She grins and gives him a cute little nod. "Awesome. Ashley, you see, Miss Jane and I aren't actually..."

"No!" I yell, much too loud. They both turn their heads to me in shock. I clear my throat and add, "The couples' massage package sounds perfect." I can feel his eyes on me, but I refuse to give him the satisfaction of me looking back at him, so I just continue staring straight ahead at Ashley, hoping he gets the hint.

"Oh my God, yay! I'm so excited for you guys! I'll show you where to undress."

Our new friend Ashley turns to lead us into the spa. She keeps listing all the wonderful things that are going to be taking place, but of course, I can't hear a single thing she's saying, because my mind is now fixated with the realization that I'm going to be butt-naked in a room with Noah Riley.

As she continues chatting away in front of us, I turn to him and whisper, "I need this massage, okay? But no funny business, you hear me? No peeking. I swear, Noah, if I catch you sneaking a peak at my ass...Oh, you'll be sorry. I'm only doing this for the hot stones. Got it? The hot stones!"

He nods his head and smirks, "Sure, Jane, *hot stones*."

Just then, Ashley opens the doors to the most serene room I've ever seen in my entire life. Warm, dim lights, gorgeous stone floors, a trickling water fountain in the corner. Ambient music encompasses the entire room, and I feel it start to take hold in every part of my body.

Noah pauses at the threshold and with an outstretched arm, he ushers me into the room. "After you, Mrs. Schwartz."

Chapter Twelve
Then

B ESIDES MY FACE ENDING up in the sand and Noah's stupid little comment about my swimsuit, the rest of the afternoon has been really great. After Jordyn reassured me that I look fine in my suit, and then also confirmed that Noah is a jerk, we let loose and started having some fun.

We played some volleyball, made a few new friends, and have been laying out together for the past hour. There's nothing better than talking and laughing with your best friend, while soaking in the last of the warm days before fall comes.

After a while, the sun starts to feel too hot on my face, and I become all too aware of all the places the sand is sticking to my skin. I squint into the sun and look out at the lake. The dark blue water is calling to me.

"I'm gonna go cool off for a bit," I tell Jordyn, but the only response I get is a light snore. She's out. I huff a little laugh and shade her with the umbrella. No one's getting burnt while I'm around.

I slowly wade into the water and the coolness of it against my hot skin takes my breath away. Noah said the water would feel great, but now that I feel it, I'm not so sure we would agree on what the word *great* means. By the time it's up to my middle, I have two choices. I can either play it safe and stay at this level or dip all the way in.

Counting to three, I take a big, deep breath in, then sink low into the cold water. Swimming deeper into the lake, I feel the weightlessness of my body start to calm my mind. Resurfacing, my hair falls into a heavy curtain down my back.

Wiping the water from my eyes, I see Noah swimming right in my direction. My initial reaction is to swim away from him, but I throw that idea out the window because I realize that would have me swimming deeper into the lake and farther from the shore. Not smart.

So, I make the entirely more awkward decision and just turn around. I'm treading water and blankly staring at the sky, hoping to God that maybe he'll just swim past me. I hear his strokes getting closer and closer. Just as I think he's going to pass me, his swimming stops, and I hear his ragged breath behind me.

"Hi, Jane."

I turn around and face him. Beads of water slip off his brown hair and slide down his face. His big smile makes him look like a little kid. I don't think I've ever seen him this happy. Not that I've seen him much anyway, but he's usually so...I don't know, arrogant, smug, self-righteous...Definitely not like this.

"Um. Hi," I say tentatively.

"So, how's it going?"

"Fine."

"Have you been to Horsetooth before?"

"No."

"Have you ever been to *any* lake before?"

"Yes."

"Do you usually respond to questions with one-word answers?"

"No. But for you I do," I say, starting to swim toward the shore.

"Wait, why? Don't you like me?" he asks with a big, puppy-dog pout, catching up to me.

I turn to face him again. "No." *Maybe.*

"Woah, that stings, Jane Robins. What have I *ever* done to you for you to not like me?" He puts his hand against his chest feigning offense.

"It doesn't matter what I think about you, Noah," I say, shaking my head. "We're not friends. We don't have to like each other."

A moment passes. I'm looking at the beach, but I can feel his gaze on me. I'm getting hot even with my body submerged in the cool water.

"Do you like debate?" His question takes me off guard.

Why does he care if I like debate or not? I open my mouth to say something but close it again.

"How long have you been doing it? I haven't seen you at any tournaments before this year," he says, water lapping against his chest.

"Yes, I like it. I love it actually. It just sort of clicks for me. I did it last year, but this is my first year competing in the tournaments."

Now that I gave him something, I can tell by the look in his eyes that he's going to take more.

"So, you like arguing then?" he says, lazily swimming to my other side.

"Yes. Yes, I do. What about you, Mr. Fossil Ridge Debate Team Captain? Do *you* like debate?"

"Yeah, of course I do. That's why I'm so good at it." He winks. "Did you know that I actually beat our rival school's debate team captain just a few weeks ago? I'd heard rumors that she's pretty good, but honestly, I think I flustered her a little bit." He looks at me through the sides of his eyes. "That's what I like most about debate. I love pushing my opponent right to the edge. To unsettle them."

I didn't know it was possible, but the look he gives me makes my already racing heart beat even faster. Clenching my jaw, heat rushes through my entire body. I don't know how he does it. I barely even know him, and yet somehow he has this innate ability to make me so entirely unbalanced. I don't like that he continues to get a reaction out of me. I don't like it at all.

"No, you didn't! You didn't fluster me! I was…sick. Just ask my coach. He'll even tell you that I was 'under-the-weather' that tournament." I splash his chest. "Besides, do you want to know what I heard? I heard that *SHE* beat you in the next debate. I heard that *you* were sweating up on the stage and that *you* even went over time on your last argument. What about that? Huh?"

He lets out a little laugh.

"What? Why are you laughing? I made you sweat, Noah Riley!" I swim closer to him and point my finger at his smug face. "Admit it!"

"You're pretty cute when you're flustered, Robins."

Chapter Thirteen

Now

*O*H. MY. GOD. *THIS feels so good.* I never would have thought that such a small woman could have such strong hands. *Oh, yeah. Right under my shoulder blade. Oh, that's nice.*

Move over, Jordyn, I think Anya might have just become my new best friend. Jordyn would probably put up a fight, but at this point, I don't even care. Also, it pains me to say it, but I'm one-hundred percent sure Anya could take her.

The earthy smell of lavender and the rhythmic movements of the massage guide me deeper and deeper into total tranquility. She's doing an outstanding job and will be getting a very large tip. All of my tips. Take all my money, Anya, you deserve it.

I don't think I've ever felt this relaxed in my entire life. I may have come somewhat close to it once when I accidentally fell asleep in my Nan's lap when I was nine. We had just spent an entire day pulling weeds in her backyard and when we came inside, she played with my hair until I fell asleep. I honestly think that's the only other time I've even come close to this level of calm. I feel like a big loose puddle.

My new best friend maneuvers her strong, tiny hands up and down my spine in such a way that it coaxes a small, satisfied moan from my lips.

It is of course, at this moment, that I'm reminded of the very male, very present, and very naked Noah Riley lying on the massage table directly next to mine. He clears his throat.

My head whips to the side. He's still face down in the donut-hole-face-thing and, from what I can tell, isn't about to move anytime soon.

I watch him, waiting to see if he does or says something to embarrass me, but he just lies there quietly. Maybe he just cleared his throat for a normal bodily function reason, not because I just happened to let out a very intimate, sexual sound, while I also happen to be butt naked.

I watch as Sven works the strong contours of Noah's back. Each muscle is carefully paid attention to and kneaded, like he's manipulating clay. My hands start to tingle. They're itching to replace Sven's hands, moving and touching each part of Noah's perfectly sculpted back. The massage oil glistens on his tan skin.

I'm losing myself in this image when I see Noah's head gently tip to the side and look at me. His eyes are glazed over with pure relaxation.

For the first time in years, we hold each other's stare. Lost in our past? Lost in our present? I'm not sure where we are, but we're here together.

Suddenly, the small sheet covering my bum lifts away and Anya's quiet, accented voice whispers, "Turn over, please."

Noah's heavy eyes stay locked onto mine. My entire back side is out on show for the world to see, but he doesn't break our eye contact. I see the muscle in his jaw tick, and the muscles in his shoulders expand as he takes a deep inhale. He opens his mouth to speak, but something stops him.

Closing his eyes, he continues his deep breaths. When he opens them again, he licks his lips briefly and gives me a quick little wink before placing his face back down into the headrest.

My entire body feels charged. The hairs on my arms prickle, and my heart begins to beat out of my chest. I suddenly feel as though all the blood has left my body. I'm trying to gather my thoughts when Anya gently taps on my shoulder and repeats, "Turn over, please."

Trying to turn from my stomach to my back on a little massage table, bare ass naked, after my muscles are all loose, is already hard. But add in the fact that I'm extremely lightheaded because Noah winked at me, then it basically becomes an extreme sport.

I feel like one of those newborn baby giraffes trying to stand up on its long, gangly legs for the first time.

At first, I try to turn too quickly, and my left leg completely misses the table and dangles off the side. Okay, then. Slow and steady seems to be the game. I can work with that.

I fumble around and struggle for what seems like an eternity, until I'm able to find a comfortable position. Anya carefully (and much too casually, in my opinion) places the sheet back on top of me. I close my eyes, trying desperately to regain my composure.

Please, almighty God above, please tell me Noah didn't see that embarrassing show.

I chance a quick peripheral glance in his direction, and to my absolute horror, he, too, is now facing up. *Shit.*

He's staring at the ceiling with the biggest fucking grin on his face. I can see his eyes have changed from calm and relaxed, to something more bright and full of wickedness.

"Sven, did you know that Mrs. Schwartz and I have known each other for almost fourteen years now?" He says merrily.

I hadn't realized it before, but I don't think I've heard Sven even say one word since we've been here. This is made more obvious when I feel his low gravelly voice vibrate through my chest. "Congratulations, you two. That is quite an accomplishment. Being together for fourteen years isn't easy." He continues kneading Noah's calf. Noah looks at me and smirks.

Sven continues, "I would know, I've been married for twenty years now, and my wife drives me nuts every single day."

His booming laugh engulfs the room. "I'm only joking, you know. She's the very best part of me. Even if she does take all the blankets every night." He smiles. "I tell her, I say, Birgit, even though I am big man, I still get cold," he says joyfully.

"I know what you mean, Sven." Noah chuckles playfully, clearly enjoying this little game. "I will tell you one thing though, fourteen years now, and that was the first time I've ever seen her all the way naked."

My mouth falls open in terror. *He saw me.* He saw me totally naked and all oily trying to shift around on a teensy tiny table. Oh, God, he saw *everything.* The palm of my hand finds my forehead, and Anya gently taps my thigh, hinting at me to put it back down on the table.

Sven's deep roaring laughter fills the spa. "You are very funny, Mr. Schwartz! I tell you, look at her naked all that you can while she is so young and pretty! My Birgit is very beautiful in her old age, but there is nothing like a woman in her, what's the word? In her prime, you say? You look and look and enjoy it while you can."

"Oh, I plan to. Since I've finally seen her in all her glory, I personally cannot wait until she gets to see me naked. Fourteen years is too long a time to wait, don't you think, Sven?"

A chuckle escapes my lips, despite the complete embarrassment coursing through my body. I hate how funny he is, even when I'm the butt of the joke. I wish I could ignore him, I wish I could block him out and...Anya moves to my calves and she starts a mind-numbing deep tissue massage on them. *That helps.* That helps push the thoughts of Noah out of my mind.

I focus on Anya's mighty little hands as she continues to release all the tension from the different parts of my body. The knots in my neck, the tightness in my jaw. It feels so good to finally give in, to let myself surrender.

I honestly can't tell if Sven and Anya are buying the poor charade of us being married, or if we've already been found out. As they finish up our massages, neither of them gives anything away.

As Anya gathers her things, she quietly says, "You two have the room to yourselves for the next forty-five minutes. You may choose to use it as you wish. Some couples lay in their separate beds while holding hands, some choose to lay together, or you're also welcome to move yourselves to the private shower in the adjoining bathroom. I hope you both feel a renewed sense of love and passion in your...marriage." She smiles warmly, then shuts the door. *Anya knows.*

The only sound I hear is the pounding of my heartbeat in my ears. What do we do now? Do I get up? Does he get up? Do we play rock paper scissors and decide who gets up that way?

I can tell you with one-hundred percent certainty that I will not be the first one to stand up. I will not chance him seeing me without my clothes on ever again.

I tap my fingers on my thigh, anxiously playing an invisible piano. I know only a few minutes have passed, but it feels like hours. The silence is unbearable.

Time painfully stretches on with neither one of us making a move to get up. I feel myself trying to use mind powers to will him to stand up. *Come on, Noah, please get up first. Just turn your body away from mine and stand up. Just move, damn it.*

Nothing. Absolutely nothing happens.

I shift in my bed, take a deep breath, and recenter myself. Okay, then, I will calmly just wait until he moves first. No matter how long it takes. I will not break. Seconds tick by with no movement. Maybe he fell asleep? I let out a huff, hoping he'll be startled awake, or maybe he'll finally get the point and start the process of getting out of here. The huff does nothing. He doesn't move a muscle. More time passes with no movement at all, so I decide to loudly clear my throat.

"The ball's in your court, Robins. I can do this all day."

I look over and see him resting his arms comfortably behind his head as he gazes happily at the ceiling.

"Ugh, why do I have to be the one to get up first? It makes much more sense if you get up before me, and then leave the room while I get changed. That's the gentlemanly thing to do, right?" I stare at him waiting for his rebuttal, but none comes. "Noah, honest question, do you even know what it means to be a gentleman?"

"Jane, I was taught that gentlemen always let ladies go first."

He's impossible. Fucking impossible. "Fine," I say gruffly. "Close your eyes and face the other wall." I watch and wait until I see him roll his eyes dramatically and comply with my demands.

I grab the light sheet covering my body and wrap it tightly around myself as I stand up. I peek over my shoulder and see that he's still facing the other direction. Good. I quickly put on my super special spa slippers and walk into the bathroom.

Along the far wall are two cubbies where we left our clothes before we started the massage. I go to my cubby and start to put on my panties when I gaze longingly at the stunning spa shower in the corner.

The floor is tiled with river rocks and beautiful stone benches line both sides of the walls. I can count a total of five different showerheads at various heights, pointing different directions, and I also spot some dried eucalyptus hanging from a hook. I can feel it calling my name, beckoning me inside.

There are only two problems. Problem number one is that there's no curtain or even a door to this shower. It's floor-to-ceiling glass, with a small opening that you walk through. Open concept. Very Scandinavian.

This brings me to problem number two, it's a man-sized problem who could/probably would walk into this bathroom at any moment and see me.

I tiptoe to the edge of the massage room and crane my neck around the corner to see if Noah is still lying there, and I'm pleasantly surprised to see that he is. It doesn't look like he's moved at all. I don't think I have much time though, so I quietly retrace my steps back into the bathroom and yell from my spot at the cubbies. "I decided I'm going to take a quick shower. Don't you dare come in here. Seriously, Noah. Don't even think about it."

I start the water before I hear a reply. It quickly hits temperature, and I can smell the eucalyptus coming alive. Right as I'm about to step in, I hear a slight chuckle coming from the massage room.

"Me thinks the lady doth protest too much." *Shakespeare? Since when does he quote Shakespeare?* "But it's okay. Don't you worry, Jane, I won't bother you. It's not like I haven't seen you naked already today anyway."

What an asshole. "What did you say? Sorry, I can't hear you over the sounds of the heavenly bliss waiting for me."

"Oh, good, then I guess you can't hear me when I tell you Sven told me those stone benches are heated."

I lift my foot and set it on the bench closest to me. Holy shit, he's right. What kind of magical sorcery is this? I sit my perpetually cold bum onto the heated stone and let the warm water envelop my skin. This is perfect.

To my astonishment, Noah didn't even bother me once while I was showering. There was no peeking, no funny quips about seeing me naked, and no pushing for me to hurry it along. Also, there was no more Shakespeare, so I'll take that as a win too.

As I dry myself off with the fluffiest towel, I bring it up to my face and breathe in the warm vanilla scent. Man, I feel good. Like a whole new woman.

I put on my clothes and reach up to the mirror to wipe away the steam with my hand. It has taken me years to like what I see in my reflection, but I have truly grown to love the woman who's staring back at me.

It took me until I was a full-blown adult to really understand that beauty looks different on everybody. I know, I know, we've been spoonfed the lines, "Everyone is different, everyone is beautiful," since we were in elementary school, but let's be honest, no one really believes it until we get older—or at least I didn't.

Standing barefoot in the spa bathroom, I hold my gaze in the mirror, my big, blue eyes that I got from my Nan staring back at me. I love my long, blonde hair that has a slight wave to it when it's wet, the light brown freckles that dust the bridge of my nose, and the small scar above my eyebrow I got from an intense game of beer pong in college. All things that, at one point, I desperately wanted to change, but now are the things I hold most dear.

Grabbing my bag, I put on my sandals and walk back into the massage room. Noah is lying on his side fast asleep on his massage table, his hand resting under his head. He almost looks sweet when he's sleeping. But alas, I'm no fool and know that there's a brooding jackass simmering just below the surface.

I move closer to his table and listen to his soft breathing. This man holds the trophy for the only person in the world who has ever been able to get under my skin.

The only person who has ever challenged my thinking and made me question my own stubborn opinions. He has this power to enrage me and, annoyingly, turn me on all at the same time. It's confusing and frankly, I don't have time for it.

It took me an embarrassingly long amount of time to get over him in the past, and it's so frustrating that he gets to walk back into my life and mess things up again.

Here I am, staring down at a peacefully sleeping Noah Riley with furrowed brows and an angry look on my face, when tiny Anya peeks her little head in to tell us our time is up.

From the look on her face, I'm positive I look like a homicidal maniac who's contemplating the murder of her sleeping husband.

I turn toward Anya, and she peers at me with narrowed eyes that are practically screaming, *I knew it!* I subconsciously put my hands up in surrender. "Hi! Yes! We will...um... be out in just a minute...my...husband...is sleeping, and I was just about to wake him up." I bring my right hand down and slap him in the chest.

"Ouch, what the hell, Robins?" He gets up and rests his body on his elbow. "What was that for?" He rubs the sleep from his eyes and looks at me standing next to the bed, my hands weirdly up in the air, and an awkward smile plastered on my face. He furrows his brow in obvious confusion, so I nudge my head in the direction of the door. As soon as he spots Anya, he sits up and dons his most charming and charismatic smile.

"Hi, Anya!" He clears his throat. "My, uh, wife and I were just about to get out of here. Sorry, we took a bit longer, I was just so relaxed I fell asleep. We'll just need an extra minute or two for me to get dressed, and then we will head out." He stands up and wraps the sheet around his lower half and tucks the corner in. It rests low on his hips, those perfect V lines on his abdomen are just begging to be touched. *What? No. Definitely not.* I shake my head. This is the exact reason I need to stay away from him.

Anya's eyes dip for a brief second as she, too, traces the V lines that disappear deep into Noah's makeshift toga. She catches me watching her and instantly recovers. "It's okay. No problem. Just leave the sheets on the beds when you leave." If I wasn't already watching her, I would have missed it, but I see her eyes dart quickly to Noah's body once more before turning and softly closing the door.

"Anya thinks you're hot," is the only thing I manage to say as the door closes.

"Does she?" he says nonchalantly as he turns to make his way into the bathroom. Just as he reaches the door, he drops the sheet to the ground, and I catch a glimpse of his perfect ass.

My cheeks flush, and I turn away. Facing the wall behind me, I act as though I'm admiring the various spa stock images framed on the wall. Oh, what pretty rocks. That's a beautiful creek. What an interesting flower...

Just then, Noah appears to my side already fully dressed.

"That was fast," I mutter, pulling my purse up higher on my shoulder.

"Yep. I didn't have one of those amazingly blissful showers that I was hearing so much about. I seemed to have run out of time for that."

"That's a shame. You really missed out," I say, patting his back.

We both move toward the door in sync. It's little things like this that make me so upset. It's like, somehow, we're always on the same wavelength. Making all the same moves, being at all the same places, liking the same things. Statistically speaking, it doesn't even make sense, but yet, here we are again.

"What are you going to do for the rest of the night?"

His question catches me off guard. "Um...not sure. Probably just go back to my room and sleep some more." I laugh nervously. "I don't remember a time when I haven't had any work to do, so I'm living it up while I can. Why? What are you going to do?"

"Eh, I'm going to grab some dinner, and then head back to my room to get some work done. Unfortunately, I'm not in the same boat as you. I have a lot of work to do tonight and tomorrow, so I'm afraid that means no rest for me." He reaches for the door again and opens it for me. "Do you want to come grab a quick bite with me before you...sleep?"

I've never claimed to have a poker face and judging by his reaction to whatever my face is currently doing, it proves that I most definitely do not have one. "Woah, don't be so offended, Jane, it's just an invitation. I know you said we should stick to ourselves and stay far away from each other or whatever, but I thought that since we just spent the whole afternoon together, and the fact that I saw you naked twice today..." *TWICE?!* "I thought maybe you'd want to just finish the night off strong, and then resume our six-foot social distancing order tomorrow."

Noah has work to do, but I don't? I don't understand this at all. Have the partners asked him to do something special? Or maybe Dumont called and gave Noah a few tasks? I feel my anxiety start to take hold of me. My thoughts begin to spiral.

I have to get back up to my room and check my emails to see if I have work that needs done. I don't want to drop the ball with this client. I don't want the partners or Mr. Dumont to think I'm lazy or that I'm not up to the task. I don't want

Noah put in charge of this account. I'm a damn good attorney, and I need to make sure that everyone knows it.

Walking through the door that he's so graciously holding open for me, I start walking down the hall, speaking quickly. "No. Sorry. I can't come to dinner. I um...I totally forgot, until you mentioned it, that I have a ton of work to do tonight too. I'm just going to order some room service and buckle down." I pick up my pace. "Besides, Noah, I really do think it's best if we steer clear from each other for the rest of our time here. You do you, and I'll do me. Remember?" My words come out choppy through my quickened breaths. I don't even look over my shoulder to see if he follows.

Chapter Fourteen
Now

A S SOON AS I get into my room, I throw my purse onto my bed and storm through, trying to find my work bag. Thoughts crash through my mind. *What work does Noah have that I don't? What if I've had important things pop up in my email folder, and I haven't even bothered to check?* I hate feeling like I've dropped the ball. I pride myself on being the person who gets things done the moment they're asked. I rush, I expedite, I priority ship.

What if I open my computer and don't have any work to do? That would mean, for some reason, they must have forwarded everything to Noah. I shakily take my laptop out of my bag and set it on the desk. I stare blankly at the screen, nerves buzzing, waiting for it to come to life.

The newly loosened muscles in my neck begin to tighten back up, and my right leg bounces up and down impatiently. Before I can log in, a prompt pops up on the loading screen.

Update required. Estimated time: 28 minutes.

A wave of nausea washes through my body, and I bury my face into my hands. My heart rate accelerates, and my breathing becomes shallow and quick. The ringing in my ears is the telltale sign that I'm on my way to officially losing control. Control of my body, control of the situation, control of my life.

The rational part of my brain fully understands that a computer update is nothing to have a panic attack about. However, in these moments, all rationality gets buried deep by all the fears and failures that rush up to the surface. It's not about the update. It's not about Noah or work. It's all about my lack of perfection.

My emotions are circling on themselves, and I feel the familiar loop of hopelessness starting to take hold.

I am not proud of myself.

I am not capable.

I am not enough.

These are the mantras I'm more used to. These are the ones that have a deeper hold on me than the ones my therapist has me say. These are the ones that have been on repeat in my mind ever since I was a kid.

In these moments, they're truer than any other words in the world. *I am not enough. I am not enough. I am not enough.* These four words feel as if they are permanently etched into my heart.

I push myself up from the desk and walk over to the balcony. The glass door slides open effortlessly and I step outside. The humid night air blankets me from head to toe, and the salty smell of the ocean rushes into my nose.

I rest my elbows on the railing and try to get a hold of myself. Deep breath in. Count one, two, three, four. Hold it for seven. Exhale one, two, three, four, five, six, seven, eight.

Again.

Inhale.

Hold.

Let it all out. A slight tingle begins in my arms as I feel the breathing exercise working. I've had panic attacks for years now. Spurred on by my parents' high expectations and demands of excellence, and then continued by my incessant need to ensure that everyone around me thinks I have everything figured out all the time.

Since I began therapy, these attacks have chilled out quite a bit. They're happening less than they used to, which is good because they got really bad for a while. I really am trying to fix myself. I wake up every day, repeat my positive affirmations, and try to force myself to alter my negative thoughts. Every day I attempt to improve something, even if it's small.

A lot of the time this works wonders, but if there are times when I find myself overwhelmed or not in complete control of a situation, or if my self-perceived perfection is put into question, I rapidly fall back into these pits of worthlessness.

I could blame everything on my past, my Type-A personality, or I'm sure there is a granola girl with a nose ring out there who would tell me that I could trace it all back to my star sign. But at the end of the day, I've come to accept that it's just the way I'm built.

Star sign aside, I do understand that I cannot afford to keep spiraling out of control, and I have to stop letting my negative self-image take over. I know it doesn't serve me, and it actually always ends up making things so much worse, but it's still hard sometimes.

The fog in my head begins to clear, and the tightness in my chest eases. I haven't lost myself like this for a while now, months even, so all of it feels so stupid and confusing. Noah telling me that he has some work to do shouldn't have sent me into this tailspin of panic and self-doubt. *Why did I let myself do this?* I shake my head, marinating in the disappointment.

Closing my eyes, I try to coax out some positive thoughts. So what if Noah is working tonight? So what if he has a ton of work to do and ends up working every day this week? Maybe he's behind. Maybe he's just bad at his job.

I feel a small smile tug at the corners of my lips. I don't actually believe that though. If he's anything now like he was when we were younger, I know he's good at what he does. *Damn, this isn't working.*

I lay everything out. Let's say that our bosses did in fact give Noah some important work to do. I don't know what this could implicate, but maybe it's not as damning as it seems.

I shouldn't automatically assume that just because they called him here to Hawaii at the last minute and gave him some extra tasks to do, it means they think he's better than me and want to take me off the account.

Breathing in deeply, I continue to work through my emotions. Let's go even further. Let's say that *is* the case. What if our bosses do decide to take me off the account? Would that really be the end of the world for me? Do I not think I would be able to re-evaluate things and recover? Of course I would. I know I would.

This is something I've always wanted. For as long as I can remember, I've made it my goal to become an attorney. But I'm the first to admit that as often as I love it, I dislike it just as much. The long hours. The constant preparations and research. The endless amount of red tape and workarounds. It's a lot to handle. To make matters worse, it was only a few weeks ago that I was so upset at being looked over for making partner, and now I find myself questioning if I'm in this career because of my love for it, or if I'm only doing it because once I set my mind to something I have to see it through.

God, I'm so confused. Why am I like this? All my thoughts are so mixed up. I rub my eyes with the palm of my hands. It all feels like too much. I grab the railing with both hands and gaze out at the vast moonlit ocean. The rhythmic in and out of the silvery waves calms the unsettled feelings gripping at my chest. The predictability and balance of it all eases the worry that's threatening to take hold.

I don't want to do this right now. I don't feel like deconstructing all of my life choices and possibly redesigning my entire future at the moment, so I close my eyes tight and shake my head. I can't have these thoughts bury themselves too deep; I just need them to go away, I just need to do what I always do—shove all this worry deep inside and convince myself that I will work it out later.

My computer chimes from inside my room. *Finally*. Taking one final deep inhale, I open my eyes and put on my happy face. Walking back into the cool air-conditioned room, the computer screen is the only light on, so I stare at it like a moth to a flame as I attempt to make my way across the dark room to the computer desk.

Just as I'm about to reach the desk chair, my foot finds the strap of my work bag and sends me flying face first into the ground. The worst part is, that stupid coffee table that I moved earlier to this very same spot, tries to catch my fall and the corner of it slams hard into my left thigh. A hilarious mixture of laughter and pain is forced out of my body as the absurdity of the day's events, coupled with the sudden adrenaline rush, punches me in the gut.

Wiggling myself up into a sitting position, I rest my back against the desk behind me. I look down at my leg and see a gnarly bruise already starting to take shape. *Shit, man, this really hurts.*

A breathy chuckle escapes from my chest, as I picture the graceful show that I just performed. I'm so glad that no one's here to see it.

Reaching my hands behind me, I blindly feel around the desk for my laptop. I locate the corner and carefully bring it over my head and set it on my lap. Opening my email folder, I see that my inbox does have a few new messages, but at first glance, they don't appear to be anything special.

I read and reread each new email thoroughly. Everything that has been asked of me is unimportant and could definitely wait until I get home. Nothing is pressing. Nothing is urgent.

Although I may be unsure about what I want for my future, I do know with full certainty that right now, I want to beat Noah Riley. I will do everything in my power to make sure I'm number one. This is going to be fun.

Tonight, I'm going to complete all my pending tasks, even the ones that don't need to be done for weeks. Then, I will re-examine all the work that I've already done for Dumont and go through every single detail with a fine-toothed comb. I'll rework and improve it every way I possibly can. Then, with any time I have left, I will detail and plan some other useful projects that are sure to further cement me into the forefront of the partners' minds as a proactive team member and strong leader.

A loud growl comes from my stomach. Holy moly, I haven't eaten anything all day. My mind has been so preoccupied with going to the beach, seeing Noah, getting the massage, seeing Noah again, and then coming back to my room to work, that I honestly haven't remembered to eat at all.

I move to get up and am promptly reminded that my left leg is still completely dead. Well, that sucks. Looks like this is where I'm going to stay for the rest of the night. I feel that gnawing sensation grow in my stomach from hunger.

Grabbing my work bag from where it rudely decided to trip me, I dig around, hoping to find something inside. A pencil, my charger, some loose change...aha! I feel the wrapper first and pull out an ancient protein bar that has been floating around in the bottom of this bag since God knows when. It's so old that the label is all worn off and smooth, like river rocks that get polished from centuries of getting tossed around in the water.

Hesitantly tearing off the corner of the wrapper, I give the bar a quick inspection. It *looks* fine. Good. Next, is the sniff test. Okay, thank God, it has no smell. I'm going to take that as a good sign because naturally, I assume that if it is rotten, it would probably smell bad, right?

I bring the bar up to my mouth and take a small mouse-sized bite. Surprisingly, it's still chewy. I can't entirely distinguish the flavor, but if I close my eyes, I can *almost* pretend it tastes decent.

Once my dinner is finished, I get down to business. I pull out my charger, don my headphones, and dive headfirst into my work.

I am going to *win*.

Chapter Fifteen
Now

*D*ING, *DING*. I SLOWLY peel my eyes open one after the other and attempt to focus them on my surroundings. I see...a shoe? It's my shoe, resting about six inches from my face.

Ding, ding. There it is again. The awful sound that started this mess. I sluggishly turn onto my back and assess my present situation. Exhibit A, the shoe. My right brown sandal to be exact. Exhibit B, I seem to have my swimsuit cover-up draped across my legs like a blanket, and my work bag is acting as some sort of makeshift pillow. Exhibit C, I spot a protein bar wrapper sitting next to the little trash can, which clearly suggests that I tried to throw it away, missed the can, and was too lazy to pick it up and try again.

My stiff body objects to any movement as I struggle to work myself into a sitting position. The floor around me looks like a war zone. Apparently, while in my rushed haze of adrenaline-spiked work, I made the floor my substitute home and didn't bother moving for the rest of the night.

Ding, ding. Who keeps texting me? What time is it? Where is my phone? I search around in my little nest but come up empty. I don't even remember the last time I used it. I don't think I talked to anyone since before the massage yesterday. *Ding, ding.* Okay, now it's mocking me.

I slowly make a move to get up and I feel a throbbing sensation radiating from my left leg. Ah, that's why I didn't get up last night. The memory of my clumsy little mishap pops into my head. I hesitantly remove my "blanket" to assess the damage and immediately see that an ugly purple bruise has bloomed overnight on top of my thigh. *Yikes.*

I tenderly put my weight on my unhurt leg and try to stand up. Man, getting off the floor used to be so easy but ever since I hit my thirties, I'm not nearly as limber as I used to be.

Spotting my phone on the entry table by the door and amusingly hobbling my way over to see what all the hullabaloo is about, I tap the screen and see that I have four different texts from Carol.

Carol

Hi Jane. This is your mother.

How is work?

> Call me today.

> This is the number you can call me on.

You know, you'd never be able to guess that my mother and father have had the same phone numbers since they first got cell phones sixteen years ago. The two of them act like they're cycling through numbers as often as they go to the grocery store. It's ironic because both of my parents each hold a number of degrees, but I'm still not entirely convinced that either one of them could tell the difference between a smartphone and a walkie talkie.

I shoot her a quick "I'll call you in a bit" text and hop myself to the bathroom to mentally prepare. Every time I have an upcoming conversation with my mother, I feel this impending sense of doom, like I suddenly have a super important test that I forgot to study for.

Our relationship has always been complicated. We've never had that traditional mother/daughter bond where we go have fun together, laugh with one another, or show any type of love to each other at all.

No, our relationship has always more closely resembled that of a teacher/student, boss/employee, king/lowly peasant.

Conversations with my mother always follow the same outline. They're so similar that I've come to think she might have printed out a list of guidelines she uses every time we're on a phone call. They usually go like this:

Step one: begin with polite pleasantries. Acceptable topics include but are not limited to the weather, current events, a new recipe etc...

Step two: slowly transition into heavier subjects. I.e., questions pertaining to work, dating/marriage, finances.

Step three: finish off strong with some heavy drawn-out sighs of disappointment, reminders of past and current failures, and top it all off with lengthy lectures about not living up to expectations.

Anyone can see where my insecurities come from. It's taken me some time to unravel these feelings of resentment and disappointment. My therapist has helped me reach an understanding that my mother acts like this out of love for me, not because she thinks I'm stupid and worthless.

Her mother taught her that education and career were the most important things in life and everything else should come second–or third. Essentially, Carol is just passing down to me what her mother passed on to her.

I'm not going to sit here and lie and say that this immense pressure is all bad. It has gotten me far in life by teaching me that I can do whatever I set my mind to. It's taught me to never give up and always put my all into everything.

The bad part is that it also happened to cement into my brain that love is conditional. I learned that people's love for me is dependent on how well I'm doing in life, and if I'm unsuccessful with something, their love for me will be put up for debate and questioned.

Countless hours of therapy have tried to help me understand that this way of thinking is wrong. It's wrong for me to believe that my worth is solely based on my success, and it's *also* wrong for my parents to demand excellence and withhold affection when I'm anything less than perfect.

Thoughts of last night's panic attack move into my mind, and I'm quickly reminded that obviously I haven't quite internalized all of this yet, but I'm trying.

Since I started working on myself, the relationship with my parents has started to improve. It's not great, but I do think it's getting better. The moment that I felt things start to shift is when I was finally able to realize that at this point in my parents' lives, they aren't going to change. It's me who has to do the changing.

It's made my life so much easier to release their expectations of me and stop placing so much importance on what they think about my life. Letting go of that burden has lightened my load and has made our conversations a lot smoother and happier.

However, sometimes when we're talking on the phone, I can feel things start to shift. If it gets heated, I've started playing this game of changing the topic as many times as possible with super random things to see where the conversation goes.

Usually, it ends up in a comically intense discussion about something completely arbitrary.

The last time we talked, I was able to derail the conversation so entirely that my dad went on a thirty-minute rant about the politics of the potato industry and the problems farmers today face in America. It was absolutely hilarious and surprisingly eye-opening.

I brush the taste of stale protein bar out of my mouth and wash the sleep from my eyes. The cold water instantly revitalizes me. I feel awake, clean, and ready for the day. I towel off my face and go back into the main room.

Holy hell, I don't know how I was able to make such a mess last night. At first glance, I can ascertain that I emptied the entire contents of my work bag onto the floor prior to making it my pillow. Loose change is scattered about, charging wires of various shapes and sizes are strewn all around, and gum wrappers and receipts litter the carpet.

I gingerly bend down to begin the clean-up when I spot the Dumont client folder peeking out from underneath my swimsuit-cover-turned-blanket. The level of planning and organization I've put into this folder gives me so much joy you'd think it was full of money.

I'm not going to lie, that would be awesome; but alas, it's just a simple legal expanding folder that has been magnificently color coded, expertly date arranged, and printed on the best paper that an office supply chain delivers. It makes my heart swell with pride. I love organizing things and making them beautiful; it's honestly one of the best perks of my job.

Next, I grab my laptop to see if any more work has popped up this morning. But I'm happy to see that my inbox is still empty. My shoulders move up and down to the beat of imaginary music as I do a happy little dance celebrating my win. *Hell yeah.* I did it.

I feel a strange sensation prickling through my body. There's absolutely nothing that I *have* to do. Nothing is waiting for me to sign off. No one needs me to check on anything. No one is counting on me to get back to them. I got so much work done last night, work that didn't even need to be done yet, mind you, so now I'm completely open. I'm free. I can rest. To make it even better, I know that per our agreement, I won't be seeing Noah anymore.

My heart twinges. A positive twinge? A negative twinge? I'm not sure. Eh, either way, it doesn't even matter; I'm not going to see him anyway. Honestly, I'm just really looking forward to finally doing my own thing. I'm excited I don't have to worry about him crashing through my life, like a bull in a china shop, and throwing off my vibes again.

I finish cleaning up my mess and sit down on the bed. I definitely should have slept here last night instead of on the floor; my poor hips would have thanked me. I rearrange all the pillows, stretch my legs out in front of me, and dial my mom. Huh, if I cock my head to the side and squint my eyes, the bruise on my leg kind of looks like Danny Divito. A chuckle escapes from me right as my mom answers.

She holds the phone so close and high on her face that all I can see is the top of her eyes and her silver hairline. FaceTiming isn't her specialty. "Hello? Hello, Jane? Can you see me? I can see you. Where are you? It's so bright and sunny. Are you laughing?"

"Hi, Carol. Can you move the phone down a bit? I can only see the top of your head."

She moves the phone down slightly and smiles. "Is that better?"

I can't help but smile back. "Yep. Hi. What's up? Is everything okay?"

"Yes, everything is just fine. Just wanted to check in and see what you're doing. Also, I just wanted to tell you about this recipe I found for teriyaki salmon. I made it for your father and me last night, and it was delicious."

Recipe. Check.

"Thanks. That sounds great. What else is new with you?"

"Nothing much over here. Your father just spoke at a conference, and I'm still working on my manuscript. What about you, Jane? How is Rex? How is work going?"

Dating. Check.

Work. Check.

I take a quick breath, hoping to get this out as quickly and as painlessly as possible. "Rex and I broke up, but work is going really great. I just landed a remarkable client. The firm is growing substantially, and our numbers look great." Nice and simple. State the facts. *Good job, Jane.*

"Oh, thank God. Rex was a complete dolt. He was holding you back. I don't know what you saw in him in the first place, Jane. Good riddance." She's not wrong. "And congratulations on your new client. Who is it?"

"His name is Howard Dumont. I don't know if you know him, but he owns some pretty famous luxury resorts. I'm actually staying at his resort in Hawaii right now." I'm going to leave out the part where he flew to a different country before I could even meet him. That would open up far too many questions.

"Of course I know who Howard Dumont is. What an impeccable accomplishment, Jane. Having a client like him will push your career in an amazing new direction. Speaking of new directions, have you heard about making partner? Last time we talked, before your father went on that awful potato tangent—"

"Hey, I learned a lot from that tangent," I cut in.

"Jane, that is beside the point, it was insanely pointless and absurd. Anyway, you had mentioned that Mr. Schwartz was thinking about possibly growing the firm and making room for another partner. Have you learned any more about this?"

I let out a heavy breath. Here it comes.

"Yeah, the firm did decide to expand and move things around a bit. Adler is going to move to our New York office, and Schwartz will stay in Denver with the new partner."

Silence. She's waiting for me to continue.

"...Anyway, my coworker, Colin Clark, was made the new partner, and I'm excited for him. He's a great attorney, and I think the partners made a great choice."

I smile and stare at the phone. She's moved the camera away from her face, and I hear a weighty sigh come from the other side. I feel my chest constrict, knowing I have let her down, again.

She slowly returns to the camera, and her face has completely changed. Her brows are knitted together and there's a hint of a frown on her mouth.

"Well, I guess that's what's best then. Who has the time to become a partner when they're busy dating football stars anyway, right?" She says with a scoff.

There it is. That little hint of condescension and judgment. Could you imagine if she knew it wasn't even *real* football? "You let him completely derail your career. You were on track to becoming a partner, and you let everything slip away. You always do this, Jane. You stop thinking about your work, and then stumble and fall right back down to where you started. I really thought you would have grown out of this by now. You have so much potential to go far, but you just don't have the drive."

I feel the tingling of self-doubt prickling behind my ears. What she's saying isn't true, but hearing it makes it *feel* real. Rex was not the reason I didn't become a partner. It wasn't because of my lack of ability or drive either. I didn't become a partner because Joe thinks men can do jobs better than women can. That isn't much better, but at least I know it's not because of me. I have drive in bucketloads. I just completed a shit-ton of work last night because of my drive. I compete with Noah Riley because of my drive.

I can feel myself start to get carried away. "Well, it's been good chatting. Tell Dan I say hi, and I'll call you guys again when I get back in Denver. Bye."

I hang up the call before she has the chance to respond. *Whew, that was a close one.* She tried to knock me down a peg, and it almost worked. An exasperated chuckle leaves my mouth as I roll my eyes. It's almost funny how predictable she is. It feels good to finally be able to see it for what it really is and find the humor in it. Because let's be honest, if that phone call happened a year ago, it would have sent me spinning.

I unlock my phone and press Jordyn's contact. She always gets a kick out of my conversations with Carol. She picks up on the second ring. "Good morning, sunshine! How's life going in your sultry tropical paradise?" I light up as I see her beautiful face grace my screen. Her flawless brown skin and rich, bouncy curls are a stark difference to my mother's wrinkled forehead and silver locks. Her smile grows wide, waiting for my answer.

"It's amazing, J. Seriously, the most beautiful place I've ever been."

Daniel forces his way into the frame. "Hi, Janie Poo! Found any hot men you can bring home to your poor little single friends who just survived a blizzard?" A very exaggerated pout forms on his lips.

Jordyn pushes his face away. "Move your giant ass head out of my way. Daniel, you know this trip is about our friend *Jane* finding hot surfer boy vacation love, *not* about her bringing hot surfer boys home for us. Unless she wants to, then in that case, it would be rude of us to not graciously accept them with open arms." They both laugh in unison as Daniel makes a show of licking his lips seductively.

I lean my body back into the comfortable pillow behind me. "Ha, I haven't been successful on the love front yet." Their faces drop in unison. "It's actually been the total opposite. The only people who have seen me naked are two Scandinavians and Noah Riley." I wish this video call was recorded, because the look of pure shock on both of their faces is something I hope I never forget.

"Shut up, shut up! What?! When?! How?!" They both fight for control of the phone. The next thing I see is Daniel's hand ripping the phone away and his face bouncing around on the screen as he's running away from Jordyn. I see her blurry figure crawling out of a booth at the café, chasing him down. "Please don't tell me that you had a four-way in the sauna with Noah and some hairy-chested Vikings, because I will die right here, Jane Robins. You know I'm not kidding." The level of seriousness that Daniel is putting forth right now is astonishing.

I hear Jordyn quickly approaching in the background, yelling obscenities.

Daniel turns his attention away from the phone and onto her. "Jordyn, you cannot cuss in my café. I have respectable customers that eat here." He scowls at her.

Jordyn grabs the phone out of Daniel's hand, and I see her flushed face push into the screen. "Oh, duck you, Daniel." She sticks her tongue out at him before moving to the back office of the café. "Jane, it's just you and me now." She looks excited as she invites me to continue. "We will get to the part with you and some kinky Scandinavians later. I just want the nitty gritty of why the hell you were naked in front of Noah."

I laugh out loud. "Jordyn, you make it sound so much worse than it was. Him and I were forced into a couples' massage yesterday. The two gorgeous Scandinavians were the ones doing the massaging." I see her face fall. She was expecting details that were much juicer than I just provided.

"Oh, that's it? Noah peeped some side-boob? That's hardly anything to fuss about."

"Fussing? Who said I was fussing?"

"Oh, babe. It's written all over your face."

"Ha, totally not fussing. He did get more than some side-boob though. He saw it all, J. Everything…" I say the last word slowly.

"I want all the details. Every single second, Jane. My next meeting isn't for another two hours, I have time," she says, sitting up straighter in her seat.

"It was nothing exciting, trust me. He just happened to glance over at me as I was doing the awkward turn from my front to my back. It's a terrible view, and he got all of it."

The look on Jordyn's face is one of physical pain. "Oh, man, that's bad. That naked oily turnover is unsightly for anyone to make. Did he say anything?"

"I guess if you don't count teasing me in front of the people who were just trying to do their job, no. Just smiled like an idiot, and then asked me out to dinner."

"Jane," she says, swallowing hard. "Are you purposely trying to give me a heart attack right now? Because I can't tell if you're deliberately being vague, or if you just simply enjoy watching your best friend suffer."

"A little bit of both." I smile, and readjust the pillow behind my back. "But in all honesty, that's really all that happened. Obviously, I turned the dinner invitation down, because I can't think of anything worse than me going to dinner with him on days that he didn't see me naked, let alone on a day he saw me naked…twice."

"Twice?! What the hell is going on over there?" She presses her hand to her forehead, bewildered.

"I promise I'll fill you in on everything when I get home. I'm hoping that yesterday was the last of the Noah surprises. I'm seriously banking on the rest of my time here being much more uneventful."

"Oh, for sure. I get that. But...selfishly I'm hoping that in a few days you call me and regale me with spicy tales, including long walks on the beach, sexy tanned abs, and sand in places where sand should never be."

"Ha, I'm not so sure about that, but I guess we'll just have to see what happens. Oh, by the way, I originally called to tell you that I just got off the phone with Carol."

"This day just keeps getting better for me, and it's only noon. What did our little ray of optimistic sunshine have to say today?"

"Oh, you know how she is. She told me how proud she was of me, and then she went on and on about how I'm the best daughter in the world. I couldn't shut her up."

"So the usual then?" Jordyn says with a small laugh.

"Yep, just the usual." We both smile, but it doesn't quite meet our eyes.

"So, tell me...What's on your agenda for the day?"

I pull out an imaginary planner and pretend to turn through invisible page after invisible page. "Absolutely nothing."

"What, no more hot Norwegian foursomes penciled into your schedule?"

"They were Scandinavian, and no, that's not until tomorrow," I tease. "Today is chock full of nothing. I finished a ton of work last night, and now I'm as free as a bird."

"I'm so flipping jealous. I've been so busy the last few days that Daniel actually offered to start making me dinner until my workload calms down. He said, and I quote, I was 'looking extremely pathetic eating Taco Bell every night.' I just about punched him in the face, but then he made me a French dip, and I swear to God, Jane, I almost kissed him instead. It's been a very confusing time without you here, to say the least."

"Sounds like it." I laugh. "Anyway, I think I'm going to reward myself for all of my hard work and take myself on a little shopping spree."

"Yes, please! Get it girl! Remember, if you see something I can't live without, please buy it for me. I'm poor." Her bottom lip juts out in a pretend pout.

"Oh, shut up. You're richer than I am, and you know it."

"'Tis true, 'tis true. But unfortunately, Dad's money doesn't count. Also, it doesn't hurt that you have better taste than most. Don't tell Daniel, but you buy better presents than he does."

"I heard you say that, you loser!" Daniel says, making his way back over to Jordyn's phone. "I have more taste in my pinky toe than you two have in your entire body."

"You wish," Jordyn and I both say at the same time.

"Okay, I'm gonna run," I say, and I see Jordyn's smile quickly mold into one of concern. I continue before she's able to worry too much. "Not literally J, I know we don't run." I shake my head in disgust.

She wipes a bead of pretend sweat off her brow. "Okay good, I was worried there for a bit." She smiles, then continues, "I hope you have a wonderful day full of shopping and sun. Call me later?"

"Oh, for sure. Enjoy your work and your freezing cold snow," I say with a big, mocking smile.

She doesn't respond, but I briefly see both her and Daniel flip me the middle finger before ending the call.

I toss all the shiny new shopping bags onto the giant bed. Bags and bags full of everything from new silk panties to hair scrunchies. I don't think I've ever shopped so hard in my entire life. It's like I was an Olympic athlete racing from store to store. Trying things on, testing perfumes, eating delicious treats.

What a fantastic day.

I look at my hoard, and the reality of the situation starts to hit me. How the hell am I going to get this all home? I look back and forth from the bed to my luggage. There's no way this is all fitting in there. My mind is suddenly transported back to the airport when I was on my way here, and the giant box of condoms I had to stuff in my purse.

I shake the thoughts from my mind and ponder my current predicament. I might just have to leave some of my old things behind to make the new things fit. *Out with the old, in with the new*, right?

Ding, ding. I pull my phone out of my back pocket and stare at the new text. It's from an unknown number. Hmm, that's weird.

Unknown Number

> Hi Jane. This is Noah.

Shit, I was having so much fun that I *almost* forgot he was even here. Wait. How the hell did he get my number?

> Before you freak out, I got your number from that guest survey Ashley sent for our couples' massage. Your phone number was listed next to your room number.

Ashley....I curse, and make a mental note to talk to her about this later.

> I gave it 5 stars.

Okay, good. Anya and Sven definitely deserve five stars. I'm surprised Noah did something nice for a change. Hmm, maybe he has grown up.

> I wrote in the review that they deserve more than 5 stars because they let me see my wife naked and it was so thrilling and erotic that I will be a repeat customer for the rest of my life.

A little embarrassed laugh escapes from me as I imagine the poor spa manager reading the survey in innocent horror. Of course, Noah would say something so confusing and funny at the same time. That answers my question then. He clearly hasn't grown up at all.

> Anyway, how was your day? Did you get all caught up with your work?

I don't even want to respond to him, but I find myself typing my answer before my brain has time to catch up.

Jane

> It was good. I didn't work at all today. I got to have the entire day to myself. It's been great.

Noah

> Sounds like you had a good day.

Yes, I did, and I don't want it to be ruined. So that means I shouldn't respond any further. I don't know what he's doing texting me anyway. It feels strange.

> What did I do today? Oh, thanks for asking.

> Sven took me on this really awesome zipline tour that ended at a waterfall. It was phenomenal.

> You should totally do it while you're here.

Honestly, what does he want me to say? We're not friends. We're co-workers at best, and I don't even *want to be* his co-worker, long-distance or not. I don't want to do this...Wait... He said he was going to be working all day. If he was so busy, when did he have time to explore waterfalls with his new friend, Sven?

Jane

> Sounds cool. Hey I thought you said you had a ton of work to do today. Did you get everything done before you left?

Noah

> Nah. I overestimated the amount of work I had. I barely had any. I just had to finish something from a case I presented before I came here.

Okay. So, it sounds like he didn't have any work to do for Dumont at all. So basically, I freaked out for nothing and stayed up all night busting my ass doing extra work I didn't even need to do? Very on trend, Jane, very on trend.

> Is that okay with you, Boss?

He's so good at saying things that get under my skin. Well, I'm not going to take the bait this time. I move my phone across the room and set it face down on the desk. No more texting. I continue the joyful task of taking my new things out of their bags and admiring them one by one. *Ding, ding.* I pretend not to hear. I turn on the TV, hoping to fill the silence. *Ding, ding.* Nope. I refuse to give in. I will not flip that phone over until morning. I don't need to see what else he has to say. *Ding, ding.*

Fine.

> Anyway, I'm just texting you to mention that Howard called me today.

Howard?! Howard called him?! Why in the hell would our client call him and not me? Also, they're on a first name basis now? This isn't good.

> He told me to let you know that he scheduled us a snorkeling trip for first thing tomorrow morning.

Whew. Relief washes down my spine. I thought it was work-related. I still don't understand why Dumont told Noah this instead of coming directly to me. I can feel the annoyance bubbling up inside me.

Besides our quick little chat at the restaurant when he told me he wasn't even on the same island as me, I haven't even spoken one word to Dumont. Heat begins to crawl up my neck.

> Be ready by 8. Boat sets sail at 8:30. See you tomorrow, Boss.

Jane

K

And don't call me that.

Chapter Sixteen
Now

I STRETCH MY ARMS above my head and sink my head deeper into the soft pillow. I'm so glad I'm waking up in a bed right now and not on the floor.

My eyes open and find the room full of warm sunlight and the smell of briny saltwater in the air. I fell asleep last night with the balcony door open so I could let the sound of the ocean waves lull me to sleep. It was a fantastic choice, if I do say so myself.

The rest of my night was both uneventful and exciting at the same time. Well, maybe most people wouldn't call it exciting, but it was exactly what I needed. After turning off my phone to avoid any more unavoidable texts thrown my way, I moved aside my shopping bags and plopped myself onto the bed.

I ordered room service and binged the trashiest of reality TV shows until my eyes couldn't stay open any longer. The best part of the night though, was the dessert—pineapple cheesecake, a mocha brownie, *and* a triple berry cobbler. For the life of me, I couldn't decide what sounded better, so I got them all. Never once did I regret my decision.

As soon as the desserts were laid out in front of me, I'm not ashamed to say that, I may have acted like a judge on one of those famous baking shows.

First, I inspected their beautiful presentation, then I took a not-so-bite-sized piece of each. *Holy hell,* they were delicious. After all the judges' scores were tallied, it was clear that the brownie was going to be the winner of the night. I scarfed it down faster than I care to admit, then put the other two remaining desserts in the mini fridge to eat for breakfast.

You can think what you want, but I happen to be a firm believer that while on vacation, you can do whatever you want. You want to eat two desserts for breakfast? Go for it! You want to spend copious amounts of money on fabulous new lingerie, swimsuits, and clothes? Do it! You want to stick with kale and avocados to meet your fitness goals? You go girl! When in Rome and all that.

A big yawn escapes my mouth and all this thinking about dessert has my stomach growling. I open the mini fridge and both remaining desserts sit there staring at me.

I choose the cheesecake and move back over to my spot on the bed. I spear a piece of the pineapple on my fork and pop it into my mouth. I don't know how it's possible, but it tastes even better today.

Licking my spoon clean, I glance at the clock on the nightstand. Shit, I only have half an hour before I need to be at the boat.

I get up from the bed to rummage around my luggage and new shopping bags. I have to find exactly the right thing to wear.

I'm embarrassed to say that yesterday the soft Hawaiian breeze convinced me that I needed to buy three new bikinis. My brain knew I brought two in my suitcase, but my heart was listening to what Hawaii wanted. What can I say, Hawaii brought the fight and Hawaii won.

Quickly putting on the top of one new suit and the bottom of another, I stare intently at the third option lying on my bed. No one ever tells you what to wear when you go snorkeling. Or maybe they do, but Noah Riley sure doesn't.

I peel off the mismatched suit and slip on the third. Hot damn, this is the one. Of course, it also happens to be the one I debated returning right after I bought it because of the hefty price tag. But alas, it's the one that hugs my body most and the all-white color shows off my *also new* spray tan.

I rip off the tags, tie a cute little sheer white wrap skirt around my hips, and finish getting ready.

On my way down to the pier, I begin ruminating over possible scenarios on how this day could go. I've always wanted to go snorkeling, but never in a million years did I think I would be going with the person in the world that I dislike most.

There is one benefit to it though. Since we're underwater, we won't have to talk to each other. Which is good, because talking with Noah is where all hell breaks loose. My mind gets all turned inside out and my words don't come out right. I guess another possible benefit is that he could drown and then be out of my life for good. *Yikes, Jane that's morbid.*

"Hi, Boss." I hear from my left. "When did you get the Danny Devito tattoo?"

Drown the man.

"Ha very funny." I roll my eyes. "This *bruise* was given to me by an inconveniently placed coffee table in my room. It was dark, and I tripped over my bag. The corner of the table got me."

"Ouch, that sucks. What were you doing roaming around in the dark?" He asks, not breaking his stride.

"Not looking to get a giant bruise shaped like Danny Devito, I'll tell you that much."

We reach our boat, and the other hopeful snorkelers are gathered around, waiting to board. I feel him stop right behind me.

Honestly, can't he go stand somewhere else? I fold my arms across my chest and tap my foot in annoyance. It's hard to pay attention to the instructor's speech about the dos and don'ts of snorkeling when I can feel Noah's presence pulsing behind me.

It's like there's a fly buzzing around in the room. The constant invisible buzz is irritating and distracting.

The air around me changes as I hear his breath come close to my ear. The hairs on the back of my neck stand up as he bends down and whispers, "By the way, I like your suit."

My entire body erupts with tiny little goosebumps. I suddenly feel overly exposed. Memories of the first time he said these words to me flood into my head. I'm transported back to being seventeen at the lake, surrounded by other teenagers, and feeling extremely self-conscious in my ugly one-piece swimsuit.

My face feels hot as I continue staring forward. I don't know what to say. Does he really like this suit or is he just being an ass again? "Oh...um, thanks. I've had it forever. I don't even really like it anymore. I was actually thinking about getting rid of it." *Well, that's not true.* Why does he make me do this? I bring my hand up to play with my necklace, hoping to hide the flush creeping up my neck.

A brief minute passes with neither of us talking. I wait for him to say something, anything, but it appears he's finished with our conversation.

I breathe out a sigh of relief. Then, I feel the warmth of his body press into my back. His muscles tense behind me as he bends his head down, inching closer to my level. The heat of his breath tickles my ear as he quietly whispers, "That's fine. I like you better in the little red one anyway."

Apparently, Wednesday mornings are the least busy time to go snorkeling because our boat isn't nearly as full as I would have expected. The flat-decked boat isn't very big, but there is more than enough room for everyone to find a nice place to sit. A cute couple situates themselves in the rear corner, and a pleasantly plump elderly woman sits in the front chatting the ear off a middle-aged single dad who's here with his two sons. I'm not sure where Noah is, but at least he isn't by me.

I take my seat in the middle of the boat and stare out at the blinding sunshine reflecting off the turquoise water. I can sense everyone's growing excitement as our boat pulls away from the pier. As we gain speed, the salty spray mists my face, and the warm sun beats down on my skin.

Everything about this whole moment screams perfection, but I can feel a part of myself that's not willing to let go. That part of myself keeps replaying the sentence Noah murmured into my ear. What did he mean when he said that? *I like you better in the little red one anyway.* The words are obviously clear, but I don't know what they could mean coming from *him*.

I hear his laugh before I see him. Noah is unsteadily making his way in my direction with a crew member following close behind him.

Straightening myself, I pretend not to notice, although my heart starts to pick up pace.

"Thanks, Zeke, I'm sure sitting here will help with the motion sickness." He plops his butt down on the bench seat right next to me and rests his arm on the cushion behind my head.

"No problem, my friend. Sometimes it takes a while to get your sea legs." Zeke crouches down and gently moves my feet to the side. He reaches under my seat and takes out a small trash can. "We just ask that if you do vomit, you either do it in this or off the side of the boat." Zeke laughs. "The fish would enjoy some extra lunch anyway." He pats Noah on the shoulder and retreats to the back of the boat.

"Don't you dare throw up on me," I say, picking up his heavy arm from behind me and dropping it onto his lap.

"Oh, don't worry, I already feel much better," he says, setting the trash can aside.

"That was fast," I say with a sideways glance, not at all believing his sordid tales of motion sickness.

"So, are you excited to go snorkeling?" He asks, placing his arm back behind my head.

My eyes narrow on him. Is he seriously going to pretend like his body—his *hard* body— wasn't just pressed up against my back while whispering very hot and very confusing things into my ear?

"When Howard called me yesterday to tell me he booked this trip for us, I was so fired up. I've always wanted to go snorkeling," Noah continues.

Yep, he's definitely ignoring that anything happened. Okay, then. Two can play at that game.

I turn my body to face him as much as I can, but since we're sitting on the same bench seat, it doesn't take much before our knees press together. I shouldn't have butterflies, I shouldn't be feeling this way right now. I'm hyper-aware of that small part of my body touching his. Actually, that's the only thing I'm aware of right now. Every other thought is out the window—gone like smoke in the wind. That little touch is like an itch I need to scratch. I see him glance down at our touching knees and from the look in his eyes, I sense that he feels it too.

I watch as the loose fabric of his linen shirt dances with the breeze of our moving boat. The top two buttons are undone, and parts of his toned chest peak through from underneath. His shoulders are relaxed, and his face is...*happy.* He's perfect.

I want so badly for this to be easy. I want to be able to let go, to have a simple, friendly conversation with him. But I just can't. He broke my heart once, and it feels impossible to forget that fact. It's especially hard when he makes stupid comments like he did earlier. It's so unfair.

My brows knit together, and he looks at me with concern. "You okay, Robins? Do you need this?" He thrusts the trash can into my lap.

Here it is. This is my in. The way we can talk, the *only* way we know how to talk, is to bicker. I can argue and debate with him until the cows come home. This is how it works for us. Here we go.

"I'm fine. I was just thinking about whether I'm excited to be snorkeling or not." I turn away from his gaze as I make this brutally untrue statement. In reality, I'm so freaking excited. I'm genuinely thrilled to check something off my bucket list, but that unavoidable urge to compete with him always bubbles up to the surface. "I mean, it's awesome to see all the stunning marine life, but you can't dispute the fact that it's extremely unethical."

"Wait, what? Where did you hear that from?" He scoffs.

"Basically everyone." *Ouch, Jane.* What a terrible argument. I'm an attorney, but I just used the equivalent of a child sticking their tongue out at you.

"Ah, *everyone.* Sounds plausible." He raises his eyebrows. "Really, what makes you think that snorkeling is *extremely unethical,* as you put it?"

A few years ago, I went on a marine biology kick and absorbed anything and everything I could about the topic. I read countless books and watched some outstanding documentaries about controversies surrounding snorkeling and scuba diving. Some argue that regularly invading these natural ecosystems negatively impacts the animals and organisms there. While others insist that these practices, if done properly, are actually beneficial. I know this, but am I going to let Noah in on this knowledge? Nah, not right now. I want to see where we can get with this. Let the debate begin.

"Okay, let's start with the coral. Did you know that coral is one of the most diverse ecosystems in the entire world? There are so many different types of animals that depend on coral for their survival. Even some groups of people rely on coral reefs for their livelihood, their jobs, for their food, etc...And when stupid people come in and mess it all up in the name of a *'good time,'* it affects everything."

Noah's face doesn't show any indication of whether or not he's heard anything I just said. He just continues staring at me, so I continue with my arguments.

"Another thing we have to think about is the mass amounts of people these experiences draw in. More people equals more things that could go wrong. There are so many instances where some uneducated snorkeler will touch the animals when they shouldn't, or feed them, or heaven forbid, even take them out of the water entirely, and each of these things cause such a disturbance in the natural behaviors of the reef. It's terrible. Sometimes people are meant to stay away from things we don't understand," I say, shrugging my shoulders.

He pulls in a breath and folds his arms across his chest. "But there are many people who do understand them. To be fair, they wouldn't understand them at all if they didn't go snorkeling or diving in the first place, right?" He says, slightly agitated.

"Okay, Noah, so you're saying that just because some people are educated enough or have trained their entire lives to research and experiment on marine life, that means anyone and their dog should be able to disturb the precious habitat whenever they want to?" I cock my head, and raise a brow.

"No, of course not. The point I was trying to make is that since there are people who, as you pointed out, work their entire lives examining the underwater environment, we rely on them to guide us in the right direction when we want to take part in the experience. We follow their rules and use best practices, which ensures the safety of marine life and minimizes the human impact on the delicate ecosystem." He sits up straighter, which takes away his knee from touching mine. The sudden absence of it feels strange.

Trying to distract myself from his missing touch, I sit up straighter in my seat as well. "Do you really think people on vacation, just wanting to snorkel for a good time, *actually* listen to what the experts say?"

"Yes. Majority do. These excursions exist to bring awareness of the reef's importance to the native population. When people come to have these experiences, it draws more attention, more mindfulness, and more funding to the reef. All of this is aimed at the actual problems that these habitats face. Sure, sometimes there will be stupid people who do stupid things, but the overwhelming benefit they have for preventing damage and bringing awareness significantly outweighs the few things that stupid people do."

Damn. He's right.

He's staring at me, waiting for my rebuttal. My mind is scrambling to find something to say, but nothing comes. He wins—again.

"Regardless," he continues, "I don't care what anyone says, if I see a clownfish, I'm bringing it home." His mouth twitches up in a smile.

"Did Finding Nemo teach you nothing?" I say to him, feigning offense.

"Nope." His knee finds its place touching mine once more, and this time, neither of us moves away.

The couple sitting in the back of the boat, starts to make their way up to the middle and sit down opposite us. They're both so young and gorgeous it's hard to look away. The woman has on a cute little yellow bikini, and her long brunette hair falls down her back in big loose curls. While her sandy blond, tall, beefy husband looks like he could pick her up with one finger.

"Hi! I'm Lauren! This is my husband, Justin." Her heavy Southern accent is not what I was expecting. "We got so bored alone in the back of the boat. We decided to come see what's happening up here! Are y'all married too?"

The answer rushes out of my mouth like a dam letting loose. "No, we are *not* married. Definitely not married, we're not even friends, really." I see both Lauren and Justin's eyes glance down at our touching knees.

They quickly bring their eyes back up and smile in unison. "Well, we are! We were hitched just four days ago." She brings her left hand up to her face and wiggles her fingers, showing off her giant diamond. "We're on our honeymoon. I'm so excited to be here. I've never dreamed of doing anything like this before, I've never even seen the ocean besides in movies. I'm from a teeny tiny town in southern Alabama, so all this here is just so exotic that I can hardly believe it. I've never been snorkeling before. I don't even really know what it's all about. Justin here planned everything, so I'm just along for the ride." She beams with pride as she looks at him. "I'm mostly excited to see a snorkel. What are they like?"

"What?" Justin asks, staring at his new wife, utter confusion written all over his face.

"I've never seen a real live snorkel before. I don't know what they look like," she says with such childlike amazement that our shock feels unwarranted.

"Lauren..." Justin starts slowly, "what do you think snorkeling is?" He gently puts his hand on her thigh.

She stares at him happily, still wearing that great big Southern smile. "It's like whaling right? My aunt Tilly went whaling once in Alaska and she got to see a bunch of whales."

Noah covers his laugh with a cough, and I bite my lip, trying to stifle my own.

"Honey," Justin starts, "snorkels aren't fish. They're the tube thing we breathe through when we're underwater."

Lauren's eyes grow wide, and her perfect little nose crinkles. I think she's about to cry, but instead, she lets loose the biggest laugh I've ever heard. "Are you kidding me? This whole time I thought we were going to be looking at some little crazy fish called a snorkel, and you're telling me that a snorkel isn't even a fish at all?" She throws her head back, laughing harder.

Once he saw that his wife wasn't crushed by her newfound information, Justin let his own laugh burst through.

That gives Noah and I permission to do the same. All four of us laugh heartily together as Lauren shakes her head and repeats in joyful amazement, "A snorkel isn't a fish."

When we reach our destination, the water is the perfect temperature. My body feels weightless as I float on the surface of the brilliantly blue water. My goggles are crystal clear, and it only takes me a minute to get the hang of breathing through the snorkel.

The magic I see under the water is unlike anything else I've ever experienced. The rough coral looks like a cityscape as vibrant fish swim in and out of the various structures. I take a deep breath and dive down. The water gets cooler the farther down I go, and the sereneness I felt on the surface is amplified the deeper I get. It's not exactly silent, but it's quiet. It's calming.

Resurfacing, I take of my goggles, and deeply inhale the sweet ocean air. I feel a sting in my nose as I float up and down in the water. Feeling overwhelmed with so much peace and happiness, tears begin to run down my cheeks. I'm basically full-on sobbing when I hear Noah swimming toward me.

"Robins, don't tell me you're crying because you already killed a fish." He laughs.

"I'm fine, Noah. Go away." I replace my goggles, hoping they will mask the full extent of my crying. "And no. I didn't kill a fish. I'm not the one who's willing to break the rules if they see a Nemo, remember?"

"Hey, I told you that in confidence. I thought we could go in on it together. You know, like partners in crime?" He circles around me, and we end up face to face.

I stretch my goggles and rest them on the top of my head. "Besides, I don't think they live in Hawaii anyway, so it looks like you're off the hook." He bobs up and down in time with the waves. It doesn't seem possible that such a large man could float with such ease, but I guess he's proof. "Hey, did you see the humuhumunukunukuāpuaʻa?"

"What? The hoo moo koo noo what now?"

"Ha, the humuhumunukunukuāpuaʻa. It just swam over by that rock. It's Hawaii's state fish. It's pretty cool."

"State fish? May I ask how you happen to know what Hawaii's state fish is? Do other states have state fish?" I poke.

"Yes, almost every state has a state fish." He smiles, and I can tell he's quite pleased with himself.

"Okay then, what's the state fish of Colorado?"

"Please, Jane. Don't treat me like a child." He scoffs.

"Oh, so you don't know. That's fine." I shrug my shoulders and turn to swim away.

The boyhood pride takes over his face as he says, "I've known the Colorado state fish since I was three years old, thank you very much. The *greenback cutthroat trout* are super hard to catch because they hang out under the ice most of the time, but I caught a handful of them myself before I moved to New York."

"Okay, fish boy," I say, facing him again. "What's the state fish of Rhode Island?" I see the gears moving in his mind as he starts to think about this question.

His mouth twitches before blooming into an adorable lopsided grin. "The striped bass."

"Oh, good Lord, you're a nerd."

He laughs. "Ha, I am not! I just like fish."

"Exactly. Nerd. Are fish your favorite animals?"

"Maybe yes, maybe no. What's it to you?"

"Nothing at all. I was just trying to have a friendly conversation for once." I float on my back and look up at the cloudless sky.

"He swims toward my head. "Okay, that sounds nice, I'll play. My favorite animal is actually a mouse."

Water washes up my nose, and I think I'm about to drown. After my small coughing fit, I look at Noah through stinging eyes. He's seemingly undisturbed and maybe even a little smug. "A mouse? Noah, you're joking."

"Oh, I don't *joke*, Robins," he says, attempting to appear stoic.

"Your favorite animal is a mouse?"

"Yep. No one likes them, so I do."

"Gosh, Noah. You get weirder and weirder every time I talk to you."

"Okay, Jane, what's your favorite animal then?"

"A dog. Like a normal person."

We bob in the water, both of us with smiles on our faces. This feels good.

"Okay, next one," he says, "What's your favorite food?"

"Easy. A brownie."

"That's a dessert, Robins, not food."

"Prove it," I say, my turn to be smug. "I happen to know that it's the best food that exists in the entire world. It's warm, gooey, and chocolatey. Basically the holy trinity. What more could you need? You can eat it for breakfast, lunch, or dinner. It's far superior to any other food there is."

"Are you done?"

"Shut up, I'm making a point."

"Oh...I see your point. You're an insane person who thinks that eating a brownie for breakfast is alright."

"Not only is it alright, it's heavily encouraged," I say, and he chortles, shaking his head. "My turn." I try to think of a question. "Um...Do you have a nickname?"

"Nope. Just been Noah since the day I was born. My dad always loved the name, but my mom hated it. Said she thought I'd turn out to be a crazy animal lover with a name like Noah, you know, because of the namesake and all that."

"Well, you do love mice...so maybe she had a right to be worried?"

He lightly splashes the water into my face. "What about you? Any nicknames?"

"What, you mean besides Robins, Boss, or let's see...what else have you called me?" I bring my finger to my chin, pretending to think.

"What can I say, Robins, I have a knack for it." He pauses and rakes his hand through his wet hair. "But really, do you have a nickname?"

"Yeah." My lungs fill with salty air as I take a deep breath in. "My Nan called me 'Bird.'" Memories of my favorite person fill my head, and those tears from earlier threaten to return. I turn away embarrassed that my emotions turned so quickly. She's been gone for a few years now, but it's still hard.

"Let me guess, she calls you Bird because your last name is Robins?" He says, trying to bring me back. "Seems like we had the same idea. She's one smart lady." I hear the smile in his voice, begging me to turn back around.

"Yeah. She *was*." I wipe my eyes and turn to face him again. "She passed away a few years back. She was really, really great. Taught me a lot about the world, made me feel safe. So, that nickname means a lot to me. It's like my own little magic word for feeling loved." I pause, feeling vulnerable. I've just revealed too much. "Sorry, woah, that got heavy..." I let out a pathetic attempt at a laugh.

"She sounds wonderful, Jane. I'm sorry you lost her." I see the earnestness in his eyes, and my heart starts to warm.

"Me too."

We float in heavy silence, both lost in our heads. After a moment, his eyes grow wide as he slaps the water with his hand. "Okay, I've got it. It's not a nickname, but I will tell you my very...very unfortunate middle name. But, if you tell anyone, Robins, I will have to kill you."

"Oh, come on. It can't be that bad."

"Horace."

"Excuse you."

He laughs. "I told you it was bad."

"Horace? Noah Horace Riley? Woof, that *is* rough."

"Right? My mom said since she didn't get to pick my first name, she got to pick my middle name."

"And she picked *Horace?!*"

"Yeah, it was her grandpa's name. Poor guy."

Just then, the captain calls for all the snorkelers to return to the boat for the trip back to the island. We look at each other. There's something in the air between us now. It feels both old and new at the same time. I don't know exactly how or why it feels so different, but it's definitely here. It changed; and it changed fast. I can sense that neither of us want to leave.

The captain whistles again, breaking the spell.

"After you, Horace," I say, casually motioning with my hand.

He rushes toward me and playfully pushes my head underwater.

I come up gasping for air.

"I warned you, Robins," he says, racing toward the boat.

My hair whips around my face as the boat heads back toward civilization. I shift around in my seat and feel the tightness from the saltwater drying on my skin. I lean my head back, the heat of the bright sun beating down on my face.

The two small boys and their dad are regaling each other with tales from their adventure. The younger boy is buzzing with excitement as he exclaims to his dad that a sea turtle swam right up to him. "Dad! I'm not even kidding! He almost bit my finger off! He came right up to me, and I could tell that he thought my finger was, like, a baby carrot or something! So, I just put my hands in my life jacket, and he swam right away! Like I took his lunch, Dad! It was so funny." His little-boy enthusiasm and laughter fill the boat. I hear Noah laugh along as the family continues with their stories.

Lauren and Justin are once again sitting at the back of the boat, her head resting on his lap. Justin gazes out over the water as he lazily plays with her hair. Periodically, I see him turn his attention on his sleeping wife, and I can see that his face is full of love and contentment. What a feeling that would be. To feel so comfortable and in love.

A warm feeling blooms in the center of my chest at the hope of it. I haven't had much luck in the love department so far, but at least I'm still hopeful about it. Even if I'm in my sixties when love finally knocks at my door, the wait would be worth it.

I look at Noah sitting across from me on the opposite side of the boat. His head is leaned back and his eyes are closed to the hot sun up above. A small smile is still playing on the edges of his lips.

My next inhale is shaky and goosebumps roll across my skin. I don't know why or how he's able to do the things he does to me, but it's becoming harder and harder to ignore.

We get to the pier and begin disembarking. The dad and two boys are off first, followed by Lauren, Justin, and some of the crew members. I'm still gathering my things when I see Noah helping the elderly lady up from her spot at the front of the boat. I linger behind a bit, watching their interaction.

"I didn't go on this trip to actually go snorkeling. Heavens no. I was just in it for the boat ride! Ha! Could you imagine this old bat squeezing into a bathing suit? Nope. Not at my age. I told Clyde, I said, Clyde I'm going to go on a boat ride. I'll be back when I'm back! And he said that he'll probably be sitting in the same place on the beach when I return." She slowly slips her feet into her sandals.

"When you've been together for fifty years, you can do that, you know. Just leave each other to do things you want to do, and then just come back together when you're done. That's one thing I like about getting old. It's not all good, but that part is." One of her hands is resting in Noah's, while his other hand is on her back, helping keep her steady on the rocking boat.

"Well, Evelyn, I hope that one day I get to experience that myself."

My heart constricts at hearing this. Hearing his hope for the future.

"Oh, you will, dear boy. Anyone that has a mug like you doesn't have to worry about finding love at all."

I see Noah's eyes fall briefly, but then quickly recover. He smiles as he says, "You think I have a nice mug, Evelyn?"

I let out a quiet laugh.

"Don't kid yourself, son. You're good-looking and you know it." She hits his hand gently. "To be honest, I didn't even need your help getting up from my seat. But when I saw you coming my way, I thought, what the hell, it's not every day you get to walk arm in arm with a handsome young man." They both laugh in unison.

"Oh, Evelyn, I would walk arm in arm with you any day." They reach the bottom step, and I see an older man, whom I assume is Clyde, striding happily toward his wife.

"Hello, my Dear." His voice is low and gruff but full of affection.

"Hello, Sweetheart. This kind young man was just helping your fat, old wife off the boat."

Clyde laughs. "Thank you—"

"Horace," Noah interjects as they shake hands.

"Horace? Now that's not a name you hear every day," Clyde says, eyebrows raised.

The corner of Noah's mouth lifts up into a smile. "No, it's not." He chuckles.

No, it's not. My cheeks burn from smiling so much today.

"Well, thank you, Horace, for helping my fat, old wife off the boat. I'd be really sad if she was stuck up there forever."

Evelyn hits him on the back of the head playfully. "Oh, shut up, Clyde, and take me to lunch." They all say their goodbyes as I step off the boat.

Noah turns and his gaze finds mine. We look at each other for a moment, slow breaths, and heavy blinks. Then, I see the corner of his mouth lift and one of his perfect dimples pops through. "I'm hungry. Wanna grab some lunch?"

I'm *supposed* to say no.

I'm *supposed* to be staying far away from him.

I'm *supposed* to be doing this on my own.

"Sure," I give in, and we walk up the pier.

Chapter Seventeen
Then

"So, what exactly are we doing for your birthday?" Jordyn asks, balancing her soccer ball on her forehead.

I look up from my book and shrug. "First off, I cannot take you seriously with that ball on your head. Second, we're doing nothing.

I have a debate tournament on Saturday, and I have to finish reading *To Kill a Mockingbird*, then write my report for English by Monday. So, as you can see, no time for birthday stuff.

Besides, my parents are out of town for two weeks for a conference, so it's not like they have anything planned for me either." I return to my book.

"Nope. Sorry, Jane, but that's not how this is going down." She drops the ball, pulls me from the grass, and plops my book down to where I was just sitting. "You've already read this book twice. You know it by heart, so that means your report could basically write itself. Also, I know for a fact that you already have your debate notes memorized and all marked up in that special little notebook you have, so the tournament will go perfectly. Also, for the record, your parents don't need to be home for you to have a party." She wiggles her eyebrows up and down. "Come on, we have to do something. Turning eighteen is a big deal, Jane. You're going to be an adult; a freaking grown up. You have to go out with a bang, right?" She grabs both of my hands in hers.

"Fine, fine. What should we do then? Wanna just come to my house, and we'll watch a movie or something? We can go over to Blockbuster and rent a few. Fridays are rent one, get one free."

Just then, our friend, Joshua, walks up and throws his arms around Jordyn and says, "What's all this about Friday? Are you two coming to the Fossil Ridge party that night? Matthew and Patrick both say it's going to be so sweet. It's at this kid named Landon's house. It's right up against a private lake and apparently, his house is so big that they have an entire arcade room downstairs. It's going to be epic."

"Ooo Josh, that sounds fun and all, but I've recently learned that the people at Fossil Ridge are not my cup of tea, so no, thank you." I reach down to pick up my book.

Jordyn, again, grabs the book out of my hand and throws it back down on the ground. "Jane, I swear to God, I *cannot* with you. Friday is your birthday. Friday is also the day that super rich kids are throwing a huge amazing party. You were just invited to said huge amazing party. On your birthday. Yes, Josh, we will be going."

After Jordyn finishes her rant, she bends over and picks up my twice-discarded book, dusts off the cover, and shoves it in my hands. "I'm sorry for putting this on the ground. Twice. But it was for your own good, Jane. I promise that one day you will thank me for pushing you out of your comfort zone." We start walking back to the school building.

"Maybe you'll meet some rich Fossil Ridge hottie and hit it off. Then, you two could double with Tyler and me." She playfully pats herself on the back. "Perfect plan, Jordyn. *Thank you,* Jordyn."

"As long as a certain someone isn't there, I'll be fine."

"Well, I have good news for you then. I can assure you of that, because I know for certain that Tyler and Noah will be out of town this weekend. Their parents are divorced, and Ty told me that the two of them are going to visit their dad in Denver for a few days. So...that means party time?"

"Okay, Jordyn. Party time."

Chapter Eighteen
Now

B EADS OF SWEAT GATHER on my cold glass of water. I catch one with the tip of my finger and bring it to my mouth. "You know, you could just lift the glass to drink the water?" He says with a small smile. I stare at the man sitting across from me and question my mental stability. I actually agreed to have lunch with Noah, for no other reason than temporary insanity.

"Oh, wow! Thanks." I don't break eye contact as I lift the glass to my mouth and take a sip of the ice-cold water.

"There you go, Robins. Good job." He winks at me and returns his attention to the giant burger and fries piled onto his plate.

I look at my salad but quickly turn away. My stomach is all topsy-turvy. I have so many questions running through my mind. Why am I here? What made me think that coming to lunch with him was a good idea? Suddenly, snapshots of the snorkeling trip flip through my mind. Noah's strong body floating in the water, the playful way he splashed my face, his big, bright smile as he laughed with Evelyn while helping her off the boat.

"Where did you go, Robins?" I look up from my plate and see Noah staring at me intently with his rich, brown eyes.

"What?"

"Where did you go? You were just looking at your food, and then you started smiling at it. Like this." He opens his eyes wide and stares at his food with a giant grin on his face.

"No, I wasn't. I did not look like that!" I throw my napkin at him, trying not to laugh.

"You went somewhere in your thoughts, I can tell." He dips his fries in some ketchup. "So, where'd you go?"

"No. Nowhere. I was just thinking about this salad. It's really delicious." I load up my fork and shove it in my mouth. I try to smile through my awkward chewing.

"There's no salad on Earth that is good enough to smile the way you were smiling. Come on, Robins. Spill."

Why does he care what I'm thinking about? Why does he care why I'm smiling? For all he knows, I was picturing having sex with a seven-foot tall basketball player. Or brownies. Or puppies. But, I wasn't....I was smiling because I was picturing *him*.

My face flushes. *Shit*. I have to change the subject, or this could get worse. "Question for you, Noah." He brings the burger down from his mouth, his brows knitted together. "Do you like doing dishes or doing laundry more?"

He chokes on his food as a laugh tries to escape. "Excuse me?"

"You heard me. Dishes or laundry?"

"Oh, I heard you, I just don't understand what this has to do with you having a love affair with your salad."

I laugh despite myself. "Just answer the damn question."

"Dishes. I would do dishes all day, every day if it meant I never had to do another load of laundry again in my life."

"Woah, there, buddy. You feel deeply about this topic then?" I say, this time taking a smaller bite.

"I do. I despise laundry."

His tone is so matter-of-fact, that I can't help but raise my eyebrows at his surprising intensity. "Okay, wow. I didn't know I was opening up such a can of worms."

He brings his glass to his mouth, and I watch as he takes a sip. I stare intently as the column of his throat moves up and down as he swallows. I look back down at my plate, trying to distract myself. Stabbing a piece of lettuce with my fork, I point it at him. "However, you're completely wrong."

He sets his glass back down on the table slowly. "Oh, don't go there with me, Robins. You will not win. I have years of real-world experience, plenty of case studies, and I'm sure I could line up some expert witnesses who would be willing to back me up on this."

I'm completely aware of the fact that this is a silly topic. One that doesn't matter in the grand scheme of things at all, but nevertheless, the thrill of debating with him has me in a chokehold.

"You could arrange all that, sure. But that won't help you win. Laundry is far superior to dishes in every way." I straighten up, ready to plead my case. "I acknowledge that both must be completed in order for a household to function properly, but if we're looking at what chore is quantifiably worse to achieve, dishes win that argument every time. For example, when you do dishes, you have to touch the cold, soggy food bits that are on each dish." I gaze at him, a disgusted look on my face. "That's just gross. Also, I'm sure that there are *actual case studies* about how bending over and doing dishes for too long can give you neck and back problems. Furthermore, no one likes pruney fingers or that stupid wet line you get on the bottom of your shirt. Laundry is easy. It's calming and smells nice. Don't even get me started on the beauty of folding it and organizing it away into nice little predetermined spots." I pretend to swoon.

He looks up at me over the rim of his glass. "Get a dishwasher, Robins."

I purse my lips, trying to come up with a rebuttal, but all I can think about is the way the sheen of sweat is glistening off his Adam's apple. I follow the muscles down his throat and see the tick of his heartbeat in that soft spot above his collarbone.

"Jane?"

I come back to the present. "True, a dishwasher would help eliminate all these things, but...I stand by my earlier argument. Dishes suck, laundry is better."

He smiles and shakes his head in dismay. "Agree to disagree then?" He holds his hand out in a truce.

"Deal." I reach across the table, and we give a simple shake. The way his strong hand engulfs mine is suddenly all I can think about. It makes me feel protected and safe. It makes me feel small, but not inferior.

I quickly remove my hand from his and pick up my fork, hoping to get rid of the electric current surging through me right now. "Have we ever just 'agreed to disagree' before?"

"Nope. I think we just made history with that one." I see him drum his fingers on the table, like he's trying to expel something too.

"I'm surprised, I mean we're both attorneys, and we just ended a debate in a calm and pleasant manner. That never happens," I scoff. "How long have you been an attorney anyway?" I ask, taking a bite of my salad.

"For quite a few years now. I was at a smaller firm up until about eight months ago when I was hired at Schwartz & Adler."

"Do you like it so far?"

"What? Schwartz & Adler, or being an attorney?"

I shrug my shoulders. "Both. Either."

"Well, I've always known that I was good at arguing. After all, that's why I was in debate. But honestly, I thought I would use it to go into business. When I was a junior in high school, I had everything all squared away to go into business school, but that all changed after I read *To Kill a Mockingbird*. So, I guess I can say, I have you to thank for that."

"What? Me? I don't think I ever told you I liked that book."

"No, you didn't. I saw you reading it at the debate tournament the first day we met. After we finished the debate, I went right to the bookstore and picked up a copy. I read it cover to cover that night and decided I wanted to go into law." He moves his hands from the table and into his lap, and I see his neck start to flush.

"I pick it up at least once a year to remind myself why I'm doing this." I see the muscle in his jaw work. "Atticus made a difference. He changed lives for the better. He used the law for good and for justice. That's what I want to do, it's what I've wanted from the beginning. Sometimes though, I wonder if I got a bit sidetracked along the way."

"What do you mean?" I have a feeling that I know exactly what he means, but I want to hear him say it. I want to hear someone else put into words the way I feel about this topic.

"Sometimes I just wonder if my drive to climb the ladder left me blind to where the ladder was taking me. I never wanted to do corporate law. I never wanted to represent large clients who have piles of money and can win any case, whether they deserve to or not." The flush creeps higher up his neck. "But then, there are other times, when I'm able to look back and see how far I've come and all the things I've accomplished. That's when I come to the conclusion that I must have ended up here for a reason. I know I'm good at my job, even if I don't always agree with everything it entails." He pauses briefly, and I watch as his smile returns. "Also, I'd be lying if I said the money isn't nice." He brings his clasped hands from under the table and places them behind his head. He's trying to look breezy and carefree, but his eyes don't seem to be on the same page as the rest of his body. They look like they're working through some invisible puzzle that only he can see.

I agree with every single thing that Noah just said. It's like he plucked the thoughts right out of my mind, then read them back to me word for word.

I've been having this internal struggle for years now, and he just said that he feels that same tug of war with it too. I shake my head. How can two people be so similar but so damn argumentative at the same time?

"Enough about me, Robins, tell me some more about you. Do you have a boyfriend?"

The sudden change in topic startles me, and I choke on the piece of lettuce in my mouth. It takes me a minute to clear my throat. I take a big gulp of water, soothing down the last of my fit. "Sorry, I'm sorry. That was gross."

"Why do you always apologize? It's not like you did it on purpose." He pauses. "Unless, of course, you did." He playfully raises his eyebrow, eyes on me. "Unless, of course, you just pretended to choke, so you could avoid answering the question I asked you. In that case, you could apologize." He nods his head. He's so happy with himself right now.

"No, I didn't do it on *purpose*." I glare at him. "I have absolutely no problem telling you that I don't have a boyfriend." I see a slight change in his eyes. I can't pinpoint what it is exactly, but something changed. "I don't date much. I'm happy just having little flings here and there. I'm far too busy to have any real relationship."

"Do you want one?" There it is, that thing in the air that keeps resurfacing.

"I mean, yes. I actually want nothing more than to be married and have kids. I want to be a mother so much that I feel it in my body as real as I feel my own heart beating." I've said too much again. Embarrassment surges through my body. I try to distract myself by twisting my cup on the table. "I just don't know if I'm cut out for it. I sure as hell didn't grow up in a functional family, so I don't really know if I'm capable of creating one." I bring my glass up to my lips and take a small sip. "So, I end up putting everything I have into my work and just hoping that maybe someday it will happen."

He looks at me, brows knitted. "A husband and kids aren't just going to fall into your lap, Jane."

"No, yeah, I know that. Another problem is that I always seem to end up dating the worst guys ever. Like, do I want my kids to have their own fantasy football leagues memorized by the time they're three? Or would I rather them know their ABCs? Ya know? That's what I've been up against."

"That's specific." He laughs.

"You have no idea." I take my fork and place it on my plate. "What about you, are you dating anyone?" My heart rate picks up again, not knowing what answer I'm hoping for.

"Not a soul." He folds his napkin and places it gently on the table.

"That's it? That's all you're going to give me? I just admitted to dating fantasy football's number one fan, and you're just going to leave it at 'not a soul?' So not fair."

He lets out a soft laugh. "What can I say, Robins, we can't all be as complex as you are."

"Bullshit. Tell me about the last girl you dated."

He throws his hands up in mock surrender. "Okay, geez, Robins, you can be scary when you want to be." He brings his hands down and crosses them against his chest. "The last girl I dated was named Hannah. We only dated for like six weeks. It definitely wasn't anything deep or exciting. Very surface-level. Then, the night of my sister's wedding, she was extremely rude to one of the servers who worked at the venue. I broke it off with her immediately. There's nothing I hate more than people who are rude to waitstaff. It's a really big turn-off for me."

My core tightens at those last few words, and my breathing becomes quick.

I think he senses the change because he narrows his eyes, and that same lopsided smile reveals itself again. "That's just one of my turn-offs though." His smile grows. "Also, I do, of course, have quite the list of *turn-ons* as well." His dimples pop, and I know exactly what he wants. I don't understand it, but I want to give into him. I want to play and see where this goes.

"I'll show you mine, if you show me yours first." I bite the inside of my cheek, waiting for his response.

His smile doesn't falter for even a second, but his eyes grow dark and his pupils dilate. "Name the time and place, Robins, and I'd be happy to show you."

The tension between us is broken as our server comes to take away our plates. I'm sure she was only there for seconds, but it felt like she was taking her merry little time.

Once she gives us our check and leaves, the atmosphere has noticeably changed and all the tension has dissipated. We gather our things and head toward the exit.

"Hey, I'm thinking about going down to the beach for a while. Would you want to come down and read or something?" He asks, but I don't say anything. "We can sit six feet away from each other and everything." He smirks and softly nudges me with his elbow.

"Okay, yeah. That sounds great, just let me go grab a few things from my room first. I'll meet you down there in about an hour."

I seem to be breaking all my rules today.

Getting into my room, I'm dialing Jordyn before I even take off my shoes. I hear her sing-song voice without even bringing it to my ear. "Hey, girl, hey! What are you up to?"

I help myself to a little bottle of tequila from the fully stocked minibar. "Nothin' much. Just got back from a fabulous snorkeling trip and now I'm just enjoying myself until I go down to the beach in a bit."

"Wait, what suit are you wearing?" I pan the phone down my body and show off my new bikini. "Holy smokes. You're such a babe."

I hear Daniel whispering from off screen, "Let me see, let me see." I repeat the panning action as Daniel whistles the cutest little whistle I've ever heard. "Jane, you look totally hot right now. I personally would have chosen a copper color, but the white docs make you look super tan, so that's a bonus."

"Gee, thanks guys." I blush, smiling wide.

"Please tell me you look so hot right now because you just spent the day being arm candy for your new love interest," Jordyn asks, regaining control of the phone.

Noah pops into my mind.

"Not exactly. But...I did go snorkeling with Noah, and then we went to lunch together..." I race through the sentence, and then close my eyes, ready for the assault of questions coming my way.

"I'm sorry, that's funny. I swear that I just heard you say that you spent the day with Noah Riley while looking smoking hot in a tiny, white bikini, and then got lunch with him...But, that can't be what you said, because you would never do that."

I slowly reopen my eyes. "But I did, and it wasn't that bad."

"Wow. I'm shocked..."

"I know, right? I mean, he's still an ass, but he also has his moments of...something else. I can't quite put my finger on it, but I think I've learned that he's not an asshole all the time. He's funny, J. Like really funny."

"That's good, really it is." Given her placating smile, I feel my heart drop a bit. "Jane, it's just that we both know what happened last time. It wasn't good. I really don't want to see you go through that again." Her smile falls, and I see the hurt in her eyes. Hurt for me at age eighteen going through something I wasn't prepared to go through.

"Yeah, no...I get it. I don't want that either." The smile that finds its way to my mouth isn't real. It's one of those smiles you give your parents when you've had something fun planned, but they cancel at the last minute because something more important came up. You smile because you don't want *them* to feel bad, even though inside *you* feel awful.

"I totally get it. I honestly did have a good day with him, but I do know what kind of guy he is. I don't need that level of drama in my life right now," I say with a small laugh. "I don't know what got into me today. Maybe it's the humidity. It's doing something with my brain." I say, trying to lighten the mood.

"Oh, I don't doubt it." Jordyn winks. "I think anyone gets horny when they're in paradise, running around in bathing suits half-naked all the time. Just try your best to turn your attention away from the toxic asshole guys and onto the ones who are actually good men."

"I hear you loud and clear. Thanks, J." I give her a genuine smile, thankful for the hard truth. "Oh, speaking of *actually good men*, Daniel, are you still there?"

The phone is ripped out of Jordyn's hand, and my screen lights up with the face of my other best friend. "I was summoned?" He has the best smile.

"Daniel, I just had to tell you that I ate a fancy mocha brownie last night that was forty-eight dollars, and it doesn't even hold a candle to the ones you make. Seriously, you have a talent that goes underappreciated far too often, my friend."

EMMA NORMAN

He pretends to wipe a nonexistent tear from his eye. "Oh, Janie. That means a lot coming from the person who has eaten more brownies than vegetables in the entire seven years I've known her."

"Just honoring my civic duty," I say with a salute.

"You're such a wonderful little nerd. We miss you. Come home and bring us lots of things. Oh, and don't do anything I wouldn't do. Especially if it has to do with Noah. Deal?" Daniel says, pointing his finger at me.

"Deal." I blow them each an exaggerated kiss. "Bye, guys. I'll call you tomorrow." I end the call and toss the phone onto my bed.

Hmm...Now what do I do?

I told Noah I would be down at the beach in an hour, but after talking with Jordyn, I don't think I should even go.

No. Of course I should go. I'm not going to run away from him. He doesn't scare me.

I'm a grown ass woman who was just temporarily blinded by horny humidity or something. I can go down to the beach; I can even see Noah and not give into his stupid charms.

I will take my book, some headphones, and will thoroughly enjoy my time, even if he's sitting right next to me. It's not like we *have* to interact.

I finish my mini tequila and load my bag with all the things I want at the beach. I'm just about to walk out the door when I stop in my tracks because my heart does this weird little flip.

I turn around, drop my things, and go straight to my suitcase. It's just waiting for me with an open lid, beckoning me to rummage through it. *Ah, found it.* I slip into my old, red bikini. You know, just in case.

Chapter Nineteen
Then

T HERE'S CLEARLY SO MANY more people at this party than Josh had initially let on, because cars are lining the street for what feels like miles as we drive up to the party house.

I honestly don't know how she does it, but Jordyn was able to talk me into wearing a pair of too-high heels that she just got last week. They haven't even had the opportunity to be broken in. My poor feet hurt already, and we haven't even made it to the street the house is on yet.

As we walk, I try to casually do an outfit check in the reflection of every car that we pass by. Right as we're about to reach the party, I become aware that I happened to pick out the brightest yellow top known to man, and so tastefully paired it with a wide, black stretchy belt cinching me at the waist. This top with the black pleather leggings, Jordyn so kindly coerced me into wearing, is definitely giving busy-bee vibes. So far, it's not looking good for me on the *don't let Jordyn pressure me into doing stupid shit tonight* front. Jordyn: two. Jane: zero.

We walk into the party as people are yell-singing, "Apple Bottom jeans, boots with the fur..." Red solo cups line every square inch of the house, and the smell of weed wafts through the air. People are coming in and out of the rooms, and I'm suddenly met with the fact that I don't recognize one single face here. I start to feel that strange anxiety that happens when you feel alone in a room full of people.

"I'm going to get us a drink from the kitchen, okay?" Jordyn says, as we walk farther into the house.

She walks away before I have the chance to protest, so I start scoping out the room for a nice quiet place to wait, while also trying to make myself as small as possible. I only make it about five steps when suddenly the music turns off.

Under the upset and confused groans of the partygoers, I hear a guy yell, "Oh, chill out! The music will come back on in a bit! Everyone, come in here! Come into the living room!" The guy making all of the fuss ushers people into the room, while impressively managing to not spill a drop of the drink in his hand. Once everyone is in the room, he makes his way over to the coffee table and stands on top of it.

"Okay, as some of you know, the party tonight is not just any ol' house party like we have every weekend." The room laughs as the "bros" around me chest bump each other, like giant fish out of water.

"It's a fuckin' birthday party!"

All of the blood leaves my body. My head starts swimming, and my vision begins to tunnel. I spot Jordyn on the other side of the room with two drinks in her hands. I stare at her red-faced and wide-eyed.

She shakes her head and shrugs. I can see her mouth the words, "I didn't tell anyone, I swear."

The guy in charge of the situation gazes in my direction and says, "Come on up here! Let's all sing happy birthday, then get back to the party!"

The room erupts into loud cheers, but my heart races, and I look for the door.

Just then, Jordyn reaches me. "Jane, I seriously don't know how anyone here found out, but you better go up there!" She gently shoves me toward the center of the room.

As I climb onto the large, heavy coffee table, the guy responsible for this mess has a look of absolute confusion on his face. My fight or flight kicks in, and I go over my exit strategy. The room goes awkwardly silent when I feel someone else step up to the coffee table behind me.

"Um...Hi, Jane. It's your birthday too?"

Noah Riley steps onto the coffee table right beside me.

You've got to be joking.

Chapter Twenty
Now

T HE WALK DOWN TO the umbrellas is long and hot. Before coming to Hawaii, I don't think I understood the amount of effort it takes to walk in deep sand. By the time I get to the chairs, I'm out of breath, and the hairs on the base of my neck are sticking to me.

I spot Noah right away. He's lying back in the farthest chair on the right, shirtless, and reading. What a sight. There's nothing I like more than a tall, attractive man, half-naked and reading. But God, why does it have to be this man?

The shirt he was wearing earlier is draped across the back of the chair to his left, saving it for me. He looks up from his book and smiles. "Hey, you made it."

I run through the conversation I just had with Jordyn. Noah is attractive. Noah is funny. Noah and I have a past that should stay in the past. Noah broke my heart.

I smile at him cooly and toss the shirt onto his lap. He closes his book and sits up straight. "Hey, are you okay?"

I set my things down and fan my towel out onto my chair, trying my best to appear disinterested. "What? I'm totally fine. I think I'm just going to stay here on the beach and get some sun." I clumsily attempt to move my chair out from under the umbrella. It's heavy and extremely awkward to maneuver in the sand.

Noah looks at me with a tickled expression. "Want some help?"

"Nope. I got it," I manage to say through my exertion. "You can read. Or, you can go do something else."

"Excuse me, Miss?" I hear a deep voice from behind me say.

I drop the chair and turn to see a drop dead gorgeous man with long, beachy strawberry blond hair staring at me, just waiting patiently. *Perfect.*

"Oh, hi. Yes? What can I do for you? By the way, you can call me Jane." I calm my breathing and whip out my brightest and most flirtatious smile for this poor unsuspecting man.

"Okay, then. Um, Jane. I was wondering if I could get you something to drink?" He brings one of his hands up to his chin and rubs the stubble there.

I can't believe this worked out so well. I couldn't have asked for a better time to have someone hit on me. I look at Noah and give him a big, confident smile before turning my attention back to my admirer.

"That's so nice. I would absolutely *love* one. What are you going to have?"

"Oh, sorry. Um, I'm not having anything. I'm the server on duty, and I was just wondering if you would like anything from the bar? I'd be happy to bring you something?"

I feel my eyebrows raise. "Ha, of course you're the server." I clasp my hands together. "Well, in that case, I'll take a mojito, please. Yes. A double mojito. I'll take two double mojitos, please." I turn to look at Noah and see he's wearing an amused grin. He's clearly enjoying this very unfortunate misunderstanding. "Do you want anything?" I say in a clipped tone.

"Nah, I'm good, my man. Maybe later." He winks at his new friend and turns back to his book.

An exasperated huff escapes my mouth. *Whatever.*

I lift my coverup over my head and feel Noah's attention shift to me. I pretend not to notice the way his eyes scan my body up and down, trailing slowly over every inch.

He lets out a heavy sigh, and I turn my gaze to him. The corners of his mouth turn up as he meets my eyes.

"What?" I say, but it comes out weaker than I want it to.

"Nothing," he says with smug satisfaction.

Seconds tick by, but eventually, he's the one who breaks our stare. As he slowly reclines back into his chair, I see him stealthily attempt to readjust himself, and a white-hot wave of vindication washes over my entire body. *Got him.*

I only know that I drifted off because I'm awakened by the sound of Noah rummaging around in his bag.

I open my eyes and turn to see him taking out his laptop. I lower my sunglasses and glare at him. "You brought your laptop to the *beach*? What are you?"

"Ha, what?

"What kind of crazy person brings their computer to the beach?"

"The kind of crazy person who has work that needs to get done."

"Well, have fun with the sand that's going to get stuck in it and never come out," I say with a superior shrug.

Then, I feel a tickle of something trying to work its way into my mind. Work. Did he just say that he has *work* to do?

"Hmm. Work. Did *Howard* ask you for something? Anything I should know about?" I'm trying to act like I don't care, but I feel the worry start to prickle on the back of my neck.

Noah must sense this, because he responds to me like he's talking to a toddler throwing a tantrum. "Calm down, it doesn't have anything to do with the firm, Robins. My nephew has a presentation for school about what he wants to be when he grows up, and much to my successful neurosurgeon brother's dismay, his son wants to be a lawyer 'like Uncle Noah.' I promised I would help put some things together while I'm here."

The worry in my chest subsides. It's not work. I'm not dropping the ball. "Wow, an attorney and a surgeon in one family? You guys sure turned out alright, huh."

He gives me something that looks like a smile, but it doesn't quite make it to his eyes. "Sure, I guess you could say that." He turns his attention back onto his screen.

"Huh, I never would have tagged Tyler as a neurosurgeon type. I always thought he would end up doing something with soccer," I say, resting my head back onto my chair.

"I did too. We were all shocked when he said he was going into medical school. I still don't know how he could be smart enough for something like that, but he's doing well for himself, so I guess he's doing something right." He raises his brows. "We don't really talk much anymore, so I don't know much more than that." He shrugs and continues typing.

I'm stunned. When we were in high school, Noah and Tyler were as close as two brothers could be; they were best friends.

"We had a falling out after I graduated high school, and we just kinda went our separate ways after that. We still call each other on our birthdays, and I see my nephews a couple times a year, but other than that, I don't really know him anymore."

My chest aches at this admission. This isn't how things were supposed to turn out for him. "Noah, I'm sorry. Family shit is hard," I say earnestly.

"Yeah, no kidding." We sit in silence as those last few words float in the air between us.

"Well, maybe by telling your nephew how crappy being an attorney actually is, your brother will thank you for helping him dodge the bullet of his son choosing a terrible career. Then, maybe you two will start talking again."

Noah looks at me through narrowed eyes.

"I mean, really, we both know that becoming an attorney isn't all it's cracked up to be. Right?" I say, raising my brows.

"Continue," he says, coaxing me with his hand.

"Okay, so we both agree that the money is good. But is that all there is? There are more days than not that I wonder if it's worth all the ethical turmoil we face. I mean, you just told me at lunch that you question if you're in the right place with your career, and I feel the same way."

I shift in my seat, the sun suddenly feeling too hot on my skin. "I got into law to make a difference. To represent people that really need me. And, I'm not going to lie, it's the career choice that makes the most sense because of my innate arguing abilities and my amazing organizational skills, but I don't think I'm in the right place to do those things in the right way, ya know?" I'm feeling flustered, and my words are becoming jumbled and repetitive, but I started the word vomit, and it's going to keep coming out. "Okay. So, I guess I like Schwartz & Adler, even if they're sexist. I even like the new partner, Colin, but I don't think I like corporate law. Atticus Finch wouldn't do corporate law. Right? He would do something like immigration or family law. He wouldn't be caught dead helping big multi-billionaire companies squash the little guys. Right?"

The words keep rushing out of me like an unstoppable river. "For example, last year I represented this large corporate chain, who had just put one of their sandwich shops on one of the busiest streets in Denver. A month after they opened, they noticed that this little mom-and-pop shop across the street had more business than they did. Oh, did I mention that this little shop also sold sandwiches, and they had been in that building for over thirty years? I digress, the corporation took the little shop to court, claiming that the building they were in wasn't up to current code and should be turned into a parking structure instead. After months of back and forth, we, of course, won. We closed their little business, and I got a huge bonus." My shoulders fall. "I don't want to do that anymore. I don't want to have to walk these morally gray lines every day. I want to be in front of a judge and know that I am on the correct side of the argument standing up for what's right. That's what I want."

"Okay, Legally Blonde." He stops me from responding by putting his hand up to my mouth, shutting me up. My eyes go wide with anger. "Logan, my nephew, is only six, so I don't think I need to go that in-depth about the ethics and morality of what we do." I start to object, but he puts his other hand up, stopping me again. "Even though I one-hundred percent agree with everything you just said."

I'm speechless. He agrees with me. He looks at me and asks with his eyes if he can remove his hands from my mouth, or if I'm going to bitch him out for calling me *Legally Blonde.* I nod signaling that he's safe.

"Logan told his dad he wants to be a lawyer because he thinks it's funny when I argue with him."

I laugh, despite myself. "Well, Logan and I have something in common then." I make a show of wiping my lips with my napkin.

"Jane, tell me, is there anything at our firm that you do like?"

"Yes. I told you. I like our bosses, sort of."

He laughs. "Is that it?"

I pause, thinking hard about this question. I go through the past few years at the firm. All the hard work, the late nights, and long days in court.

It took me years of dedication to get me to where I am, and I can't even answer the simple question of what I like about it. "I don't know."

"Well, maybe you should figure that out?"

"Maybe I should, maybe I shouldn't. Who knows, maybe while I'm here in Hawaii I will find my one true love, we'll get married and have babies, and I can start my own pro-bono firm that helps the little guys." I shrug my shoulders.

Noah cocks his head and gives me a quizzical smile.

I feel my cheeks start to heat, so I look away attempting to divert my attention. "But that's enough about me. You go ahead and tell Logan how fun it is to argue for a living, while I sit here and continue to contemplate my entire future."

He sits up straight, and I can feel his gaze burning a hole through my body. "Why are you always so worried about everything?"

"What?"

"Why do you over-analyze every single thing that you do? I mean, even when we were younger you were like this, and I was really hoping that after...what...fourteen years, you would have been able to stop trying to control everything, and maybe see some good, or I dunno, hope or something?"

I feel the world around me start to spin. The sting of embarrassment hits me, and a lump begins to form in my throat. "Wait, what? You're really going to bring up the past now?" The tremble in my voice is noticeable. "I overthink and try to control things because I *have to*. I've always had to." I hold his gaze. "And you of all people have no right to tell me not to." I still myself, the pain of the past squeezing my chest.

"Honestly, Noah, what you did that night, all those years ago, showed me that I can only count on myself. It proved to me that if I let my guard down, bad things happen." A single tear escapes my eye and trails down my cheek. *"You left me."*

Chapter
Twenty-One
Then

THERE'S NO WAY IN hell this is really happening. I'm currently standing on top of a very large, and probably, very expensive coffee table, in the middle of a room full of people I don't know, with Noah's arm slung around my shoulders.

Everyone in the room is gathered around the table, merrily singing happy birthday to both of us, because of course, we just so happen to share the same birthday. That makes total sense.

When they get to the part of the birthday song where you're supposed to say the person's name, the room shamelessly erupts with, "Noah and *that girl*," then happily continue their off-key performance through the end.

As soon as they're done, I rapidly jump down and start searching the room for Jordyn. I'm on a mission. A mission to strangle my so-called best friend for making me go up there. I've never felt more embarrassed in my entire life, and she's going to hear about it.

I spot her on the other side of the room, giving her very-present-not-in-Denver boyfriend a hug. I zero in on my target, ready to give her a piece of my mind, when someone tugs on my arm and stops me in my tracks. I already know who did the tugging before I even turn around.

"Noah, what do you want?"

"Happy birthday, Robins," he says with a smile on his face.

"Thanks. Bye." I quickly turn around and continue my pursuit.

"Woah, where are you going?" He asks, walking on my heels.

"I'm getting Jordyn so we can leave. I would say goodbye, but with the way you keep showing up in my life, I'm sure I'll see you again later tonight. Probably in my bed or something, because at this point, that might be the least surprising thing to happen."

Just then, he tugs on my arm and brings me to a stop again. He turns me around to face him, his smile grows wider, and his dimples appear on his cheeks. "Robins, was that an invite into your bed?"

"No!" My already flushed face gets even hotter. I rip my arm away and small beads of sweat form on the back of my neck. "No! I was just making a point! Noah, you're literally the only person in the world I don't want to run into, but for some godforsaken reason, I seem to run into you all the freaking time! Particularly in the moments when I'm already stressed, and you just so happen to stress me out even further."

He lets out a small laugh. "Jane, that's the nicest thing you've ever said to me."

He's trying to be funny, but I notice something else is there too. A small blush starts at the tip of his nose and slowly creeps to the apples of his cheeks.

"Noah, why are you even here? Jordyn told me you would be in Denver?"

His shoulders fall, and his brows knit together. "Nah, didn't work out." He takes a breath, and the corner of his mouth lifts. "But, you know what? I guess it ended up being a good thing anyway, because if I was there, I would have missed *our* birthday party."

I do my best to continue acting annoyed, but it's hard when he looks the way he does. The way his shaggy brown hair flips out over his ears. The way the corners of his eyes lift when he smiles. It's really hard to hate someone when they make you laugh.

I get to the spot where I saw Jordyn and Tyler hugging, but of course, they've moved on and now are nowhere to be found.

I throw my hands up in frustration, scanning the room, but I can't see them through the sea of bodies. I need to find Jordyn. I need to get out of here.

Continuing my search, I wind my way through the rooms of the massive house, Noah closely tailing me around every corner.

"Don't follow me. Shoo. Go away," I say, still walking.

"Jane, I'm not a puppy. I'm looking for Tyler. And let's be honest, wherever Jordyn is, Tyler is too. Sorry, Robins, looks like we're stuck together."

Fucking great.

We locate the love birds in the kitchen. Jordyn turns to me with wide eyes, a look of apprehension written all over her face.

"Hey, thanks for leaving me alone up there. I really appreciate it." I stare at her, my embarrassment from earlier returning.

She links arms with me and leads us into the next room. When we have reached a safe enough distance, she faces me. "As you have now very publicly noticed, Ty and Noah did *not* end up going to Denver. I had *no idea*, I swear. Tyler totally surprised me by being here."

I look at her for a moment. Not saying anything.

"I know what it looks like, but I swear I wouldn't have had us come if I knew they'd be here." I can see a silver line of tears start to form at the bottom of her eyes. "Really, babe, I'm so sorry. I was just in the kitchen getting us some cake to take home. I told Tyler we were going to leave because I know that was the worst thing that could have ever happened to you." She tries a smile, but a tear escapes. She's telling the truth.

"Don't worry about it, J. I mean, having an entire party sing happy birthday to me was nothing compared to the complete mortification I felt having Noah's arm around me for the entire thing."

"Yeah, um....we could all tell. I was sure at one point you were actually going to vomit all over yourself."

I laugh and gently push her away. "Ew. I didn't look that bad."

"Babe, I'm being completely honest, you looked like someone just told you your cat died, and then told you your house burned down, then after all that, Noah Riley put his arm around you, while a room full of drunk strangers sang you happy birthday. That's how awful you looked. And I'm telling this to you as your friend." She gently puts her hand on my arm, and we both burst out laughing as Tyler and Noah walk into the room.

"Wait, whose cat died?" Tyler asks as he puts his hand on the small of Jordyn's back. This earns another round of laughter from both of us. "Okay? Well, while you two are losing your minds, Noah and I will go get us all some drinks, sound good?"

It takes me a minute to regain my composure. I think the adrenaline mixed with humiliation has given me a weird case of the giggles. "Nah, I'm good. I'm going to head home. I think I've had enough 'fun' for the night."

"Oh, come on, Robins! The party literally just started. You can't leave now, that would be a major party foul," Noah says.

"Party foul or not, I'm going to call it a night."

Before I even finish my sentence, Noah stops me short. "At least come up to the balcony for a bit and check out the view of the lake before you go. You won't regret it, I promise."

I try to think of something that will get him off my back, but nothing comes to mind. "Fine. One quick check of the view, then I'm leaving."

"Deal." Taking my hand in his, he vigorously shakes my hand, like we just made the biggest business agreement of the year. We stay shaking hands a beat too long, and the moment grows unsteady. We break apart, and he turns away. "It's this way, follow me."

My hand feels all tingly. His touch, although brief, sent an electric current right through me.

The feel of his rough, warm hand in mine was unexpected but felt good. Too good.

I follow closely behind him, trying my best to shake all the muddled thoughts out of my head.

Noah seems to know everyone. Passing through various rooms of the massive house, fellow party-goers wish us both happy birthday more times than I can count. They're giving him high fives, asking him questions, fist bumping at every turn. They're all so happy to see him, and he's happy to see each of them.

Weaving in and out of the rooms, with so many people coming and going, gives me a vague sense of being in a maze. "Noah, you sure you know where we're going?" I say, willing my short legs to keep up with his long strides. "I feel like we should start leaving a breadcrumb trail to make sure we can find our way out of here at some point."

He laughs. "I know exactly where we're going, thank you very much. I basically live here. Besides, the last time I laid a breadcrumb trail in here, Landon's dog Milo ate it before I could make my way out. I found this crazy witch in a house made of brownies, and she fattened me up and told me she was going to eat me; it was this whole thing. Clearly, I made it out, but it was touch and go there for a minute."

"It was candy." I manage to get out through my laughter.

"Excuse me?"

"It was candy. The house in the story is made of candy, not brownies."

"Jane, I distinctly remember that you were not there. The house was definitely made of brownies. I know because I love brownies. I hate candy."

He loves brownies. I bite my lip, trying to hide my smile.

We finally find the balcony, and Noah opens the wide doors. We walk over to the edge and lean up against the railing.

I stare down at the lake below and take a deep breath in of the crisp night air.

"It's pretty awesome, right?"

"Meh, it's not bad, I guess," I say, trying to act indifferent.

"Not *bad*?! You *guess*?! Jane, is this the moment you've chosen to tell me you're blind? Are we even looking at the same lake right now?" He narrows his eyes at me.

"I'm joking." I laugh. "It really is beautiful." I continue staring out at the water. A light breeze brushes past, and my body erupts with tiny little goosebumps.

I wrap my arms around myself, trying to retain some warmth, as we both stand in the quiet of the night, listening to the lapping waves against the shore.

Noah notices my chill and tosses me his sweatshirt. He doesn't gently give it to me, he chucks it at my head. But, hey, it's the sentiment that counts, right?

Pulling his sweatshirt over my head, I can't help but notice it smells so freaking good and is still warm from being up against his body. I swallow hard. Trying to appear unphased, I rest my elbows on the railing and put my hands on my face to hide my blushing cheeks.

I look out and really notice the beauty of this place. The silver moon lighting the surrounding trees, and the dark waves moving in time with the cool breeze. I can see why Noah wanted me to see this, it's gorgeous.

"My dad and Landon's dad were best friends growing up. So, when Landon and I were little, they would bring us fishing here, like all the time. I mean, when we weren't at Horsetooth, we were here."

I look over at him as he gazes out at the water, and I don't think his smile could get any bigger. You know when someone is really happy, and they smile a different kind of smile? It's like they smile with their whole body, not just their mouth. That's the smile Noah has right now.

My insides start to flutter. He bends down and leans heavy on the metal railing as he stares at the lake, an invisible scene playing that only he can see. After a moment, I see his smile change and this time, I notice it isn't quite reaching his eyes. I want to ask, but it feels intrusive. I also suddenly remember that Noah Riley and I are not friends. I feel a tightness pinch in my chest.

I'm just about to excuse myself when he continues. "Landon and I would swim for hours. Literally from morning until night while our dads just sat on the boat and fished. They would pack the cooler full of beers and ham sandwiches for them, and Sunny-D and PB and Js for us kids. It was awesome."

He pauses, still watching the lake. He wants to keep going, and I'm not sure why, but I want him to also. I want to know more. "After a while, our lake days turned from lots of fishing and only drinking a few beers, into drinking many beers and not even taking out the fishing poles. Landon's dad tried to talk my dad into not bringing the cooler anymore and just fishing, but as you can imagine, that did not go over well. I mean, if you don't even listen to your own wife and kids when they ask you to stop drinking, then who's going to listen to their old fishing buddy, right?"

He turns his head and looks at me, as if I will give him an answer.

I don't. I don't know what to say, so I just stare at him, hoping he will continue. This part of Noah is new. I can tell that he needs to get this off his chest. He needs to talk to someone, to let his guard down, even for a minute.

As if reading my mind, he speaks again. "Growing up, me, Tyler, and my dad were inseparable. We were out all the time doing something cool. Fishing, hiking, sometimes we would even just sit in the back of his car while he drove up and down College listening to music. My mom was so happy when she had my younger sister, because she finally had someone she could do all that girl stuff with." He pauses for a moment, beaming. "I mean, we did *everything* together, and then it all just stopped. He started drinking too much, then he just left. They got divorced, and he moved to Denver. It felt like it all happened so fast." He pauses for another moment, and I see his eyes are glistening. He shakes his head. "Woah, Robins. I'm so sorry. I don't know why I got into all that. Sorry." He furiously wipes at his eyes, and I can tell he's embarrassed. He places both hands back on the railing and stares blankly at the water.

I gently rest my hand on top of his and give a little reassuring squeeze.

He doesn't face me, but his shoulders relax as he turns his hand over, so that we are now palm to palm.

My heartbeat picks up as he interlaces our fingers and gently returns my squeeze.

"We were supposed to be in Denver this weekend for my birthday, but he called Tyler yesterday and said for us not to come. He said he was feeling, as *you* would put it, 'under the weather.'" He raises his free hand in exaggerated quotation marks.

"Excuse me? That first debate against you, I was 'under the weather.' I mean, I wasn't sick, but there was *something* making me not quite myself." My cheeks start to heat.

He meets my eyes for a brief second, then turns away with an unsteady breath. "What about you, Robins. What's your story? Any alcoholic dads in your life?" He says this as a joke, but I can sense the hurt behind his words.

I don't know what he wants me to say. I don't share things with people. My life is private, and I like to keep it that way. Buttoned up. Perfect.

In my house, if there is any notion at all that something is not okay, things go wrong. My parents showed me that life is only valuable if things are flawless. So I do everything in my power to make sure every single thing I do is damn near perfect. If I admit to Noah right now that maybe my life isn't ideal, then he's probably going to run away.

He begins tracing my knuckles with his thumb. There's something about this boy in this moment though, that's making me feel safe. Safe enough to admit that sometimes things are hard.

I take a deep breath. "No alcoholic dad here, but my dad *is* absolutely addicted to his work and only pays attention to me if I do something wrong," I say through a forced smile. "Which I never do, so I honestly don't think he even remembers he has a daughter."

I shrug, trying to push away this feeling of being too exposed. It feels like I'm standing here butt-naked.

Jordyn's the only one who knows anything about me, and honestly, she doesn't even know much. I hate talking about myself, but for some reason, right now I feel like I can. Noah makes me feel like I can get some of these things off my chest. It's in his touch. It's in the way he let his guard down and showed me his pain; his tears. It's in his admitting that not everything is perfect, but it's still okay. Maybe I can do the same?

"My parents are extremely strict. Like, they literally won't accept anything but the best. I have to get perfect grades, I have to be the top in all my classes, I have to get all the finest scholarships. Basically, if I do everything right, then they ignore me. Which is honestly better than the other option, which is them constantly scolding me for not living up to their expectations." I drop my head, feeling the release. "They've always said that if I mess anything up for myself, they'll just write me off."

"What do you mean? Like, kick you out?"

"Oh totally. They've said that if I don't respect their rules, then I can find somewhere else to live."

"No way. Jane, that's not—that's awful."

It feels good to hear someone say those words. Because I know it's not right for your own parents to tell you their love for you is conditional. It's not okay for them to say they'll basically abandon you if you're not perfect.

"Yeah, it's hard. It makes it hard to trust anyone, I guess. It feels like if the people who are supposed to love me no matter what are willing to just let me go at any sign of a mistake, then why would anyone else want me? I try so hard to do everything right, but it's not always easy."

He looks at me with soft and understanding eyes. "Jane, it sounds like you're doing a fine job. And fuck them if they can't see it." He smiles a lopsided smile, and I can't believe it, but I smile back.

We stand together in this vulnerable silence, still holding hands. I can feel his heartbeat in his fingertips. The steady beat matching my own.

I can't believe I just told him all of that about myself. He's the first one in my entire life who has been able to crack this hard outer shell I have, and what's even more, he just listened. He didn't judge, scold, or run away from me.

I'm not sure where to go from here, and I can see in his eyes that he's asking the same question. My mind starts to race, confusion over this whole situation starting to take hold.

I try to break this spell by taking my hand from his and shoving it deep inside the baggy sweatshirt pocket. "So that's it, I try to be as perfect and as good as I can be, so they leave me alone." I shrug my shoulders, trying to make light of the whole thing.

I see his eyes grow dark, and his shoulders rise with a slow deep breath. "So, you're a good girl, Jane?"

The way he says this makes my heart feel like it's going to beat right out of my body. The look on his face assures me that he knows exactly what he's doing. I can feel his eyes on me. I take a breath and do my best to regain myself and remember who it is I'm talking to. I have to change the subject now, or things could get even more confusing.

"So, besides being a lake kid, is there anything else you do?"

He smiles, knowing what I'm attempting to do.

"*Lake kid*. Is that all you think I am?"

"I mean, no. I think you're also an asshole who likes to pick fights and argue." I'm not giving in.

"Oh, gotcha. So, you admit I'm a good debater then?" He nods his head. "Thank you."

"I didn't say you were *good* at picking fights and arguing, I just said that you do a lot of it. There's a difference."

"Okay, Robins, what's the difference? Tell me the difference."

"The difference is in the way you deliver the arguments. You're forceful, and as I previously mentioned, a complete asshole. I, on the other hand, am level-headed and calm in my debates. That's why I win."

"You did *not* just call yourself *level-headed*."

"Yes, I did."

"That's funny, because I seem to recall many times when you have been anything other than *level-headed*."

Excuse me? What did he just say? My pulse quickens in my throat. I'm soooo level-headed. I'm the most level-headed person I know...Okay, so maybe not when it comes to Noah. But that's only because he's so confusing. He's funny, he's smart, he's also surprisingly sweet. *God, this is so frustrating.*

I feel that exact not-level-headedness he's referencing start creeping its way into my body, and I try desperately to push it deep back down. "Look, I get the job done. Okay? I'm good at what I do, and I know you know that too."

This earns me another lopsided smile. "I do know." He steps away from the railing and moves closer to me.

We're so close now that I can feel the heat radiating from his body into mine.

I stare up at him nervously and watch as his heavy eyes make a trail from my eyes to my mouth.

"I'm good at what I do too," he says with one eyebrow raised.

This undoes me. I reach my hand around his neck and push up on my tip-toes. All thoughts leave my head as I feel the heat of lips press into mine.

After a moment, he slowly lifts his head, and I see the want in his eyes. He bites his lip and looks me up and down. With one eyebrow still raised, he stares at me and says, "Jane, are your pants pleather?"

I stifle a laugh. "They're not mine. They're Jordyn's. She said they matched my belt, they're tight as hell and very uncomfortable."

"I like them." He smiles and moves his hands to my hips. "But, if you'd like, I would be happy to help you take them off." And with that, he bends his head down and presses his lips into mine once more.

Chapter Twenty-Two
Then

A FTER CLUMSILY ZIGZAGGING OUR way through the labyrinth that is this house and drunken people, we find our way to a bedroom on the second floor.

"This is basically my room. I mean, it's one of the guest bedrooms, but I've stayed here five out of seven nights a week since my dad left. So, it's totally okay that we're in here. I mean, it's okay with Landon. And with me. Totally okay with *us*, I mean, if it's okay with you?" Noah says this all too fast, and it seems like his words are coming out faster than he has time to register what it is he's saying.

"Noah, are you flustered?" I crack a smile.

He's usually so put-together, seeing this side of him is new to me.

"Definitely not flustered. I just want you to know that we're not breaking any rules, since you know, you're such a 'good girl.'" He says those last two words slow, then swallows hard.

He locks the door behind him, and I move closer. We stand here, almost chest to chest, breath racing.

I look up at him, my eyes heavy with anticipation. The corner of my mouth lifts, and I slowly say, "I am."

He grabs my hands and pulls them up around his neck, then bends down to kiss me. This time, our kiss is messy and hungry. Our teeth scrape and our breaths join together. He grabs the back of my thighs and pulls me off the ground, my legs wrapping around him. We continue kissing as he moves us onto the bed.

He lays me down and moves his large body on top of mine. We're both uncoordinated as I try to scooch my head to the top of the bed.

He pushes up to his knees and takes off his shirt in that way I've only seen boys do in movies. In one swift motion, he grabs it from the bottom and lifts it over his head. It's the sexiest thing I've ever seen in my life.

My heart is beating right out of my chest as I stare at his amazing body. His tan skin contouring every inch of his lean muscles.

I'm very aware of the fact that this is the first time I've ever been in this situation. I've made out with boys in the past, but it's always ended there.

This is one of those moments in my life I know there will be a distinct "before" and "after." I have the sense that after tonight, I will never be the same.

He catches me staring and smirks. "Like what you see, Robins?"

I turn my head to the side, blushing. "I don't want to give you the satisfaction of saying yes, so I'll just stay quiet."

This earns me a soft chuckle as he bends his body back over mine. He brings his finger under my chin and softly nudges my face upward so that I'm looking at him. "Jane, I don't want you to ever stay quiet."

Lifting my chin, he brings his lips back down to mine. This time, I open my mouth to take him in. His breath hitches as his tongue gently teases against mine. He tastes sweet, and I lose myself in him. In this moment.

His hand finds my hip and he leans deeper into me. My core tightens as I feel his hard length press against my body.

Minutes pass, when I break away and push up into a seated position. I take off the baggy sweatshirt he lent me and as I start to take off my shirt, I'm rudely reminded of that stupid wide belt Jordyn had me put on. My shaky hands fumble with the buckle before I'm able to take it off.

I reach for the bottom of my shirt, hoping I can make taking it off look half as sexy as he did when he was taking his off. As I start to lift, I feel his hands on mine. His eyes bore into me, and he gently lifts the shirt over my head and tosses it onto the floor.

I slowly lay back down and stare up at him. Both shirtless, the tension between us grows. His eyes dip from mine and onto the zebra-print bra that I'm wearing, and I notice his pulse quicken in the soft spot on his neck.

He reaches toward my body and softly rests his hand on my ribs. His thumb brushes lazily over my small birthmark there. Bending down, he places a delicate kiss right on it. He slowly kisses a trail down my stomach, and then all the way back up to my mouth. We move in unison as we kiss until our mouths are pink and swollen.

We pull apart and each catch our racing breaths. He continues looking me up and down, eyes dark and lustful. I know what's supposed to come next, but I'm not sure if I'm ready. This is all so intense, and the whirlwind of the entire night is catching up to me. He continues looking at me, both eyes searching for answers.

"Noah... I...I don't..." I start to say, but he brings his mouth down to mine and gently kisses me.

He pulls away softly and says, "Shh, no need to say anything. I get it." He smiles down at me and brushes a piece of hair away from my face. He kisses me again, then pushes up off my body. He smiles at me, then takes a deep breath as he stands up.

"Hey, I'm thirsty. I'm going to get us some water, okay? I'll be right back." He grabs his shirt and quickly puts it back on, then comes back over to me. He plants another hurried kiss onto my lips. "I promise, I'll be right back. Please don't cover up, I like seeing this much of you." He winks, then turns to walk out the door.

I lay in the bed and stare up at the ceiling, a big, stupid grin on my face. I cannot believe where this night has gone. I share a birthday with Noah Riley. I just made out with Noah Riley. *Noah Riley*.

I don't understand it—how my brain has gone from totally hating that name, to liking the way it feels in my mouth when I say it. *Noah Riley*. The boy who's constantly making little digs at me, the boy who's stubborn and argumentative, the boy who decided to let me in and see parts of himself that are complicated and messy. The boy who let me open up and share things about myself. He didn't judge me. He just listened. He cared. No one has ever done that for me before.

My mind won't slow down. I keep replaying the last few hours in my mind. The terrible singing of the partygoers, the high fives and friendly faces of all Noah's friends.

Then, the intimate talk on the balcony takes the forefront of my mind. Noah trusted me with his hurt, and then I trusted him with mine. We both let our guard down tonight and that opened up something new between us.

Shaky breaths, trembling hands. My heart picks up pace as I remember the feeling of his strong body on mine, his full soft lips gently kissing the birthmark on my ribs.

Where will we go from here? I look back up at the ceiling and let out a small chuckle, bewildered. I think, and I can't believe I'm thinking this, but I think I like him. Like, really like him.

Just a few hours ago, I would have emphatically stated that I hated this boy, but now look at me. I don't understand any of this, and for some reason, that thrills me.

Hearing some movement on the other side of the door, I prop myself onto my elbows. I arrange my hair around my shoulders and wipe under my eyes, hoping my mascara isn't smeared. I glance over to the door, but no one enters. A minute or so passes by when I start to feel a sinking feeling in my stomach. He's been gone for quite a bit. My palms begin to sweat.

He was just getting a drink; it shouldn't take this long to get a drink.

I bite the inside of my cheek, and my nose starts to tingle. Did he leave because I didn't put out? Would he really do that to me?

I self-consciously cover myself and push off the bed to find my discarded shirt. Putting it on, I don't even bother to look for the stupid belt. I glance in the mirror above the dresser and try to force a smile. He probably just got stopped by one of his friends. Everything is okay. *Stop overthinking things.*

I rush down the stairs to the beat of the blaring music. My head is swimming as I make my way through the overly crowded house, trying to retrace our steps from earlier.

I look from room to room for Noah's tall broad shoulders and shaggy dark hair, but I don't see him anywhere. My throat goes dry. I find the kitchen and grab a red plastic cup to get myself some water, and that's when I see it.

From my spot at the sink, I see the back of Noah Riley—with his arm around another girl, walking right out the front door.

He's leaving.

He's leaving me.

Chapter Twenty-Three

Now

I LOOK AT HIM through glassy eyes, my chin trembling. "Noah, you left me half-naked and alone in a bed, in a house that I didn't even know." I cross my arms over my stomach, attempting to hold myself together. "You left me after I had just told you things I had never told anyone before. You left me after I let my guard down and started to trust you. I told you how hard that was for me, but you didn't even care."

I stare down at my feet, my toes pushing deep into the warm sand. "I waited for you. I waited and waited, and when I could tell that you weren't coming back, I left the room just in time to see you walking out the door with your arm around some drunk girl."

"Megan."

"What?" I ask, my eyes blinking rapidly.

"That girl I left with. Her name was–*is*–Megan." He pinches the bridge of his nose. "She was super drunk, you're right. She wasn't even supposed to be at that fucking party." He shakes his head, like he's trying to erase the images popping up in his mind. "God, Jane...I'm so sorry. I had no idea that you saw me with her." He inhales deeply and stares at me, eyes begging for me to listen. "Megan is my little sister. She was only thirteen, and Jane, I'm so sorry that I left you, but I had to get her out of there. I had to get her home and help her."

It feels like the floor just opened up beneath me. *His sister?* The drunk girl he left with that night was his kid sister? I don't understand. None of this is making sense. I can't wrap my head around it.

He grabs my hand and looks me straight in the eyes. "Jane, when I left that room, I had every intention of coming back to you. I went downstairs, and I saw some loser college kid trying to get my sister to leave with him to his house. She was only a kid...I went over to tell him to get the fuck off her, and that's when I saw she was totally wasted. I didn't have any other option. At that moment, the only thing going through my mind was making sure that she got home safe." He looks at me again with those same pleading eyes.

I bite the inside of my cheek, not knowing what to say. I stare at him puzzled.

For the past fourteen years, I've believed that Noah abandoned me. Left me for some random girl, because I wasn't going to have sex with him. The first night in my entire life that I let someone in, and then they completely shattered that trust.

I retrieve my hand from his and turn my attention to the sun dipping slowly below the horizon. The mix of adrenaline and sudden temperature drop sends a shiver through my body.

I continue mulling over the conversation in my mind, when I feel Noah softly lay his towel over my body, then sit down in the sand next to my feet. "I promise that after I got Megan home and settled, I texted Tyler right away and asked him for your number. I called you over and over that night, but it just went straight to voicemail. At that point, I figured that I blew my chance, and so I just dropped it. I felt like shit for doing that to you. I still feel like shit about it. I'm so sorry you thought I would leave you like that for someone else."

So many things are going through my mind right now. If Noah got my number from Tyler, then that means Jordyn must have known all of this. She let me cry to her about how Noah broke my heart, when all the while she could have told me the truth? I would have understood. Things could have turned out differently.

"Did Tyler know?"

"What?"

"Did Tyler know that you left me because you were taking care of your little sister?"

"No, he didn't. Megan begged for the whole situation to stay between me and her. There was so much shit going on with our dad, and my mom wasn't handling any of it well, so we decided that it would be best if no one else knew."

"So, Jordyn didn't know either?"

"No, Jane. Honestly. No one knows this except for me and Megan. And now, you. Tyler knew that I left the party, but he didn't know why. I told him I needed your number, because I had some debate questions."

The unease in my stomach begins to dissipate.

"Jane, I swear I tried to get a hold of you to tell you that I didn't mean to leave you like that. I tried."

"I turned my phone off before I even left the party. Jordyn took me to her house and stayed with me while I tried to work through everything that had just happened. I wasn't really in a good place. I really thought you left me that night because I wasn't willing to 'put out.' It hurt. I felt used."

Noah's shoulders drop even farther, and I see tears form in his eyes. "No. Jane. Never. I would never do something like that." He brings his hands up and combs them through his hair. "Look, I left the room that night because I was so fucking nervous just being around you. I was shaking so bad that I had to leave to regain my composure. I didn't want to push you. I didn't want to make a decision that either one of us would regret. I had never been with a girl like that before, let alone a girl that I actually had feelings for, so I didn't want to ruin it. Honestly, Jane, up until that point, seeing you in your bra was the best thing that had ever happened to me." He offers a small smile.

His gaze is soft and focused, and I can tell he's telling the truth. Everything I thought about that night is wrong—everything I thought about *him*. I mean, sure, it's true he left me, but if what he's saying is what really happened, then he didn't *want* to leave me. He had feelings for me.

I've based so many of my decisions on what happened that night, and how worthless I felt watching him walk out that door. It affected how I saw myself, and how I believed others saw me. It affected my relationships, and the level of trust I was willing to give. It changed me. "This is a lot," I say, trying my best to hold it together.

"I've never forgotten you, Jane," he adds softly, hanging his head down low.

My chest tightens at these words. "I hear you." I let out a shaky breath. "It's just a lot to comprehend. What happened that night....I don't know. It's hard to say out loud, but it really messed up how I see things; how I see myself. But I believe you, Noah. I do, I just need some time to think."

He looks up at me through heavy eyes. "I get that. I'm not expecting you to suddenly be able to forget everything and forgive me, I just want you to understand that I never intended for things to happen the way they did." He rests his hand softly on my foot and gives it a gentle squeeze.

We sit together in silence, watching the stars get brighter in the sky. The sounds of the soft repetitive waves attempting to sooth our open aches.

"Jane," Noah says, breaking the spell, "I understand if you still don't want us to work together on this account. I'll talk to the partners and see how we can move things around. I'll take care of it."

I'm taken aback. This entire situation doesn't feel real. My thoughts are all a jumbled mess. "Thank you." I attempt a smile, but it doesn't come out right. My feelings are all over the place. "I think I'm going to head up to my room and call it a night." I slowly stand up, my knees feeling weak and shaky.

He gently nods, still looking down at the ground.

I gather my few belongings and turn to watch as he gets up from the ground and takes a seat in my chair. He leans his head back and stares out at the dark, vast ocean.

I walk over to him and give him back the towel he placed on my body. "I've never forgotten you either." I slowly turn to begin the long walk back to my room.

Chapter
Twenty-Four
Then

HOW COULD I HAVE been so stupid?

Isn't that the typical line everyone says when they finally gain back their sense of self-awareness after a sudden total lapse in judgment? Well, I hope so, because that's what's been replaying in my mind over and over all morning long.

How could I have been so stupid?

How could I have been so *stupid?*

How could *I* have been *so* stupid?

So. Fucking. Stupid.

I honestly don't know how he did it. I don't know how he was able to make me trust him enough to open up. I never open up to anyone, but he made me feel safe, and he made me feel listened to. I thought he was different. I thought that maybe I had him all wrong, and he was a good guy after all, but he proved me wrong.

Replaying last night in my mind, for the life of me, I cannot make any of it make sense. I let him get into my head. I let him get things out of me. I let him touch my boobs!

I desperately try to work it out in my mind, to untangle all the events, hopelessly attempting to make any of it understandable, but I can't. I just can't.

Walking over to my bathroom mirror, I stare at myself with a pained expression. This hurts. This feeling of regret burns so deep, it feels like it's worked its way into my bones. I don't know how I let myself do this. Pinching the bridge of my nose between my fingers, I try to hold back tears. I don't like feeling like this. Shaking my head, I bite my lip. I don't like when things are out of my control. I don't like when I make mistakes.

Squeezing my eyes shut, I clench my fists at my sides. My chest tightens and a lump forms in my throat. Opening my teary eyes, I bring a shaky hand to my forehead. I need comfort. I need someone to tell me it will be okay. *Will it be okay?*

I reach into my back pocket and pull out my phone. I flip it open as fast as I can and hold down the number "2" button. Breathing hard, I will her to answer. Please, please, please.

"Hello? Who is this?"

A choked sound escapes from me.

"Birdie girl? Is that you? What's the matter, my sugar?"

I crumple down to the bathroom floor and bring my knees up to my chest. "Nan, I'm sad." My voice cracks. "I did something stupid, and I don't know how to fix it. I messed up."

"Oh, my darling girl. Remember, for every problem under the sun, there's an answer or there is none," she says, repeating the old adage I've heard her say many times during my life.

It has never made sense to me. Because, yes, it's obvious that there's an answer or there's none, but that doesn't help me at all. I don't like not having answers. I want answers. I need answers. Why did I let my self-control slip? Why did I let myself fall for Noah? Why did I let him get under my skin?

"Dear Birdie girl, I don't know what you did, but maybe this is one of those times where there isn't an answer?"

"I don't like that, Nan. I don't like not having an answer." I bury my face in my knees.

She lets out a soft laugh. "I know, sweetheart. No one really does. But I know you, and I know you will come out of whatever this is on top. You are strong. You are brave. You are one hell of a girl, my sugar. I want to be like you when I grow up." She huffs a small laugh. "Oh, and you tell that stupid boy to fuck off and never come back, okay?"

That does it. The paper-thin dam that was holding in my tears, breaks and tears of both sadness and laughter run down my face. "How did you know it was a boy?" I manage.

"Sugar, every girl has a moment when they feel like the world is turned upside down because a dumb boy decides to crush their spirit. But we can't let them. No one should hold that much power over you, sweetheart. It's not fair to you, or them." Just then, I hear her ancient cat let out a loud meow in the background.

I close my eyes and picture my Nan sitting in her big, purple chair, cat in her lap, rocking back and forth. The image fills me with so much warmth that it begins to patch up the heartbreak hole that Noah left me with.

"You just focus on getting what you want out of your life. You set your sights on graduating and getting into that school and pursuing your dreams. You hear me?"

"I hear you, Nan. I love you."

"I love you too, my sugar." The cat lets out another meow. "I better go feed this damn cat. I swear to God, Bird, I feed him more than I feed myself, and he acts like he's never had a meal in his entire life." She laughs. "Goodbye, sweetheart. I'll talk to you later."

I shut my phone and bring my head back to rest on the wall.

She's right, my Nan; she's always right. This whole Noah thing has left me feeling raw and cracked open, but cracks can be fixed. This is all just a tiny blip in the map of my life. I have so many wonderful things to look forward to, and I need to focus on getting what I want. I can't always let my emotions ruin everything.

I roll my head back and forth on the wall behind me, questioning how I let myself get so lost in feelings. This entire situation makes me think of my favorite quote from *To Kill a*

Mockingbird. Atticus' daughter, Scout, says, "Atticus told me to delete the adjectives and I'd have the facts."

That's exactly what I plan to do. I just need to focus on the facts and not let *any* emotions or feelings get in the way of my bigger goals. I won't let myself do anything like this ever again. No boy will ever get in the way of me achieving what I want.

I will work hard. I will finish this year strong. I will get the debate scholarship I've worked so hard to get, and I will go to an amazing university. I will reach all the goals I want to reach, and I won't let anyone stand in my way. These are things that I can control. These are the facts. I can do this.

Chapter Twenty-Five
Then

I FEEL EXTREMELY HOT and uncomfortable. The auditorium seats are old and have lost all padding, so my butt already hurts. The kid sitting in front of me keeps farting and it doesn't smell like he'll be stopping anytime soon.

It's safe to say I would rather be anywhere else right now than sitting here at this debate tournament.

My foot taps on the ground nervously, as I go over my notes. This is the last tournament of the year and if I win my arguments, I'm that much closer to getting the scholarship I need.

My nerves today have nothing to do with my upcoming debate. Strictly speaking, I have this one in the bag. My buzzing nerves come solely from the fact that today we're debating against Fossil Ridge for the last time. This means I will have to see Noah for the first time in months; since my–*our*–birthday. I haven't seen or heard one word from him since that night. He just left me there and never came back.

Whenever I think about it, I still feel the hot sting of embarrassment that washed over my entire body as I watched his back walk out the door with his arm around another girl.

Just to be clear, I'm completely over Noah. To be fair, I wasn't really "into" him in the first place. I've resigned myself to believing that maybe I had a contact high or something from the party and that's why I had a total lapse in judgment. That has to be it, because there's no other reason I could have ended up in bed with a very tan and very shirtless Noah Riley on top of me.

I cross and uncross my legs countless times, trying to find any comfortable position, but nothing is working. I'm just growing more and more irritated with each passing moment. That paired with the fact I haven't spotted Noah yet isn't helping. The debate is about to start, and I don't see him anywhere.

Just as I'm about to stand up and walk around the room, Coach Christensen gets up to the mic and starts. "Good afternoon, ladies and gentlemen of Poudre and Fossil Ridge debate teams!" The auditorium claps and whoops in response. "I just wanted to start this tournament off by saying that we, here at Poudre, are so sad to hear that your debate team captain, Noah Riley, won't be joining us today. We send our condolences to him and his family, and we all sincerely hope that we will get to hear him debate again in the future."

The next words that coach says are all muffled together, because I don't understand what he just said. My muscles tense and brows knit in concern. What happened? Is Noah okay? Jordyn hasn't said anything to me about Tyler; I would have remembered that. I have no idea what's going on, and I can feel myself starting to spiral.

I stand up in confusion, feeling the sudden urge to leave. I don't know where I would go, but it's like my body doesn't know that. My cheeks get hot, and my head begins to swim.

I peer around the room and see both school debate teams looking up at the stage listening to Coach Christensen explain the rules of the upcoming debate.

The reality of the situation comes flooding back to me. This, right here, is where I need to be. I have to compete in this debate, and I need to win it. I don't even know what's going on with Noah, so why did I feel the urge to get up? To do what exactly? To go see him? No. *Definitely not.*

I sit back down and take a deep breath. Keep my eye on the prize. Focus. I convince myself to push the thoughts of Noah out of my mind and change this confusion into frustration and channel that into my arguments. Just then, Coach calls my name up to the stage. I'm first.

The rest of the tournament goes off without a hitch. I win my arguments, and our school secures the overall win. It wasn't the best debate I've ever had, but to be fair, I'm pretty sure a parrot could have won a debate against my opponent, so take that as you will.

As I start to pack up my backpack, I overhear a conversation happening behind me.

"I'm so bummed that Noah wasn't here. He totally would have helped us win this one."

"Yeah, I feel so bad for him. I can't imagine what I'd do if my dad died. I'd be a mess."

My muscles go weak, and my limbs grow heavy as all the blood rushes down to my feet. Noah's dad *died?* My eyes become blurry as tears begin to well up in my eyes. I know they had a hard relationship, but he was still his dad. My chin trembles, and I continue to pack up my bag. What should I do? Should I reach out to him?

My packing slows to a stop as I contemplate what it is I should do. The answer that comes to me isn't an answer I like.

I don't do anything. I don't owe him my feelings of compassion or concern, it's not like he showed me those things. Me and Noah Riley are not friends. We never have been, and we never will be.

Chapter Twenty-Six
Now

I DON'T KNOW WHEN I finally fell asleep, but I do know it was after what felt like hours of mulling over the conversation I had with Noah. I laid in bed combing through different parts of the past, trying to piece them all together.

It's hard to admit that I let myself be so affected by what happened that night. It totally changed how I see myself, and others. I've never dated anyone seriously, and I've never been able to trust that things could actually work out for me. Essentially, that night rewired parts of my brain, and I wonder what would have happened if that night ended differently.

This weird mixture of emotions surges through my body. It's like I've had a burden lifted off my shoulders, but also like something new is now pressing down. I've carried the weight of that night in my subconscious for years, and now that it's gone, I feel a sort of empty hole where it was.

Instead of ruminating over this all day, I desperately need to think about something else. I don't even bother looking at the time as I pull out one of my new bikinis and decide to head down to the beach.

The mid-morning sun is already hot, but the fresh air is doing wonders for my racing thoughts. Maybe I should just move to the beach after all this is said and done. I could escape all of my problems and get a good tan while I'm at it.

This spot at the beach has easily become my new favorite place. I set down my things and move in for the day. Lathering myself in SPF, I take out my book and park my butt right on my towel for the foreseeable future. If this doesn't help distract me from all the thoughts that have plagued my mind since last night's conversation, then I'm not sure anything will.

I'm six chapters in, when someone clears their throat from above me. I turn my head and am face to, well, *crotch* of a man standing right next to my chair. It's a nice crotch. One that is topped with very tan and very sculpted abs. I trail my eyes up his body and am met with the face of a literal god.

If you were to look in the dictionary under *handsome-man-who-drips-sex-appeal*, you should find this guy, but you probably wouldn't because some girl decided to cut out his picture and hang it on her mirror to stare at every day.

I shut my book as the godlike man says in a low husky voice, "Hi, I know it's only noon, but I was wondering if I could get you something to drink?" *Oh, fuck. He even has an Australian accent.*

"Hi! Yes, sure! Um, I'll take a strawberry daiquiri please. You can charge it to my room, 417. Thanks!" I say with a happy smile and return to my book.

He lets out a small laugh and says, "Okay, you got it." He turns to walk away, and I sneakily take a little peak at his backside. Man, the men working at this resort are some of the most good-looking men I've ever seen.

My cheeks feel flushed, and I let out a satisfied sigh. That's the moment I realize just how screwed I am. If I feel all tingly inside just from *looking* at a man, I can't imagine what actually being intimate with one would do to me right now. A smile sneaks its way on my face as the last few days with Noah weasel themselves into my thoughts.

I see his easy smile; the way the left side always raises slightly before the right. I see his dark eyes and the way they light up just as he's about to say something funny. The way his strong hands held onto Evelyn as he gently helped her off the boat, and the joyful way he laughed with her when she tried to flatter him. I huff out a small laugh.

Other parts of him start to take over my mind. The subtle way his face changed last night as we talked about the past, the pinched brows, the way he chewed on the inside of his cheek. The way he tried to hide the fact that his eyes were wet by turning away and covering his face. I picture his body and the way his strong shoulders curved in with the weight of what happened.

He sure is something.

I take a breath, and my head slowly tilts to the side. Noah Riley really is something, and I don't know why for the first time in fourteen years, I feel like I want to know what that something is.

Thor returns with my strawberry daiquiri and to my surprise, with little to no effort, lifts one of the heavy beach chairs right next to mine. He even did it with a beer in his hand. I definitely need to remember to work out more when I get home.

"They were all out of those little umbrellas, sorry," he says, beautiful white teeth gleaming. "I'm Ezra. Nice to meet you." He reaches out his hand, and I bring mine up to meet his without even thinking.

"Um, hi, Ezra. I'm Jane. Nice to meet you." I retrieve my hand and take a big gulp of my drink. Through the brain freeze that follows, I manage to mutter, "So you don't work here, do you?"

His big, white smile grows even bigger. "Nope."

I literally face-palm, which makes him laugh.

"When I was walking away, I was thinking, did she just tell me to charge her room? That's when I guessed you thought I was one of the servers."

"Oh, god, I'm so sorry. I've had a really crazy few days..."

"Ha, don't worry about it." He tips back his head and takes a drink.

I feel myself watching the column of his strong neck as he swallows. The way his Adam's apple moves up and down with each gulp.

"So, Jane, what brings you to Hawaii?" He asks, his friendly lilting accent working its magic.

My mesmerized stare is broken, and I move my gaze to his eyes. "Um, work actually. Nothing too exciting. What about you?"

"Work? Ah, that's no fun," he says with a playful scoff. "I'm here with a few of my mates from home." He pauses and looks at me through narrowed eyes. "I'm here purely for fun." He says this last part with a flirtatious smirk.

"Oh, that's cool," I say extremely unsexy and take another too-big gulp of freezing cold drink. "What do you, um, what have you done for fun so far?" I can't believe this. I sound like a bumbling idiot. What has gotten into me?

"Loads of things, actually. We went ziplining, swam with sea turtles, things like that. Oh, yesterday we went on this really amazing volcano tour."

"Wow, that sounds great. I'd love to see a volcano. I didn't know you could do something like that here." I smile, getting more comfortable.

"Jane, I know a lot of fun things to do." He slowly scans my body up and down. "I can definitely show you a good time," he says with a wink.

Holy shit. He's coming on strong. This is exactly what I've been waiting for. I chew on my bottom lip. It's absolutely perfect. A drop dead gorgeous man who only wants to have fun for a few days. So, why am I hesitant? *Don't be stupid, of course I know why.*

"Ezra, I don't doubt that you could show me a fantastic time," I say, turning on my charm because this guy deserves something. He looks at me with anticipation. "But, I'm just a bit too busy to make it happen before I have to leave for home."

His beautiful smile doesn't break. "It's all good. If things change, I'm in room 212. I'd love to show you just how much *fun* we could have. Hope to see you around." He stands up and makes his way down to the water, drink in hand.

I honestly can't believe I just let that bold, gorgeous man go. I just let him walk right down the beach and didn't even touch his hair, or his abs, or anything. These past few days have been the craziest and most confusing days I think I've ever had.

I came to Hawaii thinking I was going to talk to my client, have a few meetings, and maybe get a good tan. But instead, I came face to face with someone who broke my heart and told me that we would be working together. If that's not bad enough, then he told me he didn't mean to break my heart, and the events of that fateful night were a total misunderstanding.

I'm so confused, and things are all topsy-turvy. Seeing Noah again has awakened things in me I didn't think were still inside me anymore. I'm surprised that I even want to explore these parts of me I thought were long dead.

I'm also surprised I want to explore the parts of him I've seen peek through these last few days as well. I want to have fun during my remaining time, and I think I want to do it with Noah. I close my eyes and huff a laugh, Jordyn is going to flip her lid.

Before I can change my mind, I take out my phone from my bag and go to the last message he sent me. My thumbs pause over the screen, debating if this is a smart thing to do, but then I see the hurt in his features as he apologized last night and the honesty in his eyes as he admitted he's never forgotten me. My next move becomes clear.

Jane

> Hey, Noah. It's Jane. Wondering if you have any plans for tomorrow?

My heart is racing when I press send. What if this is all too much? What if he doesn't want to spend more time with me? What if our conversation last night made him think I'm crazy for holding onto something that happened so long ago?

I'm not looking for anything, but it wouldn't be bad for us to get along, right? I see the three little dots appear on the bottom of the screen, he's typing. I watch my phone intently, questioning if I made the right decision, when his reply pops up.

Noah

> Nope. I'm free as a bird. Why what's up?

Jane

> Great! I just heard about this volcano excursion. I was wondering if you would want to go on it tomorrow?

> With me?

Yikes. I couldn't have made that any more awkward. Maybe this wasn't a good idea after all. I wish I could just delete it and forget it even happened.

Noah

> That sounds right up my alley. I'd love to.

He wants to come...He wants to come with me. My stomach fills with butterflies as I type my response.

Jane

Perfect. I'll get more details tonight.
Wanna meet tomorrow around 8?

Noah

Can't wait. See you tomorrow, Jane.

Chapter Twenty-Seven

Now

I KEEP PLAYING WITH the little burnt spot on my tongue I got this morning from my coffee. You'd think I'd know by now that coffee is scalding hot when it first comes out of the pot, but alas, patience is not my strongest virtue.

I see Noah walking toward me from across the resort lobby, and while I look like I just raided a Lululemon, he looks like he's going traversing through the Amazon. Who knew I had a thing for cargo pants and hiking boots? I don't even have time to register what I should do with this information by the time he reaches me.

"Hey, Robins. Good morning," he says with a smile that tells me he's been awake longer than I have.

"Hey, good morning." I'm trying to act as normal as I can, but I'm suddenly aware of the raging kaleidoscope of butterflies in my stomach. I'm not sure where we stand at the moment, so my feelings are all a tangled mess.

"Who packs hiking boots when they come to Hawaii?" I say, looking down at his feet.

"Well, if I looked as good as you in a bikini, Robins, I would have packed that instead." His laugh is easy, and the blush prickles at my cheeks.

We stand in silence, neither one of us knowing what to say next. There's a certain tension sitting in the air between us. It's not the same argumentative and stubborn tension that we've always shared. This new tension is charged. It feels alive with past experiences and new expectations. I don't really know how to interact with this Noah, and to be honest, it's all a bit overwhelming.

He lets out a heavy breath and brings his hand up to the back of his neck. "Hey, um...I just wanted to see if we're okay?"

The question catches me off guard. I find that tender burnt spot on my tongue again and rub it on my teeth, searching my mind for an answer.

"Oh, yeah. Um...we're good. Things are good. I'm good. Are you? Good?" I sound so nervous, and I don't like it. I don't want to be on edge all day.

He smiles that slow smile, which instantly helps ease my nerves. "Good, good, good." He huffs a small laugh and starts moving toward the lobby doors. "So, what's the plan, Stan?"

"Thanks for the new nickname, but I think you should stick with Robins."

"Ha, well, I guess we'll just have to see how the day unfolds."

"I don't like the sound of that."

"Don't worry, Stan. We're going to have a good day." His little wink at the end of this sentence makes my stomach flutter. I give him a big overexaggerated eye roll and walk out the door. I don't tell him this, but I think we're going to have a good day too.

By the time we load the bus, it's already full with a group of coworkers on a teambuilding activity. It's a group of ten men and women who would clearly rather be on this excursion with literally anyone else than the people they see at work every day.

I don't know how we ended up on this bus with them, but it's just their group, and Noah and me.

The strange new tension between us pales in comparison to the awkward get-to-know-you questions the group is being subjected to by the woman who I've learned is their boss. She's already been asking them questions for the past twenty minutes, and by the look of the papers in her hands, she isn't nearing the end.

The answers that the employees give are honest, but I can tell the majority of them answer in the quickest and most generic way so the attention can shift to the next person as fast as possible. Boss Lady isn't reading the room particularly well.

For example, one question she asked the group was, "What is your spirit animal, and how does that affect how you work on a team?" Then they'd say something like, "I'm a lion, so that means I am a good leader, etc..." Or they'd say, "I'm not sure what kind of animal I am, but I do know that I'm dependable and trustworthy," to which Boss Lady would enthusiastically follow up with an animal she thinks that person is most like. "Oh, you're totally a golden retriever!"

After a spectacular question pertaining to zodiac signs, I feel Noah shift in his seat and raise his hand. "Hi. I'm Noah, and this is my coworker, Stan. I was wondering if we could join your get-to-know-you game? We're both attorneys who have recently been assigned to the same client, so I think we could use some of these team-building exercises to help us get to know each other on a more intimate level." He gives her a big smile. "Would you mind if we answer some of the questions?"

I snap my head in his direction, desperately trying to get his attention. This is my worst nightmare. I open my eyes as wide as I can, and I know he can see me, but he won't look at me. He knows what he's doing, and he's happy about it.

Boss Lady looks at Noah with the most heartfelt smile. "Of course you can! That would be wonderful."

Only once he gets the green light does Noah turn my way. My jaw is clenched tight, and he just smiles and shrugs his shoulders. "This is going to be fun."

Boss Lady turns our way and readjusts her papers. "Alright, time for the next question. Noah and Stan, don't be afraid to chime in with your answers, okay?"

I wish I could stop the bus and get off right now.

"You got it." Noah gives boss lady a thumbs up.

Shoot me now.

The muscles in my face ache from smiling so much. The past twenty minutes have been filled with some of the funniest moments I've ever experienced in my life.

We learned that Jason, the sales bro, collects velvet black light paintings; Peggy, the accountant, thinks people who don't like cats are equal to murderers; and Boss Lady, Debbie, isn't quite a conspiracy theorist, but she also isn't entirely sure that the moon landing was real.

Noah has everyone on the bus wrapped around his finger. He answered each question, as if he's preparing for the most important interview of his life, and he even managed to fake a tear after he answered a would-you-rather question about having to eat either only pizza or only ice cream for a year.

After Debbie asks each question, everyone hurries through their answers and when it gets to Noah, they all turn around and stare at him eagerly while he gives his carefully worded answer. I honestly can't tell if he's really as into it as he's acting, or if it's all a show. Either way, everyone loves him.

The way he's able to make every single person on this bus nod their head in agreement, or laugh at all his jokes, is something that's completely unique to Noah. He's charismatic, he's intelligent, he's witty. But most of all, he's all himself all the time. His pure authenticity is so magnetic that it pulls every person around him into his orbit. Including me, despite my protestations.

We're sitting next to each other, so this entire ride I'm hyper-aware of all the places his body is touching mine. The light pressure of his shoulder leaning into me over the armrest, the way our thighs brush together every time the bus goes over a bump. His close proximity is intoxicating, and I feel any inhibitions beginning to melt away.

I want to reach out and grab his hands and interlace his fingers with mine. I want to rest my head on his shoulder, close my eyes and soak in this feeling of...lightness...happiness? I'm not sure, but I want it. I want to dig deeper and peel back the layers to see what's inside.

The bus stops, and it's time for us to disembark for our hike. As soon as I get off, I'm met with the most breathtaking scenery I've ever laid eyes on. The light sprinkling of rain is making everything vibrant and alive with color.

The guides take their time leading our group up the mountain. Telling us stories about their land and all the fascinating folklore that surrounds it. The striking beauty of the landscape is only made more beautiful by the look on our guides' faces as they talk about their history and the culture that means so much to each of them.

We cross bridges with rushing waters beneath our feet. We see flowers of every size and color blooming on vines above our heads. It's such a full sensory experience that I know I will never forget.

Noah and I stop at one of the larger waterfalls and take a minute to absorb the moment, trying to capture each of the sounds and smells to hold in our memories and take them home with us to keep forever.

"This is...gosh, I don't think I have the words." My voice is breathy from the exertion of the hike.

"Right?" He pulls out the plastic water bottle from his pack. "I feel weird using the word magnificent, but I really think that's the only way to describe something like this." He takes a gulp of his water and then offers it to me.

I immediately look from the bottle to the lips it just touched and feel myself swallow hard. Sharing your drink with someone is significant, right? I mean, you don't just do that with anyone...do you?

"Want some?" he offers again.

"Oh, sure. Thanks." I grab the water from his hand and take a sip. The water is cool and slides down my throat easily. I put the cap back on and gesture for him to take it back.

"No worries. You can keep it, I have more." *Ouch. Maybe not.*

We both stand in silence as we watch the waterfall disappear into the deep pool below. I turn to look around and see that we're the only ones here. The rest of the group must have continued up to the crater.

I take a sip from my new water bottle, then gesture to the trail. "Want to keep heading up? I don't think we have that much farther to the top."

"Ready when you are." He adjusts his pack.

I let him lead the way as we begin the next leg of our journey. The drizzle of rain has stopped, but the trail is now muddy and harder to manage. I attempt to climb over a group of rocks when my shoe slips and I roll my ankle. A string of curse words fly out of my mouth, and I don't think I say them quietly.

I sit down in the mud and hold my hurt ankle between my two hands. Hot tears begin to sting my eyes.

"Jane?" I hear Noah approaching from slightly farther up the trail. "Hey, are you okay? I heard some yelling?" He's getting closer, and I wipe away my tears, hoping to stave off some of the embarrassment.

I take a deep, shaky breath. "Hey, I'm over here."

He appears from around the bend and finds me sitting in the mud with tears in my eyes. "What happened? Are you okay?" He quickly crouches down to my level and puts his hand gently on my shoulder. Concern is etched on his features as he frantically searches my eyes for an answer.

"I...my shoes are all muddy, and I slipped on that rock...I twisted my ankle, and I...I think I'm okay, but it really hurts."

"Can I take a look? I won't move it, I promise."

I slowly extend my leg toward him, and he tenderly holds it in his hands. My ankle has already started to swell, and a light bruise is beginning to form.

"It definitely looks like a sprain. Do you think you can move it?"

I attempt to point my foot, but that shoots a pain through my leg. "No, I don't think so." I say through gritted teeth.

"Okay, no problem. Let's get you back down to the bus so you don't have to keep sitting in this mud," he says, attempting a smile.

"Yeah, that's a good idea. I can do it on my own though. You go up and see the volcano. I'll just try to find a stick or something to lean against to help me on my way down. I'm fine. Totally fine," I reply, attempting my own smile through the pain.

"Robins, you have got to be joking." With this, he helps me up to my good foot, then with his back turned, he squats down in front of me. "Get on."

"What? Noah, no! You are *not* going to carry me down the trail."

"Excuse me? You can't tell me what to do. Now, get on."

I lightly slap his back and start hopping in the direction of the bus. I only make it about five hops before I take a short break.

"It's a long way down, Robins. Just let me carry you the rest of the way."

"I can do it."

"Oh, I have no doubt in my mind that you could. But you don't have to. Let me help you."

I turn to look at him. This man, who makes no sense to me. This man, who makes me so confused and so unsettled. This man, who's offering to give me a piggyback ride all the way down a slippery mountain.

"Please?" He reaches his hand out, and I accept it into mine. He smoothly helps me onto his back, and we begin our trek back down to the bus.

The first half-hour of Noah carrying me is filled with me apologizing over and over. I'm so sorry I tripped. I'm so sorry my pants are kind of slick and hard to hold on to. I'm so sorry if I'm holding on too tight. I'm so sorry I'm all muddy. I'm so sorry. I'm so sorry. I'm so sorry.

It takes me a bit, but after I realize he literally hasn't said a word about it, and is even smiling, I decide to just make myself comfortable and enjoy the ride.

He's carrying me like it's effortless. I can feel all the muscles in his upper body move as we make our way down. His back tenses as he carefully moves over rocks in the trail, and my thighs squeeze tighter around his middle. I hear a small sound come from somewhere deep in his chest when I do that, a sort of satisfied groan. I decide to put a mental pin in this and revisit it later.

"You still awake back there?" he asks.

"I'm awake. Do you need to stop? We can take a break."

"Nah, I'm good," he protests, barely even breaking a sweat. "But an ice cold Coke does sound pretty freaking great right about now."

I feel a smile tug at my lips, I want to play. "Gross. Coke is awful. I'd take a tall glass of Diet Pepsi over a Coke any day of the week."

Noah stops moving. All forward momentum has entirely halted, and we're standing still in the middle of a tropical forest with me perched on his back.

"What happened? Is everything okay? Do you need that break?"

"No. I told you. I don't need a break. But I do need you to think long and hard about the blasphemy that you just spouted about Coke. Nobody in their right mind *actually* likes Pepsi, it's disgusting." He turns his cheek and peeks at me from over his shoulder. "I can stand here all day, Robins. Take it back."

From this close, I can see the way his eyes crinkle in the corners when he smiles. My breath hitches, and my heart picks up. "And what if I don't?"

"Oh, I'm sure I could think of something." He faces forward again and takes a deep breath in. We start moving.

One of the tour guides stayed down at the bus just in case something like this were to happen. When we reach the bus, he carefully helps me down from Noah's back and supports my other side as we get into our seats.

"Oh, man, I'm so sorry, Miss. That looks like it hurts," our tour guide Jerry says as he gets an ice pack from the first aid kit. "Unfortunately, we're going to have to stay here until the rest of the group comes back down to the bus. We don't have another way for them to get back to the resort if we leave now. There's not another tour until tomorrow morning."

"Oh, it's okay. Really. I'm totally fine to wait here until they get back. The ice will help. Really. Thanks." I nod, hoping he believes me.

"Okay, good. If you two are okay here for a bit, I'll hike up and let the others know what happened and that you made it to the bus safely. That way, they don't wait at the crater for you and start to wonder if you got lost."

"Yeah, that's fine. We're all good here," Noah says, and Jerry turns and walks out of the bus, leaving us alone.

Noah sets his bag down by his feet and sits in the aisle seat opposite me. The bus is one of those long distance buses that is all comfy chairs and bright neon fabric from the nineties. The middle aisle is wide, so the distance between us feels big. *Too big.*

I study him as he wipes the sweat from his brow. A single bead of sweat slides from his temple and down into the stubble on his jaw. I suddenly feel hot. Very hot. I take the ice pack off my hurt ankle and touch it to my chest.

He catches my eye, and I shrug. "I'm hot," I say, turning away from his gaze and suddenly finding interest in the pattern on the seat in front of me.

"So, what do we do now?" Noah says, raking his hands through his damp hair.

"I brought my book, so I'm just going to sit here and wait until the others get back. I want you to go finish the hike and see the crater. I bet it will seem ten times easier without me on your back," I say with a smile, trying to alleviate some of this tension.

"Nope. I'm staying with you. You can still read, but I'll be sitting right here while you do." He turns in his seat and rests his back on the window behind him.

So here we are. Sitting face to face, with nothing but time and ourselves to keep us company.

I can feel the air between us. The awkward silence grows the longer neither of us says anything. Eventually, we enter a game of chicken. He makes a silly face trying to make me break, and I return the gesture hoping to get him first. He grunts, I grunt. He shifts, I shift. Finally, he lets out a yell, and it startles me so bad that I let out a scream, which makes us both erupt into raucous laughter.

"Okay, you win." I put my hands up in surrender, and he makes a show of bowing to an invisible audience.

"Thank you, thank you." Again, to the pretend spectators. "Now, if only you could say that every time." He turns to me with eyebrows raised.

"Ha, yeah right. Don't get that used to it, Riley. We both know I'm usually the victor in this relationship."

"Oh, you're stealing my nicknaming strategy now?" He scoffs.

"Maybe I am, Riley. What are you going to do about it?"

"Not sure yet, but I do like the way it sounds when you say it." His voice is a touch lower. "And wait, rewind. You said relationship. What *relationship* is this exactly?"

"Oh, you know..." I feel my cheeks turning red. "This...whatever this thing is we have going. Coworkers, I guess. Coworkers who occasionally get couples massages together," I say, raising my shoulders.

He laughs. "Coworkers with benefits. I can get down with that." He shifts again in his seat, and my blush deepens.

"Speaking of coworkers," I say, changing the topic, "what are we going to do about the Dumont account?"

"I told you the other night, I'm leaving it up to you, Jane. I understand the unique situation that we're in, and I don't want you to do something that you don't want to do. If we didn't have a past and if it wasn't colored by my stupid teenage mistakes, I could see that maybe we would be able to work together, but that's just not the case. It's in your hands." He concedes.

I pause before I continue. What a crazy turn of events. All I wanted from the first night that he came back into my life a few days ago was for him to say this very thing. To say that I have the control and it's all up to me. But now, I'm questioning what exactly I want.

"Thanks, Noah. I mean, Riley. Noah Riley."

"Nah, that doesn't sound as good."

"Right?! I'll just stick with Noah. Thanks, *Noah*. I don't know. What do *you* want?"

"Hmm, not sure honestly. I was excited when I heard that we had Dumont as a client and was even more excited when they told me I would be on his account. But I don't know, being here and seeing the scale of his resort and his brand as a whole, I'm not totally sure what I want to do."

"I get it. I actually feel the same way," I admit.

"Well, then, maybe we just need to put a pin in it and keep thinking about what we both really want." He raises his brows. "But, I can tell you that if you decided to stay on the account, I would be happy to work on it with you," he says with a small smile.

"Same." I find myself saying before I have a chance to take it back.

We see the other group members come through the bushes and start heading toward the bus and just like that, our solitary moment has come to an end. He straightens himself and gives me that lopsided smile that makes my insides go all a flutter.

"It's so hot in here. Are you hot?" He asks, fanning his shirt.

"Meh, this ice has really helped cool me down."

Before I register what he's doing, he stands in the aisle of the bus and unveils a hidden zipper on the knee of his pants.

"Don't tell me those are the type of pants that turn into shorts..." I say, slightly horrified.

He looks me square in the eyes and in one swift motion, unzips both legs, and the bottom portions of the pants drop to the ground. His cargo pants, now cargo shorts.

"They sure are, Robins," he says proudly. "I always come prepared."

If it wasn't enough that Noah carried me down a mountain today, he somehow found the energy to also carry me up to my hotel room. I could get used to this.

When we get into my room, he carefully sets me down on the bed and grabs some extra pillows, while I gingerly take the shoe off of my injured foot. He gently props my foot up on the pillows and sits on the bottom corner of my bed.

He unzips his pack and takes out a water and a small bottle of Tylenol. He thrusts them both in my direction. "Take two of these every four to six hours tonight. Try to stay on top of the pain, and it should help you get some sleep."

I take them from his hands and set them on my nightstand. "Hey, thanks again for today. I really don't know what I would have done without you." I take two pills out of the bottle.

"Don't mention it."

"Really, it means a lot." I smile. "I've never had anyone take care of me like you have today." I pop the medicine into my mouth and take a long sip of water. "There was this one time during my sophomore year of college when my boyfriend at the time actually threw up on me when I had a bloody nose." A small laugh escapes as I recall the night. "We were sitting on his couch watching a movie, when I suddenly felt a drip from my nose. He looked at me with horror on his face and before we both knew what was happening, my lap was covered in vomit. He started apologizing as he ran into his bathroom and locked the door."

"No way. There's no way that happened." Noah stares at me, eyes wide with amusement.

"Oh, it totally did. I never saw him again after that night. He broke it off over text." I smile. "So, again, thank you for helping me and not throwing up on me then running away."

He laughs and stands up off the bed.

"Anytime, Robins." He puts his backpack on. "Is there anything else you need before I head to my room?"

"Nope. Thanks though. I think I'm all set." We stare at each other. Both lost in this moment. I don't know what he's thinking, but I know that I don't really want him to leave.

"Jane, I...um... I'm sorry again for everything. That conversation last night about my sister, and you thinking I left because you didn't want to have sex....God, I'm so sorry." He sighs and combs his hand through his hair. "I was up all night replaying everything that happened that night, and I should have tried harder to get a hold of you after. I should have done more. I didn't mean to hurt you." He looks at me through sad, earnest eyes. "I'm just so sorry."

My nose starts to tingle, so I clear my throat before tears can fall. "It was a long time ago. It's okay now. Really. Thank you, Noah."

He nods his head and gives me a small smile. "Okay, then. I guess I'll see you around." He turns and starts toward my door. "Oh, wait, are you going to the luau tomorrow night on the beach? I think it starts at seven."

"For sure. I wouldn't miss it."

He smiles and nods again. He puts his thumbs in the straps of his pack, and suddenly, I'm transported back to high school. He did this same thing back then, and there's something comforting in seeing him still doing it now. The past and present coming together.

"Hey, sorry again that you didn't get to see the volcano today, I feel awful about that."

"No worries, Jane." He smiles at me, hope in his eyes. "Next time." He turns off the overhead light and softly closes the door on his way out.

I lean my head back and think through the events of the day. The crazy ups and downs of everything. Of all the things that went wrong, and all the things that went so right.

I feel something warm in my chest. A certain spark and excitement that I haven't felt for a very long time. I feel myself drifting off, when a knock at the door startles me awake.

I flip on the lamp as I hear a man's muffled voice on the other side of the door. "Room service!"

"Hi, sorry! I can't come to the door, my foot is, uh, sorry, I didn't order room service." I try my best to yell as quietly as I can.

"No problem, if it is okay with you, I have a key. Do I have permission to enter the room and set your tray down on the table for you, Miss?"

"Oh, yeah, sure. But like I said, I didn't order anything."

I hear the lock to my door click open, and a hotel server holding a silver tray in his hands steps in. "Sorry to bother you, Miss. A gentleman from the third floor ordered this for you."

A smile tugs at my lips. "Oh, thank you. Would you mind bringing it here to me? I hurt my ankle, and I can't really get around much at the moment."

"No problem, Miss. The gentleman who placed the order said just as much." The kind server places the warm tray on my lap and opens the lid with a flourish. Sitting in front of me is the most beautiful chocolate brownie I have ever laid eyes upon.

A tear trails down my face. I don't know if it's because I just realized I'm starving and I'm really excited to eat a delicious brownie, or if it's because Noah remembered me saying brownies are my favorite food, or if it's because he was thinking about me and cared enough to show it. Maybe it's all these things.

I wipe the tears from my face as the server turns to leave. "Hey, before you go, can I order a cold bottle of Coke to be sent to his room from me?"

"No problem, Miss. I'll do it now." He smiles a knowing smile, then gently shuts the door behind him.

Chapter
Twenty-Eight
Now

M Y INSIDES ARE A mess. I'm so nervous to see Noah today; I feel like I could vomit. Which I would prefer not doing, because I just finished putting on my makeup. I'm sitting in front of the mirror in my hotel room, counting down the minutes until the luau. Well, really I'm just counting down the minutes until I get to see Noah.

After I ate my brownie last night, which was absolutely incredible, I couldn't stop thinking about everything he did for me yesterday.

Not only did he carry me all the way down a slippery mountain, he propped my foot up, gave me medicine, then ended the day by supplying me with chocolate. My stomach does another flip.

If you told me a week ago I would be seeing Noah Riley again, I would have laughed in your face. Then, add in the fact that it's been a positive experience, and I might have actually slapped you in the face.

Nothing about these past few days makes any sense at all, and the more I think about it, the more confused I get.

Whenever I've thought about Noah over the last fourteen years, all I remember is how much of an egotistical asshole he was. Not once have I had any fond memories of him. Not once have I thought maybe that terrible night was a misunderstanding. Not once have I thought he could possibly be a good guy.

The night he left crushed me. I had finally given myself to someone, and he took that trust and threw me away. It fundamentally changed who I was. From that night on, I was more self-conscious, more insecure, more shut off from people, and I don't think I've ever truly healed from that.

But now, hearing his apology and seeing the regret in his eyes has made me question if I *ever* truly saw him for who he is. I've spent the last fourteen years believing he was the worst kind of man for what he did. But if he didn't want to abandon me that night— if he was being a *good* man, showing up and caring for someone who needed him, just like he did for me yesterday— that changes everything. Noah is a good man, and he's been a good man all along.

Yesterday, he proved to me that he can handle hard things. He proved to me that he's kind and compassionate toward others. He proved to me that he doesn't only care about himself.

These are all things I never thought Noah Riley could be, but I've been so wrong. He helped me. He stayed with me. He laughed with me. He *cared* about me. I bite my bottom lip, trying to hold in the tears threatening to let loose.

I just want tonight to go well. Don't get me wrong, I'm not going into it expecting anything, but I do know that Noah deserves an apology from me. I want him to know that I finally see him for the man he really is, and not the man he's been in my head for the past fourteen years.

I put on my lip gloss and take the claw clip out of my hair. Letting my loose waves down on my shoulders, I stare at myself in the mirror. I don't recognize the woman staring back at me. I know it's a total cliché, but this isn't the same Jane that came to Hawaii just a few short days ago.

The Jane staring back at me is a woman who's starting to realize she may not have everything all figured out. All the control and order I force on myself doesn't mean I understand everything. It doesn't mean things can't touch me, or hurt me, or surprise me. It just means I demand a high level of perfection that's completely unattainable. It just means that I've made myself miserable my entire life by not letting myself or others be human.

The last few days have shown me that maybe it's okay if life doesn't go exactly how I've planned. Maybe it's okay if life waves things in my face and says, "What Jane? What are you going to do about this? Why are you here? What do you want?"

For the first time in my life, I don't think I have any answers for these questions. I mean, it's been less than a week, but I'm finding myself actually thinking about these things and not just shoving them away for Later Jane to handle. Maybe it's time for Today Jane to start helping Later Jane out every once in a while. Maybe Today Jane can stop pretending that everything is fine all the time. Maybe Today Jane can stop putting hard things off for another day, because those days never seem to come.

I stand up from where I'm sitting and smile at my reflection, finally able to see who I'm supposed to be, and I think I love it. There's a certain lightness in my face I haven't seen in a long time, and it looks good on me.

My blue and white floral dress is loose and flows around the curves of my body. The low-cut front is tasteful and beachy but also revealing enough to make me feel incredibly sexy. My new silky baby blue panties underneath help with that as well.

I do a little twirl in my dress, and I feel like a million bucks. Even my ankle feels better today. There's only a little bit of swelling left, and I know I only have Noah and his doctoring skills to thank for that.

On my way out, the door handle catches on my dress, and I let out a little yelp. *My dress has pockets?!* This day just keeps getting better.

Walking out of the resort, I'm met with the most vivid, colorful sunset I have ever seen. Swirls of oranges and yellows mixed with intense shades of pinks and purples blanket everything I see. It feels more like a painting than real life.

The only thing tethering me to reality is the feeling of the late afternoon breeze caressing my skin and gently tossing my dress around my legs. I'm completely stunned by the beauty of it all; I never want to leave.

I've never been to a luau before, let alone one in actual Hawaii, so I wasn't sure what to expect. However, as soon as I get here, I know what I'm seeing far exceeds anything I could have ever imagined.

Tiki torches line the perimeter and twinkling lights hang overhead. There are tables all around decorated with beautiful floral arrangements, and a large stage full of dancers sitting right in the middle. I've never believed in magic, but if I did, I'm pretty sure this is what it would feel like. The Aloha Spirit is real, and suddenly, it's all around me.

I spot Noah sitting at a table with the newlyweds, Lauren and Justin, from our snorkeling trip. Noah looks good. Better than good. The collar of his white linen shirt is open just enough so the hard lines of his collarbone peak through, and his pushed-up sleeves are showing off those thick veins that snake around his muscular forearms. My whole body heats.

Lauren throws her head back laughing at something Noah says, and Justin begins wiping away tears of laughter with the back of his hand. There's so much joy in their moment, and again, I find myself questioning how Noah does it. How he's able to make everyone around him abandon all of their cares and be totally present in the current moment. He makes everything feel so natural. So easy. So real. I can't look away from him.

"Jane!" Lauren says brightly, getting up from her seat and wrapping me in a warm embrace. "We missed y'all so much! I'm so glad we got to run into you again!"

"Same to you guys. How has your vacation—I mean, honeymoon—gone so far?" I ask.

"Oh, we've had more fun than I ever could have imagined. The snorkeling trip was just the beginning, and we have not slowed down since. What about y'all? This guy right here was just telling us that you two went to the volcano yesterday. How was that?" Lauren nudges me with her elbow and raises her eyebrows up and down as we make our way closer to where her husband and Noah are sitting.

Noah turns to me, and his face changes. The carefree breeziness that he had with Lauren and Justin has taken a back seat and in its place is something more complex, more intense. I can see the weight of my presence reflected in his stare, in the way his eyes darken as he looks me up and down. His shoulders rise as he takes a deep breath. His lopsided smile appears, and he says, "Jane, hi. Glad you made it. How's your ankle?"

He gets up from his chair and pulls out the one next to him. He motions for me to sit, and his eyes do an ever so brief glance down to my boobs, and then right back up. "You look great, by the way."

A smug smile appears on my lips, and I take my seat. "Thanks, Noah. You too. And my ankle feels much better, thank you."

"So, tell me about this volcano tour. I think Justin and I should do that before we go home." Lauren rests her hand on Justin's thigh, and he places his hand on hers. *Gosh, they're so freaking cute.*

"Well, funny story, on our way up, I twisted my ankle in the mud, and we didn't even make it up to the crater." I unfold my napkin and put it on my lap. "Noah actually carried me all the way back down the mountain."

"Nice, man. Good job." Justin raises his hand in a high five to Noah.

Noah delivers his high five and smiles.

"She makes it sound more heroic than it was." He turns to me and winks.

"So, let me get this straight, you two friends/not friends went on an exotic volcano tour together and you," Lauren says pointing her long finger at Noah, "carried her," turning her finger to me, "down a mountain, and you're *not* dating?" She looks at us through narrowed eyes. "Sure. That makes sense," she says with a knowing smirk.

Before either Noah or I could explain our confusing state of affairs, cute little Ashley from the spa makes her way over to our table, and I can tell this is going to make things so much worse.

"Ohmygod! Mr. and Mrs. Schwartz! It's so good to see you!" She says, giving me one of those awkward hugs when one person is standing, and the other one is sitting. "I'm so glad I got to run into you again. Sven and Anya haven't been able to stop talking about you two. You left quite an impression." She smiles. "I told them I've never seen a more attractive married couple than you guys. Ever. Like in my entire life." She pauses and gazes at a stunned Lauren and Justin at our table. "No offense, if you guys are also married."

"Oh, none taken," Lauren says, words dripping with sarcasm. "How do y'all know each other?" She wags her fingers between us and Ashley.

"Oh, sorry. I'm Ashley!" She reaches her hand out to shake Lauren's. "I work at the spa. Mr. Dumont, the owner of this entire place, scheduled these two for a massage the other day. We went all out for them because, I mean, they know Mr. Dumont, so we gave them literally the best couples' experience we could think of." She smiles at me expectantly.

I can't look away from Lauren and Justin. They're hanging on Ashley's every word, and I know the gears in their minds are churning with questions.

"You guys liked it, right?" She asks, worry creeping up on her face.

"Totally, Ashley," Noah chimes in. "It was by far the best massage experience we've ever had. When we talk to Mr. Dumont next week, we'll definitely tell him how amazing it was. How amazing you were. Thank you so much." Noah smiles at her, saving the day, again.

I see Ashley's cheeks blush, and it's only then that I notice how young she really is. Out of her spa uniform and in some colorful beachwear, I can tell that she's no more than nineteen. "Thank you so much, Mr. Schwartz! That seriously means so much to me." She says, voice shaky.

"No problem. Also, you can call me Noah." He offers a small nod. Still not breaking the spell.

"Okay, *Noah*. Thanks again," she says, the blush deepening on her cheeks. "Well, anyway, I'm gonna get my seat. I have tomorrow off, so I decided to bring my sister to the luau tonight to have some fun. My next day is Monday, so if you're still here, be sure to stop by and maybe you could sneak in another massage before you go back home."

"Sounds wonderful," Noah says, exuding charm.

"Okay, well, it was nice to meet you!" Ashley motions to Lauren and Justin. "And it was good running into you again, Mr. and Mrs. Schwartz." She waves her goodbyes and leaves our table to go find hers.

I don't want to look up. Somewhere in the middle of all that mess I made myself stare down at the napkin in my lap. I honestly have no idea what I'm going to find when I look up.

A few silent seconds tick by. I'm desperately wracking my mind for something to say that could sort out the confusion, when I hear Lauren erupt into a thunderous cackle of a laugh. My head snaps up and my eyes search for Noah's. He meets my gaze and his face cracks into a smile of his own. I'm not sure I understand what's happening.

"I knew y'all were hiding somethin'! Didn't I, babe?" She hits Justin in the chest, and he beams at her, totally enthralled by what's happening.

"The night we got home from snorkeling, we laid in bed, and I told him that there was no way y'all weren't dating, and now I find out y'all are actually married?!" Her laughter slows, but her face is still radiating happiness. "You know, you didn't have to hide the fact that y'all are married." Her smile is sincere, and I can tell she's meaning every word she's saying. "Y'all weren't good at hiding it anyway. I saw the way you two were actin'. I could tell y'all were made for each other the minute I saw you whisper in Jane's ear before we even got on the boat. You should have seen her face, it turned red as a beet."

I feel a rush of heat pass through my entire body as I remember the words he said to me before we got on the boat. *I like you better in the little red one anyway.* I know I shouldn't do it, but I chance a quick glance at Noah, and I see him staring at me, undoubtedly recalling the moment as well. I instantly regret my decision to look at him.

The way his eyes are boring into mine makes my core tighten and my heart race. He knows exactly what he's doing. He always has.

"Hmm, I don't recall," I say, my voice cracking.

"Y'all are too funny." Lauren grabs Justin's hand in hers. "Anyway, we'll leave you two love birds to enjoy the luau together in peace. We're gonna get some of that yummy pork I've been eyein' on everyone's plates."

Justin stands up and pulls out her chair for her, then reaches into his wallet and hands Noah a business card. "Hey, if you guys are ever in Alabama, please don't hesitate to give us a call. We'd love to have you over."

"For sure, man. Thanks. Same goes to you if you ever find yourselves in New York." I kick his knee from under the table. "Ouch. Oh, I mean Denver. If you're ever in Denver, you can call us. Or New York. We both live in both. Of those cities." He could not have been any less smooth saying that sentence if he tried.

The newlyweds look at us with such a strange fascination on their faces that I can't help but laugh as Noah takes a nervous drink.

"You two just keep surprising us. Keep in touch, okay?" Lauren adds as she links arms with her husband, turning to walk away.

With Lauren and Justin gone, it's just Noah and me at the table now. I'm not entirely sure what to do with myself. Suddenly, my arms feel too heavy, my head feels too big, and my legs can't find a natural way to just sit here.

I feel out of sorts, and I don't like it. When it's just me and him, it's like I don't know who I am anymore. Not in a bad way, just in a less organized and less aware version of myself way.

"That was rough." He shakes his head and lets out a little snicker.

"Ha, I know. I'm shocked Lauren thought it was so funny. I was scared she was going to think we were part of one of those crime rings where people pretend to be wealthy married couples and go on fancy vacations to pull off elaborate art heists or something like that."

Noah looks at me, brows knitted in amused confusion. "Excuse me? What?"

"Haven't you ever watched one of those kinds of movies? They're literally everywhere. They're usually true stories too."

"Nope. That's not a real thing." He crosses his arms over his chest.

"Oh, it so totally is, and with the way we just handled all of that, I'm sure that's exactly what's going through Lauren's head. We acted so fishy, there's no way she believes anything we just said. She definitely doesn't believe we're married. Also, Ashley let it spill that we knew the boss and that we're both attorneys. From different cities! Working on the same case! This whole situation screams covert art thieves." I look at him, both eyebrows raised.

A hearty laugh comes from deep within Noah's chest, and I can't help but feel it in my body too. "I guess I'll just have to take your word for it, Robins."

"Guess so." I shrug my shoulders. "So, if you don't watch true crime art thief shows, what do you watch in your spare time?"

"I don't really watch *anything*. I usually just read when I have any extra time on my hands, which is not as often as I would like."

"I hear that. Wouldn't it be nice if we didn't have to work at all and could just sit in a cozy corner and read all day?" I can feel the tension ease a bit and sense that we're both starting to relax. "I mean, I much prefer reading to watching TV too, but there's absolutely a time and a place for trashy reality shows, amIright?" I put my fist up to him waiting for a fist bump, and none comes.

"Robins, I think that right there is the most untrue thing you've ever said to me," he says with a completely straight face.

"What are you talking about? Noah, trashy reality TV is what makes the world go 'round. Of course, I'm the first to admit they're both equally as awful as they are essential, but that's the honest-to-God truth. The world would not function properly without a look inside at the lives of the most unhinged of our species. It's a necessary evil." He's staring at me like I am speaking an entirely different language. "I can talk about this all day, Noah." I smile.

"I don't doubt it, Robins." He puts his hands behind his head and reclines back in his chair, watching me with that perplexed amusement he always seems to have.

"Why do you always do that?"

"What?" His dimples pop as he replies. *God, he looks so good right now.* I dramatically copy his posture. "This. Why do you always sit like this."

He scoffs. "You don't like the way I sit?"

"No, it's not that, but it's like you only do it when you're making fun of me or something." I'm still leaning back in my chair, but I cross my arms in front of my chest. "Sometimes, it's like this though."

He copies me now and crosses his arms in front of his chest, but, *damn,* it looks so much better when he does it. The defined muscles in his forearms are on full display, and I know I stare at them longer than I should.

"Like this?" He raises a brow at me in a challenge.

"Yeah, like that. Why do you do that?" I sit up straighter.

"I like watching you talk, Robins. I always have, and this is the way I sit when I like what I see."

"Aloha. My name is Maya, and I will be your server tonight." My ears hear this, but my eyes have yet to look away from Noah. He straightens in his seat and looks at the waitress who just arrived at our table.

"Can I get you two anything to drink besides water?"

Noah motions to me, inviting me to answer. "Um," I begin, clearing my throat. I can't focus, my mind is racing. "Sorry, what's the question?"

Noah smirks.

Maya smiles, apparently not minding having to repeat herself. "Would you like anything to drink besides water?"

"Oh, I'll take a glass of your house white wine, please. Thank you." I grab my ice water and take a sip, hoping to calm my nerves. I'm definitely going to need something stronger.

"Excuse me, Maya," Noah says, gazing intently at the menu in front of him. "I was wondering if you have any wild snorkel on the menu tonight?" Before I know it, the water in my mouth shoots out of my face and sprays all over our waitress.

Noah looks at me with wide eyes, and our poor, wet waitress purses her lips and wipes her face. "Um, I don't think we do." That's it. That's all she has to say before both Noah and I are laughing together in unison, barely even able to take in a breath.

When I catch my composure, I look at Maya. "I'm so so sorry that I spit on you." I'm trying really hard not to laugh again, but it's like trying to keep your laugh inside when your teacher tells you to be quiet, but your friend keeps making funny faces. "I'm not laughing at you. I'm laughing at something else. I'm so embarrassed. I really am. Is there anything I can do?"

She studies me for a second, then smiles. "No, I'm okay. I've been doing this for ten years. That is not the first time something like that has happened, and it definitely won't be the last."

I take a deep breath and dab my eyes with my napkin, hoping my mascara isn't running from the tears of laughter that were just streaming down my face.

"I'll be back with your wine. Feel free to look at the menu while I'm gone to see what you'd like." She walks away, and again, we're alone.

"So...What do we do now?" Noah says looking at me, his head cocked to the side.

I fold and unfold my napkin in my lap, trying to act casual. But everything about this situation is the exact opposite of casual.

I look up, and Noah is counting silently on his fingers. "What are you doing?"

"Seeing what I owe you?"

"What? Pretty sure you don't owe me a thing. If anything, I'm the one who owes you."

"I do. I owe you..." He continues counting. "Fourteen. Fourteen Happy Birthdays."

"Oh, yeah. I guess, happy birthday fourteen times to you too." My chest squeezes, and I feel the threat of tears prickling behind my eyes. These past fourteen years have been a wild ride. It's crazy I'm now in my thirties, but inside, I still feel like that same eighteen-year-old girl standing on a coffee table, while a room full of strangers drunkenly sings me happy birthday. "God, that was so embarrassing."

"What was embarrassing?" *Oh, shit.* I didn't mean to say that out loud. Noah's confused face is quickly becoming one of my favorite faces that he has. It also happens to be appearing more and more frequently.

"Remember the night of *our* eighteenth birthday, and we stood on that kid Landon's huge coffee table, and people sang to us?"

"Oh man, I could never forget a room full of teenagers singing the line 'happy birthday to Noah and *that girl*'. That goes down in history as one of the funniest things that has happened to me."

"Ha, well I'm glad *you* thought it was funny. I still have nightmares about it. Sometimes though, in my nightmare, I'm standing on the coffee table totally naked." I shudder, just thinking about it. Noah swallows hard, clearly picturing my worst nightmare in his mind.

I throw my napkin in his face. "Hey there, Bob. Slow your roll. Stop thinking about me naked and wallow with me in my embarrassment, please."

"I'll think about you naked all I want, Robins." He throws my napkin back at me, but I spot the familiar pink flush that starts just below the collar of his shirt and spreads up toward his jaw.

He lets out a heavy sigh. The space between us grows tense again, and I know we can both feel it; this attraction that's tainted by our past. I see a smile appear on his lips, and I wish I knew what was going through his mind right now.

We go back and forth for a moment, exchanging embarrassing stories with one another, and each one gets more and more crazy the longer we go. I learn he cried in history class when they watched the Titanic. He learned that I peed my pants from laughing so hard when Jordyn cut her bangs too short right before we left for junior prom.

My stomach is killing me from all of the laughing we've been doing. My cheeks are sore, my mascara is ruined, but I've never had more fun.

The easy way we laugh together and the way I can feel us both give into the happiness of the moment is so freeing. I can't even remember the last time I laughed this hard for this long and didn't care what anyone thought about me.

As adults, we don't laugh like we did when we were kids. Where we just abandon all worry and care. This type of laughter is so unreserved and real. I make a mental note to add *laugh more* to the top of my To-Do list.

Chapter
Twenty-Nine
Now

"THAT'S IT. I'M OFFICIALLY moving to Hawaii." I use a toothpick to get a piece of roasted pork unstuck from one of my teeth. "Seriously, wasn't that the best food you've ever had?"

Noah shakes his head, and a small smile plays at the corners of his lips. "I love that you do that."

"Do what?" I drop the toothpick on the table, suddenly reminded of exactly how unsexy picking one's teeth is.

"You're always saying things like that. Like, 'This is the best food I've ever had!' Or 'That is the most beautiful thing I've ever seen!' I love that you always enjoy things so much, and you're not afraid to let people know. It's like, if life exists between the numbers one through ten, you live your life on eleven all the time, and I love that."

I instantly blush. To have him notice something like this about me makes me feel vulnerable and unsteady. Especially because it's something I've been made fun of for my entire life.

"I've been told I'm *too much* because I do that. I've had so many people tell me to stop over-exaggerating everything. But I promise, I'm not over-exaggerating, I swear. I just genuinely really enjoy the thing I'm doing. I guess, I'm just easy to please." I shrug my shoulders and take a sip of my drink.

"Are you?" I barely hear what he's said, but the way he looks at me as he says it makes me understand what he's implying. I feel my core heat, and I look away, trying to steer the conversation back on track.

"Oh, most definitely." I motion up to the dancers on the stage. "See, that is without a doubt, the best hula dancing I've ever seen in my entire life."

He laughs. "Oh, yeah? How much hula dancing have you seen, Robins?"

"Just this. But man, isn't it stunning?" I pause for a beat and really watch. The beauty and reverence the dancers portray is otherworldly.

I'm starting to feel overwhelmed, and a tear slides down my face.

"Hey, what's wrong? Are you okay?"

"Oh, yeah, totally. I do this a lot too." I bring my hands up to my face, framing my tears. "I cry too easily. Which is totally the opposite of the hard perfectionist attorney stereotype I try so hard to maintain."

He passes me his napkin, and I dab my cheeks. "Can I ask what made you sad?" I can tell he isn't asking to make fun of me. He's asking because he cares.

"I just wish I could do something like that."

"You want to...hula dance?" His adorable, confused look makes yet another appearance.

A small laugh leaves me. "No. Not necessarily hula dance. Just to be able to have the self-confidence to do something *like* hula dance. You know, to like, trust myself enough to let go a bit and not always have to control everything."

"Jane." His tone has suddenly shifted from confused to something stronger and more commanding. I'm scared at what he's going to say next. "You're unbelievable." I feel my brows knit together. I'm not sure where this is going. "You're a badass corporate attorney who just acquired one of the richest men in the world as a client. You're brilliant, you're a stupid hard worker, and you're pretty damn funny when you want to be." The way he's looking at me makes me feel exposed.

I don't know what to say. "I...um...thanks, Noah."

He nods, but I can tell he's nervous. He brings his hand up to his jaw and rubs the dark stubble that's grown longer since the first day we got here. "I get it though. I totally understand what it's like to feel like people are judging you. It sucks to feel like you never measure up, or like you should be doing more. I feel that all the time."

"What? Noah, come on, you're like the most confident person I've ever met."

"Nah. It's all a show, Robins. We're not so different, you and me." He gives a soft smile, but it's weighted.

"What do you mean? You mean you're not a perfect guy who really does have everything figured out while the rest of us are drowning in a sea of self-consciousness and anxiety?"

"You're making fun of me, but really, I feel all those feelings, all the time, and sometimes it's hard to find my way out."

I had no idea. I didn't know he felt like this at all. I always thought he was not only full of self-confidence but was entirely overflowing with it. "I'm not making fun. I'm sorry. I'm just surprised. You've always acted so self-assured, and I don't know, cocky even. I always guessed you just thought you were so much better than everyone else all the time."

He winces. I can tell this hit a nerve. "Yeah. Ouch. It's the total opposite, actually. I act that way because I've always thought it was the only way people would accept me." He takes a deep breath. "Hell, if they knew the real me, you know, like the *me* under all of this smart-ass attitude, I'm pretty sure no one would want to talk to me ever again." He laughs in an attempt at brevity, but I feel the truth in what he just said, deep in my chest. It feels so much safer to show people what we know they can handle of us, instead of the deeper parts that are harder and more difficult.

"Noah, that's not true." I reach over and put my hand on top of his. The physical touch instantly sends jolts throughout my body.

His eyes. God, those deep brown eyes are mesmerizing, as they search mine for answers. For the truth in what I'm saying. He doesn't believe me. He doesn't believe that he's more than what he thinks about himself.

"You're...you're incredible." I delicately trace my thumb up and down on the top of his hand. "Those things you just said about me, about being smart and hard-working...That's you. You're killing it, Noah."

He looks at me for a bit before raising one brow. "You forgot the part about being funny."

I lightly slap his hand. "Noah, I'm much funnier than you are."

He shrugs a shoulder. "Eh, agree to disagree, I guess."

I finish the last of my wine and sit with him in this tense but connected moment. This new tension between us that's full of honesty, sadness, laughter, and....lust, I think? It's hard to nail down exactly what it is I'm feeling with all these emotions whirling around me right now.

"Do you want another drink?" Noah motions to my wine glass.

"No. I'm good. One and done for me tonight. What about you, do you want another...wait, do you just have water?"

"Yep. I don't drink," he says, smiling at me over the rim of his glass.

"Wait, what?! Like you don't drink ever? Or just tonight?"

He laughs and sets his glass back down. I try to think of this past week to see if I remember him having anything besides water.

"Ever. I tried it a few times, but it's—complicated. It's just something I don't do." He shakes his head and brings a shoulder up, trying to make light of it, but I can feel his nervous energy peeking through.

"Oh, that's totally fine, I'm just shocked I haven't noticed you not drinking anything this entire week."

He gives me a smile, but it looks like he's debating if now is the time to say more.

I return his smile, hoping to convey that I'm right here with him, that I'm here to listen to why it's complicated. I want him to trust me enough to tell me.

His eyes meet mine for a brief second before he looks back down at the table and clears his throat. "Growing up, my dad had a problem with drinking. When I was a kid, I honestly thought that's all it was." He pauses and steadies himself. "Well, turns out, he was actually a complete alcoholic, and eventually, that's what killed him. He died just a few months after my...our...eighteenth birthday."

I don't know what to say. I remember he told me his dad drank, I remember his dad dying before high school graduation, but I didn't connect the two. I didn't know that was how he died. "Oh, Noah. I'm so, so sorry." He fiddles with the straw in his cup. "I know you two had a complicated relationship, but still, I can't imagine how hard that must have been for you."

From the way he looks at me, I don't know if anyone has ever said these words to him before. "Yeah. It was. It was really hard, but everyone just assumed since my parents were already divorced, and the fact that he lived in Denver, and the rest of us were still in Fort Collins, it didn't really affect me that much. But it did. It affected my whole family. We completely broke apart after he died." The dam has cracked, and I can tell he needs to get this out, he needs to keep going.

"My family was awesome when I was little, like everything we wanted to do, we would do together. My brother and I were as close as brothers could be, and my mom and sister were inseparable. It felt like we had the perfect family. My dad was a great dad, until the alcohol took over and everything changed. They got divorced when I was fifteen, and the years following that were really rough. My mom became a shell of herself, and my dad just kept digging himself deeper and deeper."

He stops playing with the straw and looks at me. "That's why it was so important for me to get Megan home the night of that party. She was so angry at our parents for what they'd done, and even more, she was so angry at our dad for leaving that she rebelled every chance she could. My mom wouldn't keep any alcohol in the house, so that night, she and some of her middle school friends came to that party hoping to get wasted. She came specifically to get blackout drunk as some kind of fucked-up middle finger to our parents. I had to get her out of there." He holds my gaze intently. "I promise, Jane, I wouldn't have left you if it wasn't for that."

"I know," I whisper.

"I'm just so sorry. There was so much going on, and I couldn't, for the life of me, seem to figure it all out. I was so hurt that he canceled on me for my birthday that I didn't even talk to him after that." He takes a deep breath before continuing. "It wasn't very long after that night that we got a call from my dad's landlord in Denver saying that he'd passed away. Apparently, he was late on rent, and that's how they found him. He died alone in some cheap apartment with a bottle of whiskey in his lap." He looks away, eyes wet.

Tears stream down my face. The pain Noah has been carrying all these years, it's terrible. I can see it now in his eyes, and in the way he's finally letting it all pour out.

"Literally, only two weeks after he died, we moved to New York to be closer to my mom's side of the family. But it was just me, my mom, and Megan. Tyler was in college already, so he just decided to stay in Colorado. He totally wrote us all off."

Noah moved away. That's why I never ran into him again. I try to think back to that time, to the end of senior year. "Tyler and Jordyn broke up right before your dad died. She said she tried to reach out after we heard the news, but Tyler didn't respond to any of her calls."

He nods, like he already knew that. "Yeah, doesn't surprise me. He didn't respond to *anyone's* calls. Our mom was distraught. She had just lost her ex-husband and father of her children, and then her son wouldn't even talk to her. He didn't even care that our mom was hurting. He didn't care that she wouldn't get out of bed and was basically disappearing." Tears pool at the bottom of his eyes now. "So, that left me. I was put in charge of taking care of our little sister who essentially just lost both of her parents and a brother. It was awful. Our mom really struggled. I tried, but nothing ever helped. Eventually, she passed away three years after my dad."

"I'm...I don't know what to say. I'm so sorry."

"It's okay. I'm okay now." He blinks away the tears. "It was hard, but we've made it through. That's why Tyler and my relationship is the way it is. That's the hardest part about all of this actually."

"What about Megan? How is she?"

"She's great, you'd love her. She lived with me through college, and then moved into her own apartment just a few blocks down from me once she graduated. She's so freaking smart. She just got married a few months ago to an awesome guy, and they're actually planning to start a family soon."

"Sounds like you did a great job then." I smile at him, hoping that he understands how true that statement really is.

"Nah, it was all her. She's just a really good kid. Well, woman, I guess. It's weird to think of her as married, let alone as a mom." He laughs. "She's going to be good at it though, I can tell. Tyler's a good dad too. It's like they were made for it, which is funny, because they definitely didn't learn that from our parents."

"What about you, Noah? Do you ever want a family?" This question makes me nervous. I don't know what I'm hoping his answer is.

"I love kids...but if I'm being honest, I don't know if I'm cut out for it. I would love nothing more than to have kids of my own, but what if I don't do it right?" A line of worry appears between his brows. "I don't want to be anything like my dad. It terrifies me."

"Noah, you just told me yourself that Megan is an amazing woman, and that's all thanks to you. You fought for her. You saved her. That's the kind of dad you'd be."

"Yeah. I don't know." He looks up at the sky and takes a breath. "I really would love to be a dad someday, to have my own family." I see his mouth curve into the beginnings of a smile, and I can't help but smile myself. "You know, I hold a firm belief that there's nothing funnier in this world than a four-year-old who's had too much sugar."

I let out a chuckle. I can imagine him playing soccer with his nephews and play-wrestling them while they try to wiggle free. I can picture him as a dad, brushing his kid's teeth, or reading them bedtime stories. I can see the love that he has. It's in his eyes, in the way he smiles, the way he laughs. This man in front of me is full of it.

"Wanna head down to the water for a bit?" He asks, standing up from his chair.

"I'd love to."

Chapter Thirty
Now

W E HOLD OUR SHOES in our hands as we slowly walk along the beach where the sand meets the water. The waves are warm, but the air is growing cooler as the night goes on.

"Are you cold? Do you wanna head back?" He asks, slowing his stride.

"No, I'm okay. It's at least seventy degrees right now. There was a blizzard the other day back home, so I'll take this over *that* any day of the week." I spread my arms out wide, like I'm about to take flight. Trying to feel it all over my body. "This is perfect."

"Too bad you don't have that lucky turtleneck you had when we first met. I'm sure that would come in handy right about now."

"Haha, oh *God*. That lucky SWEATSHIRT was my favorite shirt I've ever had, I'll have you know. I still have it somewhere in my parents' attic." I give him a smug little smile.

"Oh, that's right. It was a *lucky crewneck sweatshirt*, if I'm remembering correctly. Am I right?" he teases.

"Very right."

"I never did get to find out what made it so lucky." He nudges me gently with his elbow. "God, Jane, that day you surprised me by whipping it out and showing me who's boss was one of the best moments of my life. I was so proud of you for not taking my shit."

This earns a laugh. "I knew it! You did give me shit. You were such an ass." I shove him softly toward the water.

"Hey, I know. I was a dick to you but only because I thought you were cute."

I pretend not to hear this.

"Boys are so stupid. Why do you guys do that anyway? Poke fun at girls you like?"

"Don't ask me, Robins. I don't make the rules, I just do what I'm told." He slings his arm around my shoulder, and his body feels warm against the quickly cooling night.

I look up at him, his arm still wrapped around me. "My Nan gave me that shirt a few years before I met you. She got it at a K-Mart around the corner from her house. It was on sale for three dollars. The shirt itself was nothing special, but she gave it to me and told me that it was the last thing she was ever going to buy for me."

I feel myself getting swept away into the memory of that day in her home. She wrapped the small box in Christmas wrapping paper even though it was mid-July. "She gave me the box and said, 'Birdie girl, this is the last piece of clothing I will ever buy you again. You see, my sugar, I know you'll achieve all your dreams, and you'll never need anything from anyone. I know you'll go far. You'll fly high, my Bird.' That's it. That cheap oversized sweatshirt represented that someone believed in me. So, when I wore that sweatshirt, it made me believe in myself too."

At this, Noah brings me closer to him. Close enough that I reach my arm around his back and rest it on his hips. I let my head lean against his warm body as we walk along the beach. It feels so natural, so comfortable.

"I really wish I could have met this Nan of yours. She sounds like quite the extraordinary lady."

"Oh, she was. I miss her." I stare out over the ocean and try to hold it together.

"She was right, you know. You did achieve all your dreams and from what I understand, you did do it all on your own. You should be proud of that."

"I guess." I try to shrug my shoulders, but his heavy arm slung across them makes it impossible.

"What?"

"I don't know, I guess I've done most of what I've set out to do, but I'm not sure if it's what I *wanted*, or if it was just what I chose to focus on....Does that make sense?"

"Hmm, not really. Keep going."

"Like, I still live in Colorado. I don't really know why, I just never left. I know my parents are there, and of course, my best friends, but, like, I don't think I stay because I *want* to. I just stay because I don't want to deal with the change."

"Jane, what do you want?"

"What? What do you mean?"

"Think about it. What is it that *you* want? Not what other people want for you, or what you think you should want. What is it that you really want? Do you want to live in Denver? Do you want to work for Schwartz & Adler?"

I feel myself start to disappear into my head. The swimming feeling of not having control and having too many decisions up in the air is beginning to consume me.

I maneuver my way out from under his arm and cross my arms against my chest, feeling like I need to be held together or I might just come apart. "I don't know. I really don't know."

"What *do* you know, Robins?"

I think for a moment about my life and all the different working parts. My day-to-day life back home. "I do know that I love my friends. Jordyn and Daniel are the best part of my life, and I would be devastated to ever leave them."

"Okay, good. So, you want to stick around because they're there. Denver is a good fit then." I feel my chest expand slightly with this realization. "What else do you know?"

"I know that I want to be an attorney."

"That's a relief, because you already are one." He smiles. "Come on, keep going."

I try to come up with something else, but my mind draws a blank. "I...I don't know. I don't know what else."

"Try, Robins. You need to see that you're made up of more than what's expected of you, that you're more than what others think about you."

"Hi, pot, meet me, kettle," I say, sticking out my hand waiting for him to shake it.

He playfully shoves my hand away. "Okay, touché. I know it's hard, but apparently, it's something we're both needing to work on." He smiles. "Jane, I can tell there's more in there that you're not saying. It's okay though, I want to hear it. Say it."

"I know I want to be a mother, but I'm terrified because my family was an absolute mess. It's like you said earlier, I don't want to bring a kid into a messy family. I don't want to end up making the same mistakes that my mom made. I'm so scared that I would end up making a mini version of myself, who's an extreme perfectionist, and has panic attacks all the time."

I've been holding that inside of me for a long time, and it feels so good to get it out. "I've been in therapy for a while now, trying to get the panic attacks under control, and I'm doing a lot better, but I still have them sometimes. I didn't even know that's what they were until one night I honestly thought I was having a heart attack. I had just lost an important case I had done so much work for, and I just cracked. It wasn't because we lost, I'd lost cases before, it was just because I really thought I knew exactly what would happen, and it just totally went the other way. I felt like I had lost control, and I spiraled from there. Jordyn helped me through it and let me know that I wasn't really dying, just having a panic attack. It totally sucked, but at least it pointed me in the right direction for help."

"Jane, I'm so sorry. I had a buddy in college that dealt with anxiety and panic attacks, and they're no joke. There were a few times I had to help him deescalate, and it's a tough thing to do. I hate to think of you going through that." He moves closer to me and grabs my hand in his, it's so effortless you'd think we'd done it a thousand times before. It feels so right, his big hand holding mine as we stroll along the moonlit beach.

"Therapy has been the best thing for me. I'm getting so much better at getting through my attacks, and in all honesty, they're happening much less than they used to. So that's good." I attempt a smile. "Mostly I'm just realizing I have to unlearn everything I was taught about myself when I was a kid. Like, I shouldn't still be so worried about what my parents think about me, but they really did a number on me. Somehow, they always made me feel like I'm way too much and not enough at the same time." I shake my head. "I just have to be okay with the fact that I've never been perfect enough for them, and that I never will be." I shrug my shoulders.

Noah stops walking and stands in the wet sand, the water lapping gently over our feet. He stares at me intently and releases my hand from his, then turns to face me. He towers over me, so I look up at him, not knowing what's going through his head. We're so close now, our chests almost touch. He slowly brings his hands up and softly lands them on either side of my face. His dark eyes stare deep into mine. "Jane, you're already perfect. You always have been." With this, he bends down and presses his full lips into mine.

The feeling is nothing like I remember from our kiss as teenagers. That kiss was so nervous and inexperienced. This kiss is anything but that. It's full of years of longing and wanting. It's all-consuming.

It's everything.

Our lips part, and he softly rests his forehead on mine. His hands are still tenderly placed on the sides of my face, and the heat of his breath is still brushing my lips. "I'm sorry if that was...I've just been waiting for so long...was that...are you okay?"

I look at him, not wanting him to pull away any farther. "Yes. That was..." I can't seem to find the words.

"Good," he says, pulling away and looking me square in the face. "Jane, I'm only going to ask this once, and if you say no, I promise I won't ever ask you again." His rapid heartbeat thrums at the base of his throat. "Do you want to go up to my room?"

I gaze at him, my eyes heavy with desire. I slow my breathing and think for a moment. There's nothing I want more in this world than to go up to his room right now. I want to feel all of him, in every way. I nod my head, not breaking eye contact.

"I need to hear you say it. Say it, Robins. Tell me what you want."

My breath hitches in my throat. "*I want you.*"

This time, our kiss is hungry. Our teeth scrape together as I tangle my hands in his dark hair pulling him closer to me.

We stumble our way up the beach and back to the resort. Taking short breaks from walking, barely able to keep our hands off each other.

The elevator ride is an entirely different ball game though. Thankfully, an adorable little Asian lady gets in with us on the second floor, which gives us a much-needed break to catch our breaths.

As soon as the elevator door opens, he gets out and stands on the landing in front of me, just like he did on the mountain, and motions for me to get on his back. I happily oblige, and we walk down the hallway to his room, my heart pounding out of my chest.

He fumbles around in his back pocket for the room key as I playfully nibble the lobe of his ear.

"You'd better stop that now, Robins, if you don't want to end up naked right here in the middle of this hallway."

He finally opens the door, and I carefully slide down his back and stand against the wall inside the room. We stay like this for a moment, wondering what move to make next. His chest moving up and down with his rapid breaths.

He's first to move and closes the distance between us, his mouth finding mine again. The intensity growing with every breath.

I part my mouth and take him in. The first touch of his tongue on mine sends a shiver of pleasure down my spine. He tastes just like I remember.

He moves deeper into my mouth, and I let out a soft groan. This has him pressing harder into my body, and I feel him, all of him, hard against me. A white hot heat grows deep in my belly.

One of his hands is on my hip, the other finding its way up to my breast. His thumb traces lazy circles around my peaked nipple.

I lift one leg around his hip, and we move in time as his mouth tracks from mine to down my neck. His tongue traces a line across my chest.

He softly pulls down the shoulders of my dress and looks at me, my bare breasts on full display. "God, Jane. You're beautiful." He moves his mouth to my nipple and his tongue dances around it as the suction pulls me in deeper.

I move my hand to find the length of him, and *holy shit*, length there is. He lets out a low groan as I let my palm work up and down, trying to feel all of him. He moves his mouth back up to mine, and our heavy breaths join together.

He reaches down and finds the inside of my dress. He moves my panties to the side, and his fingers find my middle. I feel him smile on my lips as he says, "You're so fucking wet."

My knees buckle as he thrusts his fingers deep inside of me. I let in a sharp intake of air, and I feel a soft satisfied laugh escape his mouth.

"We're moving to the bed," he says breathlessly. He grabs the backs of my thighs, and I wrap my legs around his middle. He carries me over to the bed and gently lays me down.

He stands tall at the foot of the bed and slowly unbuttons his shirt as he stares down at me, his eyes hungry with want. "Take off your dress."

"Not until you drop your pants," I say, raising one brow and biting my lip.

"Tell me, Jane," he says unbuckling his belt, "do you enjoy always being so stubborn?" He takes off his pants, and his boxer briefs are fast to follow. It's then that I see just how perfect Noah Riley truly is. His skin pulled tight; he grips himself hard in his hand as he watches me slowly undress.

"Panties too," he says, clenching his jaw.

I cock my head to the side and give a small smile as I do exactly what he says. As I lay back down, everything on full display, he moves over me, and his lean muscles tense as he makes his way up my naked body. Just like when we were younger, he softly rests his hand on my ribs. His thumb brushes delicately over my small birthmark there. He bends down and places a delicate kiss right on it. "I've thought about this birthmark more than I'd like to admit." His lips hover over my tender skin.

"Hold on," he says, breaking the kiss. He gets off the bed and moves toward his suitcase. "I have a condom in here somewhere. Gimme just a sec."

I prop myself up on my elbows and stare at his perfectly muscular ass as he searches through his things. "If you can't find it, I conveniently have an entire Costco-sized supply of them in my room."

He turns around with one eyebrow raised, and a shiny little wrapper in his hands. "I'll need *that* story later. But for now..." the corner of his mouth ticks up as he moves back onto the bed and licks his way from the middle of my chest all the way up to my pink, swollen lips.

His entire body presses into mine, nothing between us. My back arches into him, needing to feel every inch. The way we move together is even better than I ever could have imagined. We fit together perfectly. Our kisses get deeper and sloppier as our hands feverishly trace over every part of each other's bodies.

Pushing up to his knees, he rips open the condom with his teeth and slides it on himself slowly as he looks down at my body with dark, hungry eyes.

EMMA NORMAN

Not breaking eye contact, I bring a hand up to my nipple and give a little pinch as my other hand lightly traces a line down my stomach to the wet warmth aching for friction.

He bites his bottom lip, and I see his cock twitch before he bends back down over me. He gently uses his knee to nudge my legs open wider and positions himself right at my entrance. *Fuck.* I just want him inside of me; I need him inside of me. He wants me to ask for it. "*Noah,*" I softly moan.

"Say it, Jane." He growls into my mouth. He wants me to beg. "Say it."

"Please," I whimper, then I feel him plunge deep inside me, every inch stretching me to my max. I look up at him, chest moving up and down as he stays like this for a moment, allowing for me to adjust.

I slowly roll my hips, pulling him deeper, and watch as he bites back a smile. My head bends back in ecstasy, and I grip the sheets in my fists as he thrusts deeper again, and again.

"You're everything, Jane. Everything."

I come undone. Every feeling, every emotion, everything culminates into one perfect moment, and I feel myself dive over the edge in ultimate euphoria. I've wanted this for so long. This. Right here. With the only man I've ever trusted.

He grabs my hands in his and lifts them over my head. Our fingers intertwine as I feel his thrusts grow more rapid and frenzied. His face moves close to mine, and he stares deep into my eyes.

He lands a passionate kiss onto my open lips, then completely comes apart.

We lay in bed, my chin resting on his chest as he traces lazy lines up and down my bare back. He smiles at me. The most content smile I've ever seen on his face. "You know, I've been waiting fourteen years to do that." He tucks a piece of hair behind my ear. "Ever since that day at the lake when you were wearing that blue swimsuit...I was fucked right then and there. I'll never be able to get that image of you out of my head."

"What?! There's no way. That was the ugliest thing I've ever owned! I'm surprised you even knew it was me under all that fabric." He laughs. "God, I was so embarrassed." I cover my face in my hands.

"Why were you embarrassed? I fucking loved that suit." He turns me on my back and moves on top of me. "But if I'm being honest, I really just wanted to see what was underneath it..." He plants a soft kiss onto my lips and just like that, I'm lost in him again. The way he tastes and smells. The weight of his body pressed against mine. I want to stay here forever.

He breaks our kiss and stares at me. "You're so beautiful, Jane."

I bite my lip and smile. "You're not too bad yourself."

Noah gently rolls off and hugs me tight into his body. We lay in comfortable silence, my back to his front, feeling each other's heartbeats. He rests his hand on my hip and gently drags it up and down my outer thigh. I feel him nuzzle his face into my hair and press a soft kiss on the back of my head. "Thank you."

"Ha, for what? That sex was for me just as much as it was for you." I laugh.

"No, Jane. Thank you for listening to me," he says, trailing his hand over my stomach. "I've never told anyone those things about my family before. No one knows how messy my life has been. Growing up, I wasn't allowed to talk about my feelings, at all." He swallows hard. "That night of the party was the first time I'd ever felt comfortable enough to let my guard down and shirk off this stupid cocky shell I've always had. Because of *you,* Jane. Even though we spent so little time together, you changed me. That was the first and only time in my life that I ever felt seen or heard. *You* did that for me. You make me feel like I can be myself. Like I can have feelings and be imperfect, and it's okay." He takes a deep breath. "There's just something about you, Jane Robins. There always has been."

My chest tightens, and I move in closer to him, not wanting there to be any space between our bodies at all.

He holds me close, wrapping my hands in his. "I'm so sorry about the pain I put you through all those years ago. I feel awful knowing how much I hurt you, especially after what you did for me. I never meant to..."

"Ssshhh, Noah. I forgive you." I squeeze his hands in mine, and his entire body relaxes into me.

"Goodnight, Bird," he whispers softly and hugs me tighter into his chest.

Chapter Thirty-One
Now

T HE ONLY THING PULLING me out of my dream is the weight of his arm draped softly on my stomach. It's still dark in the room when I open my eyes, so I know it's not quite morning yet. I sit in this moment, replaying the night in my head. Every touch, every kiss, every heavy breath.

I slowly turn my head to the side and wonder just how we got to this point. How on earth did I end up in bed with this truly amazing man?

I take my time as I study his long, dark lashes. The way they curl slightly at the edges, framing his beautifully intense eyes. I watch as his chest moves up and down in slow rhythmic time, in and out. In and out.

Noah Riley isn't like any other man I've ever known. He's so much more than anything I could have ever imagined. He just gave everything to me, and he doesn't even know it.

He's the first person who's ever made me feel seen and important. He listened to me as I revealed just how much of a mess I can be, and he didn't judge me for it.

The best part is that he treats everyone like that. I've witnessed countless times over the last few days when he's made everyone around him feel like he's only there to spend time with them. Every room that he walks in is just another room for him to meet a new friend, for him to make someone laugh; for him to help someone out.

He's everything I've ever wanted. He's the man of my dreams, and...he deserves so much more than me.

My chin starts trembling, and tears quickly blur my vision. *What am I doing? Why did I do this? I shouldn't be here.* I slowly lift his arm from my stomach and carefully remove myself from underneath. I gently lay his arm down on the bed where my body just was.

The room is spinning. I stood up too fast and all the blood rushed to my feet. I should sit back down, but I don't want to wake him up.

Tears begin to fall heavy from my eyes as I feverishly search in the dark room for my clothes.

I get dressed as quietly as I can. I find my shoes and slip them on, but I can't find my phone anywhere. *Shit.* Where is it? I think back to the last place I had it; I took it with me to the bathroom to check the time after we went for a second round. It hope I left it by the sink. I tiptoe my way to the bathroom and silently close the door behind me.

Not even bothering to turn on the light, I feel around to where I know the sink to be. My fingers are desperately searching for anything familiar, when I feel the grippy silicone case and quickly clutch it to my chest.

My breathing becomes faster and faster and silent sobs take over my body. *What the fuck was I thinking?* How could I have messed up so bad?

I sink to the bathroom floor and try my best to bite back the sobs, not wanting to chance waking Noah. *Noah.* The man who just gave so much of himself to me. The man who has walked into my life, twice now, and both times has left me feeling raw. The first time, raw with abandonment and shame, but this time, I'm left raw from change. From forgiveness and surrender.

I shake my head. I can't do this. I can't do this. There's too much uncertainty. I don't like uncertainty. I don't like when I can't control the outcome. I like facts. I like things that I can look at and have a clear picture of how it will end up. This isn't like that at all.

I want to escape all of this unknowing fear that's in front of me.

Heartbreak.

What if he hurts me again? What if I hurt him? There are too many bad things that could happen. There are too many unknowns. I can't do this.

Wait, just a few days ago, I said that I wasn't going to do this anymore. I told myself that I wasn't going to let myself shove hard things aside. I said I would deal with them head on but right now, I can't do that. I'm too scared.

Noah opened up things in me and now what am I supposed to do? How do I put it all back? How do I stop feeling like I've made all the wrong choices in my life, and that I'm not who I'm supposed to be. Am I in the right career? Am I a good friend? Am I a good person? Am I ready to be the woman that he already thinks I am?

My breathing becomes shallow and quick. I suddenly feel like I can't get enough air, and my chest feels like it's being crushed from the inside out. I'm having a heart attack. I'm going to die.

I close my eyes and touch my clammy hand to the cold tile floor, attempting to ground myself. I remember my therapist saying that when we're having a panic attack, it feels like we're dying, it feels like we're floating away, but we're not. We have to try to re-ground ourselves back to our surroundings. To bring our thoughts 'back to earth,' so to speak.

Letting my phone slip into my lap, I place my other hand on the tile as well. I take a shaky breath in, try to hold it, and let it out. I try again and again until I feel like I've overcome the worst of it.

My breathing finally slows, and I open my eyes to the pitch black bathroom.

I need to go home.

I need to get out of this fantasy place and back to reality. This little thing with Noah can all just be forgotten. I can move on. I have to move on.

I know he'll be able to move on. Of course he will, and he should. He needs a woman who can give him everything that he deserves; a woman who knows who she is and knows what she wants. That woman is not me. I will never be enough for him.

We don't work together. We're way too similar. We both like to argue too much. Besides, he lives in an entirely different state, and long-distance things never work out.

I need to go home.

I'll go to the partners and tell them that I have to get off of the Dumont account. He can have it. He deserves it. I'll work hard, and I know I'll get on another account. I just need things to go back to how they were before all of this.

Running my fingers through my hair, I wipe away my tears with the loose fabric of my dress. I'll figure out all this dating and relationship stuff later. It's fine. It's just not in the cards for me right now. Maybe it never will be, I don't know. I just know that at this moment, *I need to get home.*

My phone screen is so bright that it hurts my eyes. I open my emails and find the one with my trip itinerary. I try a few different airlines, but I'm finally able to change my flight home to the earliest one available. I have three hours to get to the airport.

I turn my phone back off, and the darkness of the room seems so much darker now. I stand up slowly and quietly open the bathroom door.

There's a part of me dangerously hoping that Noah is awake and stops me from leaving, but he's not.

The soft silver light of the moon is illuminating the room just enough for me to see that he's still in the same position as before. With his arm outstretched, thinking I'm still beside him.

"I'm sorry," I whisper, then softly close the door behind me.

Chapter Thirty-Two
Now

MY HEAD IS POUNDING. Hungover from the pain and hurt of this morning. My airport experience this time was a stark contrast to the day I left for Hawaii. I couldn't find my ID because my travel wallet was in my checked bag, so I had to unpack everything to find it, which made a long line form behind me, and people were pissed. Then, my gate changed right before it was about to board, and I didn't notice until it was almost too late. I can honestly say that the airport may have lost some magic for me.

I know I don't look good right now. My glazed expression and red-rimmed eyes have caught the attention of one of the flight attendants, and every time she walks the aisle, she looks at me with a sincere *I'm sorry* look on her face.

But I don't deserve anyone's sympathy. I don't deserve to have anyone look at me with any type of concern or compassion, because as I sit in the stillness of the airplane, after I had finished with my flurry of packing, scheduling Ubers, and boarding my flight home, I become painfully aware that

I just left Noah in the same way that I thought he left me all those years ago. Alone, in a strange bed, without a word.

But I wasn't being someone's knight in shining armor, like he was that night. I didn't leave him there intending to come back. I left him after we had the most incredible day together, full of laughter and connection. I left him like it was nothing. Like *he* was nothing. Like he didn't mean anything to me.

But that's what hurts the most. I wouldn't have left him if that was the case. Isn't that so messed up? Like, if he was just some random guy who didn't mean anything to me, I would have stayed. I would have stayed in that bed until morning, when we probably would have had sex again, then ate a delicious breakfast. I'd probably still be there.

But I couldn't do that with Noah. I couldn't face the fact that he changed me. These past few days, I reconnected with him, and he changed me. He stripped me down and cracked open my shell and saw the real me. He saw all of the raw and broken parts of me and what if when he woke up in the morning, he didn't like what he saw? What if he didn't like the real me? What if he *hated* me?

These fears have been part of me my whole life, and that's why I keep everything so bottled up and hidden away in the first place. I'm afraid people won't like the person I am on the inside. The person who's behind the perfectly organized attorney who has everything figured out. I'm afraid they won't like the mess. My mess. I'm afraid.

Fear. This is what I've based my life on. Fear of disappointing my parents. Fear of getting a bad grade. Fear of not being good enough. Fear of failure. Fear of mistakes. Fear of rejection. Fear of being alone.

I squeeze my hands together. I just told myself I wasn't going to let fear run my life anymore, and here I am, playing the same game yet again. I know this is not how life is supposed to work. I know life isn't so black and white. But for some reason, this is the only way I know how to do things.

I don't want to be like this anymore. I want the confident Jane back from a few days ago. The one who wasn't afraid of her feelings, and who wasn't afraid to be herself. To let her hair down and let things unfold how they may, instead of trying to control every outcome.

I want the Jane who laughed. I want the Jane who opens up to someone, and then lets them open up to her. No judgment. No worries. I want the Jane who isn't afraid of someone loving her.

Noah gave that to me. All that and more. He gave me hope. He gave me a clear future. I could see it. I could see this beautiful life filled with love. Noah is this future. He is everything. He is brave, he is loyal, he is smart, he is kind. Facts. These are facts, and I've always prided myself for using facts over feelings, and here are the facts laid out before me, plain as day. *Noah is meant for me.*

I bury my face in my hands, thinking about the mess I just made of things. I can't believe I just left him the way I did. I want to call him right now and tell him how I feel. I want him to know how sorry I am. I want him to know I didn't mean to hurt him. I want him to know that *I love him.*

"Do you want another Diet Pepsi, hun?" The flight attendant rolls by with her cart, and I look up at her through my tears. She opens a new can, gives it to me, and then also grabs a little package of tissues and sets them on my tray. "Oh darlin', I'm sorry for whatever it is you're strugglin' through this morning. I've had my eye on you, and I can tell it's somethin' fierce."

"Yeah, thank you. And, thank you for the drink. I needed it."

"No problem. Just remember, 'for every problem under the sun, there is an answer or there is none.'" She winks and gives my shoulder a little squeeze as she makes her way to the next row.

Nan. My Nan. I feel the weight of everything pressing down on me, and I know that I need to figure out if this is one of those problems that has an answer. I close my eyes. "Nan," I whisper. "Nan, please tell me if there is an answer this time. Tell me if I should try to fix this, or if I should let it all go."

I grip the armrests beside me, trying to stay here and not let myself float away into panic. That's when I hear it. I hear the most beautiful sound in the world.

On the row across from me, I hear the sound of a little girl unapologetically laughing to her fullest extent. A laugh with absolutely no inhibitions. A laugh with no care in the world. Her mother is sitting at her side, trying her best to hush her daughter, but isn't succeeding because she, too, is laughing.

"Mom, no way. No one loves mouses! No way," she says through her giggles. My head snaps in their direction. The mom picks up the picture book from her daughter's lap and reads the page out loud. "I promise nugget, that's exactly what it says! Here, I'll read it again. Okay, it says, 'Luna the cat wasn't an ordinary cat. She was a magnificent cat. You see, her most favorite animal was a mouse!'" The little girl laughs her full belly laugh again, and her mom shuts the book, and joins her daughter, both laughing in joyful bliss.

That's it. That's what I want. I want to be a mother. I want to have a family. I want my career that I've worked so hard for. I want it all, and I know I can have it. But more than anything, I want Noah right there doing it with me. *Together.*

"Excuse me. Pardon me." I'm not a violent person, but if this guy in front of me doesn't move faster, I can see myself becoming one. I run up the boarding bridge, clutching my phone in my hand for dear life. My carry-on slung heavily over my shoulder, banging against my ribs with every step. I will invest in one of those nice roller carry-ons after this.

I've had my phone off since I boarded the plane, so I hurry and turn it on and search for a signal. The second I get one, I dial Jordyn first to have her help coaching me on what to say to Noah.

"Hey, you! How are you? I miss you!"

"Hey, J, I'm...Um...Well, I have a lot to tell you. I need help."

"Jane, are you okay? What happened?"

"Okay, so... first...I slept with Noah."

"Holy SHIT!" she yells, "Oh, shut up, Evan, this is important." I hear her say to her boss as she moves from wherever she is in her office and into a quieter area. "Jane! What the hell happened?"

"Okay, wait, when you're done, tell Evan sorry from me. I didn't mean to drop this bomb on you while you're at work."

"Don't worry about Evan, I had to listen to him give a two-hour sexual harassment seminar yesterday, and he used actors, Jane. He can deal with this."

I laugh despite my situation. "Okay. So, turns out, Noah is the best man in the world. Jordyn, I swear to God he's the most amazing man who has ever walked the Earth. He carried me down a mountain, he told me he was being a good brother, he told me he's never forgotten about me, and then we had the best sex of my life—twice—and then, I left him alone in his hotel room, and now I'm here in the Denver airport asking for your advice on how I tell him that I know I fucked up, and I'm sorry for everything." I got all of this out in one breath, and now I feel like I'm going to faint.

"Holy shit, rewind all of that. I heard mountain, brother, sex, and abandonment. Is that correct?"

"Yes."

"I don't understand, babe. I need a few more details." I sit down and rest my feet on my bag in front of me and tell her everything.

I hear her let out a deep breath. "Oh, Jane. You're doing the right thing." Her voice is kind and soft. "I'm happy for you, babe. I'm so happy that you're finally figuring out that it's you who is hurting yourself. That your perfectionism is hurting you more than it's helping. I'm happy that you're letting yourself feel these things and not shutting off and disappearing." I hear the emotion in her voice. "But most of all, I'm happy that you found him. I'm happy that he makes you happy."

Now I'm crying again. In the middle of the airport. "Thanks, J. He's incredible, and I want him to know that. *I love him,* Jordyn, and I'm so scared that I fucked it all up. What do I say, how do I fix this?"

"Tell him the truth. Tell him why you were scared. Tell him what you thought you were preserving by running away. Tell him everything you told me, and if he's even half as amazing as you say he is, he'll understand. Call him."

"Okay." I take a deep breath.

"Listen, I have to get back to work, but after I help Daniel with some inventory at the café later tonight, I'm coming straight to your apartment, to hear all of the details. No matter how late it is. I'll bring a pizza. Deal?"

"Deal. See you tonight." I end the call and stare at my phone.

The colors are blurring together, and I'm suddenly not so sure I should be doing this. I could break this off now and try to heal. Try to forget everything. Try to forget him.

But images from last night move through my mind, and I know I could never do that. I have to call him, and if he doesn't accept my apology, then at least I'll know where we stand. He deserves to know why I left; he deserves to know that it wasn't because of him.

I navigate through my phone and find his message thread. I click on his number and wait for it to ring. My heart rate is picking up, and I feel my hands begin to tingle.

Straight to voicemail.

Okay. No problem. Let me try again.

I click his number again, and just like before, it goes straight to his voicemail.

Okay. That's it.

That's where we stand.

Chapter Thirty-Three
Now

T HE SNOW FALLS LIGHTLY from the gray Colorado sky. I feel so out of place with my sun-kissed skin. Everything feels so uncomfortable and wrong. I get back to my apartment, and I feel like everything has been drained of color.

I take off my shoes by the door, leave my suitcases in the entryway, and go into the kitchen. Jordyn and Daniel have been watering my plants, and my mail is waiting for me on the island. Back to reality.

Heat rushes to my face, I feel so embarrassed. I don't know how I messed up so badly. I can't believe I thought he would actually want to talk to me after what I did to him. *Fuck.*

I go into the bathroom and strip down. I feel dirty and broken. I don't even wait until the shower gets warm before I get it.

The cold water takes my breath away, and tears fall from my eyes. *I'm the worst. Why did I do this? Why did I hurt him? Why am I the way that I am?*

I get out of the shower and wrap myself in my old, tattered robe. I feel empty and alone. Moving to my bed, I pull down my covers and slip inside.

I just want to sleep. I just want to wake up in Hawaii with his arms around me. I want this all to have been a dream. *I'm so sorry, Noah. I really messed up.* Tears hit my pillow, as I drift off into a fitful sleep.

A knock at the door startles me awake. I sit upright, my room is dark and cold. The clock reads 9:16 p.m. *Jordyn.* I rush out of bed and run to my door. I need her. I need her to tell me that I'm okay.

I open my door, and Noah is standing there, small flecks of white snow dusting the top of his head and shoulders. *Noah*...In his hands he's holding a can of Diet Pepsi, a plastic-wrapped brownie, and a large bouquet of flowers. "I didn't know what your favorite flowers are, so I just got ones that reminded me of your eyes, and..."

I crash into him. My arms wrap around his neck, and I press my lips into his.

He drops the items to the ground and picks me up as I wrap my legs around his middle. I break away from our kiss, tears streaming down my face. "I'm so sorry. I'm so sorry." I bury my face into his neck.

He carries me through my open door and sits me on the island. He quickly grabs his things from the hallway, then shuts the door behind him. Before he moves closer, he studies me. I'm still in my robe, and my hair is still damp from my shower, but he looks at me like he did last night, like I'm beautiful.

He moves back to me and nestles in between my legs. I rest my hands on his shoulders, and he stares at me intently. I open my mouth, about to let it all out, to tell him everything I did wrong, when he puts his finger softly to my mouth.

"Wait, before you say anything, I just want you to know that I got your address from Adler's secretary. I told her I needed to send you some documents for the Dumont case. I promise I'm not a stalker or anything." He smiles his lopsided smile, which loosens the knot in my chest.

"Noah....I..." My mind is racing, and none of my thoughts make sense. I don't want to just give him excuses. He deserves more from me.

"Jane, when I woke up this morning and saw that you weren't there, I was crushed. I was confused. I didn't understand how you could have left me after the night we had just shared. But then I remembered...I know you, Jane Robins." He smiles. "I know that you started to overthink things. I know that you woke up scared, and thought we had made a mistake, but...I know we didn't."

He grabs my face between his hands and rests his forehead on mine. "From the very first time I met you, I knew you were something special. Your drive, your ambition, and your insane passion for everything in your life set you apart from everyone else. I haven't been able to get you out of my mind since. I know when we were younger, I messed up. I messed up so bad, Jane, and I really thought I had lost my chance. I thought I would never see you again...But then when I did, when I saw you sitting there at that restaurant table in Hawaii, something in my chest opened. Something that has been closed off and broken since I was eighteen years old. You make me feel. You make me hope. Hope for the present, hope for the future." I see tears forming in his eyes. "This morning, I wanted to give you space. I was going to wait until you got home to call and tell you that I would be right here waiting. Waiting for you to figure your shit out, but then I realized that wasn't going to be enough for me. I don't want to wait. I want you *now*. I want all of you, all of the time."

I feel his warm breath on my face, and that's when it really hits me. He's here. Noah is really here. He didn't let me run away. He didn't let me ruin this. He came for me.

He pulls his face away from mine but continues staring into my eyes. "Look, I know you don't trust me, but I want you to learn that you can. I'm here to earn that trust and prove that we can make this work."

I hang my head low, and my shoulders curve in, filled with shame.

"Jane," he says, gently tilting my chin up with his finger. "Please look at me."

I open my eyes and gaze back and forth between his. He traces my bottom lip softly with his thumb.

"I love you," I whisper through my tears.

He replaces his thumb with his lips, and I take him in. I fold into his embrace and let myself really feel all of this. All of him.

"I love you too," he says, lips hovering over mine.

"I've always loved you, Noah. I always will." He lifts me from the island and holds me close.

"It's settled then." He whispers into my ear. "I'm going to marry you, Jane Robins, and this is not up for debate."

Epilogue
Three Years Later

Noah

God, she gets more and more beautiful every day.

"What are you looking at?" She says to me, big, blue eyes narrowed with suspicion.

"Oh, nothing. You just have something on your shirt."

She looks down and rolls her eyes. "Ha-Ha, good one, smart ass." She throws a potato chip at my face, which makes me choke on my drink.

Jane is the best thing that has ever happened to me. These past three years have been the craziest and most alive years I've ever had in my entire life. So many things have changed since we left Hawaii, and I'm happier than I ever could have imagined.

Here we sit in the backyard of our home in Fort Collins, Colorado. The town where we grew up. The town where we met. The town that holds all of our past hurts and desires. The town where we went to school, where I broke her heart, where we fell in love, where I proposed, where we had our first child.

Jane sits under the large tree, shading herself as she feeds our daughter, Bird, who just turned four months old yesterday. The ease at which this mothering thing came to her is something I will forever admire.

This little girl is one lucky lady, because she's surrounded by people who love her more and more every day. Jordyn and Daniel are over basically every day, already teaching her questionable things, and Jordyn has single-handedly provided Bird with an entire wardrobe of clothes to last her until she goes to college.

Jane's mom, Carol, has really stepped into her grandmother role and is a completely different person than she was when Jane was little. She came to us when Jane was newly pregnant and told us that she was going to therapy and had since come to the realization that the immense pressure she had put Jane through had actually done a lot of damage. She apologized for everything, and they've been working on their relationship since.

Jane was so close with her Nan, and I'm so happy our daughter will get to have that special relationship with her grandma as well. Since Carol has been working so hard, she has been pushing Jane's dad, Dan, to go to therapy and start making changes too. Things are looking good for our little family, and honestly, it feels amazing.

Tyler still lives in Fort Collins, and our relationship has also started to mend. We still have a long way to go, but I can feel the positive changes starting to take shape.

I coach my nephew's soccer team, and they all come over after games for big family dinners. He's a great uncle to Bird, and I'm excited to see where our lives take us.

I sit in the shade and look up at the house, the life we have built together. This life that feels like it's only just beginning. I've opened my own firm now, and Jane was working with me right up until she gave birth.

She's giving herself some time to stay at home, but I know she's not going to stay away for long. She's going to take on clients here and there until Bird gets a bit older, and then I'm sure she will come back full time. We both love what we do, and we feel so lucky we can do it together.

Everything with the firm happened so fast. When I finally moved back from New York and settled fully into Fort Collins, I found the business card Justin had given me the night of the luau in Hawaii.

Little did I know, he was a partner at a medium-scale immigration firm in Alabama. I gave him a call, told him my proposal about us opening a firm here in Colorado, and he agreed.

He and Lauren were already pregnant by that point, a honeymoon baby nonetheless, and the three of them moved here the following summer. Our firm opened that fall, and we've been steadily growing our clientele ever since.

Their son, Jedd, is the wildest little monster I've ever encountered. They have their hands full with him, and they couldn't be any happier.

I often think about what would have happened if I would have let Jane run away in her fear of the unknown. We would have missed out on this wonderful life we have created.

This life where she does the laundry, and I do the dishes. Where we dance together in the kitchen and sing off-key during parties. Where we argue like cats and dogs but lay with our bodies and limbs tangled together each night.

We would have missed out on this life of joy, this life of laughter, this life of love.

I watch as she smiles brightly at our daughter. The light in her eyes shining so strong and vibrant, I feel like they could light the world on a dark night.

She rocks Bird back and forth, singing a song, and kisses her softly on the forehead.

She looks at me and catches me staring. "I know I don't have anything on my shirt, so seriously, what are you looking at?"

"You, Jane. It's always been you."

"Atticus, he was real nice...."
"Most people are, Scout, when you finally see them."
-Atticus Finch, *To Kill a Mockingbird*

Acknowledgements

First, I would just like to start by saying thank you! Thank you for giving this silly little book a chance!

To Cord. The man with the silly name, and even sillier dad puns. I wouldn't have been able to do any of this without you by my side. Thank you for the early mornings, late nights, and all the time in between. You are my rock, my love, and my best friend. I am blessed to have you by my side during this journey called life. High school sweethearts forever.

To my four hilarious and wonderful children. You have made me who I am. I am so thankful for each one of you and your little perfect and unique personalities. Thank you for letting me take the time to write. Thank you for encouraging me and celebrating with me all along the way. I love you, forever and always.

To my mom. Thank you for always being willing to help me find the time to get this book completed, or even just making me take some time for myself. My kids are so lucky to have you as their Granny. Thank you for always being there for me. I love you.

To my in-laws. Thank you for the long Sunday dinners and all the days full of smiles and laughter. I love our little Montana family, and I am so happy that we all have each other.

To Alix & Kaylie. My other high school sweethearts. I am so lucky that at age thirteen, I got to meet such wonderful girls that turned into such amazing women. Thank you for standing by my side, even through all of my questionable hair, makeup, and fashion choices throughout the years.

To Christina Hill. This book wouldn't be a reality without you. You are such an incredible woman, mother, and author. I am so grateful that I took the chance that warm sunny day in a little Montana town, bought your book, and messaged you. You inspire me in so many ways, and I am so grateful for our friendship. Thank you!

To Danielle Morris. The best beta reader, hype-woman, and all around amazing author extraordinaire. You encouraged me during this entire process, and I am so grateful for all that you have done for me. Thank you, thank you, thank you!

To all the wonderful ladies at Mountains & Manuscripts. Your friendship and advice has been invaluable to me. I have learned so much from each of you, and I feel like I have been blessed to have met you. You're some of the most spectacular women on this planet, and I know I wouldn't be where I am today were it not for the retreat we went on. Thank you for the kind words, the extremely useful advice, and of course, the impressive karaoke skills.

To my beta readers. Thank you for the time and attention you put into my book. Thank you so very much! I promise I deleted most of the "that"s in the book.

To Krys. Thank you so much for taking the time to read and edit my book. Thank you for working so hard for me and helping me make this the best story it could be.

To Graham. The coolest Colorado guy I know. Thank you so much for putting up with all of my Fort Collins questions and always going above and beyond when doing it. You helped make the process so much easier, and so much more fun. Thank you so very much.

To all of my Colorado family. Thank you for always believing in me. Thank you for always being there for me, and for always knowing the right things to say. I love you all, and I wouldn't be who I am without each one of you.

Lastly, to all of my amazing readers. At the time I'm writing these acknowledgements, the book hasn't been released yet, so I'm not entirely sure how it will be received, but if at least one of you found something in Jane and Noah's story that resonated with you, then it's a win for me. I can't thank you enough for picking up this book. For giving it a chance. I know there are so many other novels out in the world, and I am so incredibly blessed that you decided to read mine. Thank you.

About the Author

Emma Norman is a Montana-based author who loves warm sunny days and cooking for her family. She is married to the most perfect husband who loves all things outdoors, but also has a soft spot for learning and literature. Emma also has four amazing and rowdy children who are her pride and joy. When she's not writing her novels, you can catch her homeschooling her kids, reading to her kids, or playing with her kids. Basically it's all kids, all the time, and she wouldn't have it any other way.